I0703760

TAKEDOWN

ANDREW HUDAK

WORKBOOK PRESS LLC
187 E Warm Springs Rd,
Suite B285 Las Vegas NV 89119 USA

Website: https://workbookpress.com/
Hotline: 1-888-818-4856
Email: admin@workbookpress.com

Ordering Information:

Quantity sales. Special discounts are available on quantity purchases by corporations, associations, and others. For details, contact the publisher at the address above.

Library of Congress Control Number:

ISBN-13:   978-1-965732-07-6   Paperback Version
                978-1-965732-15-1   Digital Version

REV. DATE: 01/24/2025

Dedication

For my two wonderful parents, Jim and
June Hudak, from whom I got my love of
reading, writing, and storytelling.

ANDREW HUDAK

CHAPTER 1

SARAH KOLCHEK KNEW it would be a cool night. She thought about this very fact as she planned out her jogging outfit for the evening. In warmer weather she'd favor a pair of shorts and a tank top, but tonight would have to be a more dressed-up affair. She decided to go with a midweight polyester shirt over the tank top and a new pair of thermal running tights. *Sure,* she thought to herself, *this outfit doesn't show off as much as the other one would, but I still look sexy.*

Looking sexy was key for that evening. As Sarah put on a light jacket and grabbed some gloves, she got butterflies in her stomach thinking about the assignment that lay ahead of her. The city had been plagued in recent weeks by a man the local press dubbed the River City Rapist. He was a nasty piece of work—five rapes in the past two and a half weeks, all around a local park where families gather in the day. The evening hours were more for joggers or young lovers on an after-dinner stroll. Late at night, the park turned into a denizen of homeless, drug pushers, and drug addicts, but the River City Police were pretty good about cleaning them out by dawn to make the park safe for families once again.

During the day, however, police presence was not strong. The River City Rapist was not active during the day, so children and families needed not worry. He only attacked in the evening. He had a type as well. He sought out only fit women jogging in the park with age ranges from midtwenties to midthirties. The description of the perp was consistent among all of the women when they talked to the police after each incident: about six feet tall, late thirties to early forties, and he had a potbelly. He used a weapon of some kind to inca pacitate his victims—a blunt object like a club or a bat. The Rapist hid in the bushes along the trails in the park and cracked the women in the back of the head as they ran by. After they were on the ground, he'd drag them into the bushes where they were out of sight and do his business, then take off. The whole incident was typically over in less than three minutes, leaving the victim stunned, disoriented, and in pain.

The River City Police Department took these incidents seriously and beefed up police presence in the evening starting right after the first rape was reported. The problem was that the park was big, and they didn't have the extra officers to spare because of budget cuts and a mayor that publicly stated he was not on their side. Two extra officers were assigned to patrol the entire fifty-six-acre park from 6:00 p.m. to midnight, but it did no good. Their patrol pattern was easy to predict even after it was altered following the third rape, plus there was too much ground to cover. After rape number five, the lieutenant in charge, Lieutenant Maxwell "Buzz" Busby, decided the only way to nab this pervert was to send someone undercover. He needed to select a female officer who would essentially be used as bait. This decision sickened him, but he was left with no choice. At the very least, he would select a woman who could handle herself when the going got tough.

That's where Sarah came in. Busby knew that before joining the police force, she had some mild success as a professional mixed martial arts fighter. Sure, her fights were all against other women, but it was training that he knew would come in handy in any scrape up, even with a man who was taller and heavier than her. Lucky for him, Sarah was up for it. She hated the idea of the young women of this city living in fear every evening and unable to go to the beautiful city park for fear that some scumbag would jump out of the bushes. Indeed, foot traffic in the park after dusk was little to none. This actually worked in the police's favor, since with fewer targets the River City Rapist would have to go for Sarah.

The only problem Sarah really had with the assignment was the jogging at night. As an athletic woman she could handle it, but she never liked long-term, steady-state cardio, instead opting for more high-intensity training during her fighting days. For three consecutive nights, she'd gone for a jog in an almost completely empty park with no sign of the rapist. It was getting old, and now it was getting colder out. She didn't really want to go, but she thought of the victims as she grabbed her cell phone and a pair of earbuds and headed out the door. This was for them.

Waiting for Sarah in an unmarked police car parked outside of her house was her partner and friend Jill Ronkowski. Jill was in her early thirties, a few years older than Sarah, who was twenty-eight. Both women regarded police work as a calling, but the similarities ended there. Jill didn't have an athletic bone in her body, instead preferring a more sedentary lifestyle. The only time she got on the treadmill was when she knew she had a mandated police physical coming up. Jill was lucky to be blessed with a naturally high metabolism, so the sitting around and eating junk food never really caught up with her. She was a bit plump, but not severely overweight. She couldn't run if her life depended on it, though, and it was this thought that gave her relief that Lieutenant Busby didn't ask her to go jogging too. She was happy staying in the car and waiting for the call from Sarah. Something had to happen soon.

Sarah opened the passenger side door and got into the car. Jill greeted her with a smile. In spite of their differences, the two women chose to focus on what they had in common, and they genuinely liked and respected each other. Sarah smiled back, only with less enthusiasm.

"What do you think?" asked Jill. "Is tonight the night we nab this creep?"

Sarah shrugged her shoulders and let out a sigh. "I hope so. Let's go to the park and find out." Jill turned on the engine and put the car in gear. She stepped on the accelerator a bit harder than usual. Her desire to stop working every evening and get back to spending some time on the couch with her husband and pet beagle overwhelmed her. The car sped through the suburban residential neighborhood as the last remnants of the sun shone off in the distance, headed toward the city, and toward the park.

CHAPTER 2

J ILL SLOWED THE car down and crept along the sidewalk next to the park. Getting a space wasn't too difficult since most folks were too scared to go to the park this time of night, but nevertheless, she didn't want to draw attention to herself. She found a convenient spot near a gate to the wrought iron fence, and without too many trees to obstruct her view. As she put the car in park, she looked over at Sarah.

"Tonight's the night. I feel it."

"I hope you're right," replied Sarah with a sigh. "This jogging at night is getting real old, real fast."

"Well, it's keeping you in good shape," said Jill with a wry smile and giving Sarah a friendly punch on the shoulder.

"Oh yeah? I think I'm in good enough shape already. How about you go for a run, and I'll sit on my butt in the car and listen to podcasts."

"No, thank you," Jill said adamantly—in case Sarah was even the least bit serious in her suggestion. She knew that sometimes people can say serious things in a joking way. "I am more than happy staying right here with nothing but the stars in the sky and Joe Rogan in my earbuds to keep me company."

Sarah stared at her partner. The incredulity was unmistakable.

"Really, I'll be fine," Jill blurted out before things got too awkward. "Don't you have laps to do and a potential rapist to lure into a trap?"

"Just the way I love spending my evenings," Sarah retorted as she pulled the handle on the car door and stepped out on to the sidewalk.

The sarcasm was not lost on Jill. She could have made some snarky reply but decided against it. After all, Sarah was the one putting herself in danger on this assignment. She just gave Sarah a nod as Sarah headed through the gate and into the park.

As she entered the park, Sarah thought about how Jill could be a real pain in the neck but meant well. These evening assignments weren't only difficult for her; they were difficult for Jill too. Then again, Jill had been married for ten years and had already fallen into the routine monotony of married life. Sarah had a fiancé at home— Dale—whom she loved spending her evenings with and wanted to be with now more than ever. But when duty called, it was loud and insistent. She knew she was doing this for a good reason. Plus, in spite of all of the grief she gave to Jill, this was a good time to catch up on podcasts. There was one about a hunter who encountered a Kodiak bear and killed it with a six-inch hunting knife that she thought sounded interesting. Sarah found it on her phone, put in her earbuds, pressed play, and started jogging.

By the time Sarah began her run, the sun had completely gone down. The only lights in the park were the bright fluorescent ones that shone her way along the jogging path. The coolness of the air penetrated her lungs as she breathed heavier and heavier during her run. It was starting to get uncomfortable, but she knew she could manage.

Sarah stopped. She hated this part of the park. The path led under a dimly lit tunnel. She knew it was too early in the evening for a vagrant or a drug addict—or drug dealer—to be there. Nevertheless, it was more than the air in the evening that gave her chills up her spine. What if *he* was in there and this is where it all went down. She wouldn't have a lot of room to maneuver in a fight and only two directions to run away. But this is the job. *Go hard or go home*, she thought to herself.

Catching her breath, Sarah sprinted through the tunnel. Her peripheral vision picked up that no one else was in the tunnel except for her. Sarah smiled as she arrived at the tunnel exit. She breathed a sigh of relief that she made it out just fine. Then, just when she was at her most calm and relaxed coming out of the tunnel—

Whack! Sarah felt an impact on the back of her skull like she'd never felt before. Dizzy and dazed, she hit the ground hard. Luckily for her, the path veered off to the left as she got hit and she fell off to the right, on to the grass lining the sidewalk. She would have had raspberries all over her arms and face if it wasn't for this bit of good fortune.

Barely conscious and lying facedown in the grass, Sarah heard a loud metallic sound off to her left. She glanced over and saw a crowbar. Sarah then started piecing it together. Someone just cracked her in the back of the skull with that thing. Then she heard heavy breathing and footsteps coming toward her.

A large pair of hands roughly turned her over and on to her back. Getting some more clarity in her vision, Sarah made out the silhouette of a large man standing over her. Before she could make a sound, the man got to his knees and fell on top of her. She could feel his large potbelly moving over her lower abdomen as the man wrestled with the tie on his sweatpants.

It was at that moment that she knew it. This was him: the River City Rapist. Sarah looked down at what he was doing and saw the manifestation of the man's excitement poking out. Sweatpants do a poor job of hiding such things. With this as her focus and panic setting in, Sarah had an involuntary knee-jerk reaction—a literal one.

The potbellied man howled in agony as Sarah's hard, bony kneecap connected directly with his crotch. She was just as surprised as him that she did that, but it worked. Sarah gained some of her cognition back after the weight of the man was off her. She was well enough to roll away and stand up. The man was still on the ground, clutching is lower abdomen in pain. Not only did she get him by surprise, she got him pretty good in a very painful spot.

On her wrist, Sarah was wearing the latest in communication technology. It wasn't really the latest—federal government officers had been using wrist communication technology for years. It was new to the department, however. The feds had a surplus they were selling and there happened to be enough money in the police department budget to buy some wrist comms—as the department called them—that could be used on special assignments like this one. Sarah held the wrist comm up to her chin and pressed the button on the right side of it.

"Kolckeck to unit four-oh-nine. Come in, four-oh-nine. Jill, are you there?"

Jill of course was there. Having gotten bored with staring at a lamppost while listening to a podcast, she was starting to doze off. She would have totally been in dreamland in another few minutes if the crackle of the radio and Sarah's voice didn't jolt her wide awake. It took around two seconds to come to complete awareness and regain her composure. Once she was with it again, she grabbed the communicator on the console.

"Hey, Sarah. Yeah, I'm here. Are you okay?"

"I got him, Jill!"

"Great news, Sarah! Way to go!"

"Thanks. The only problem is that he's a handful and a half. I'm going to need some help."

"All right, I'm coming. Where are you?"

"I'm just outside the tunn—"

Jill jerked her head at the abruptness with which Sarah's message was cut off. This was troubling to say the least.

"Sarah, I didn't catch the end. What was that? Where are you? Sarah? Sarah? Oh crap!"

Jill slammed the communicator back on the console, threw her door open, and leaped out of the car. She almost barreled over a middle-aged woman walking a small dog on the sidewalk as she rushed into the park entrance. The middle-aged woman gave her a "watch it lady" look, but Jill was too frazzled and in a hurry to notice.

Outside the tunnel, the potbellied man had regained his strength. He just got finished interrupting Sarah's call to Jill by giving her a hard push that sent her right to the ground. He made a move for the crowbar but was too slow, and Sarah was closer anyway. She grabbed it first and took a swing at him as she got to her feet. His protruding belly was a good target, and she almost hit it. If only he didn't scooch back so quickly when she wound up to swing at him. He was a surprisingly nimble man for someone of his girth around the midsection.

Seeing that she had the crowbar and was getting up, the potbellied man did the only sensible thing: he ran. Unfortunately for him, he was too big and slow. Added to this was the fact that Sarah was athletic and had been practicing running every night for the past three days. Taking advantage of her second wind, she caught up to him in no time.

Sarah dive tackled him, and he landed right on his big potbelly. He tried to get up, but Sarah swiped at his legs, catching a brief hold of his ankle. This was enough to trip him up and he went headfirst into a nearby tree, splitting his forehead open.

Enraged and with blood dripping into his right eye, the potbellied man charged Sarah as she got back to her feet. He got her in a bear hug. The grip was tight. Sarah could feel the air being forced out of her lungs. She longed to take a deep breath of the cool, evening air, but her upper abdomen was so constricted from the vise-like grip that she couldn't.

Sarah thought back to when she was ten years old and first learning karate. Her instructor, a kindly man in his late fifties with a mustache who seemed to always be wearing a headband named Sensei Okuno, taught her and her classmates a very important lesson. He used to say, "Find your enemy's weakness—and exploit it." It was a lesson not just for martial arts, or for sports, but for life as well. If not for the wind being knocked out of her at the moment, Sarah would have managed a smile at the thought that it was in that class that she first learned the word exploit and what it meant. It's a funny thing, the how and why human beings pick up words throughout their lives.

Focusing on the potbellied man's brand-new, wide-open flesh wound, Sarah took her old sensei's advice. She took her free left hand and pressed her thumb right into the wound. The potbellied man let out a deep, guttural scream. With her right arm she arched back and then delivered an open-handed chop to the side of the man's neck. This dazed the man and caused him to drop Sarah instantly.

Sarah fell on her butt as she was dropped and stayed there for a few seconds, gasping for air. The potbellied man had his own pain he was dealing with, so she had the time, and she took it. When she felt like she could stand and fight again, she got up.

This time, she had him right where she wanted him. Sarah rushed over to the squirming man—who was doubled over in pain, holding his bloody head in his hand, and trying his best to compose himself. Any attempt at composure was in vain, however, as Sarah, showing no mercy, delivered a front kick to the potbellied man's head while he was doubled over. This sent him reeling back. He slammed against a tree, back first, shaking a few of the already loosened leaves off it.

Now that the man was upright, blinded, and had his back against a tree, Sarah moved in for the final blow. She grabbed the potbellied man's shoulders to hold him in place, and with lightning-quick precision kneed him with all of her might in the upper abdomen. The target was a ripe one, given the man's protruding gut. The thick layer of fat on the man's belly did not protect his diaphragm from such a forceful blow. The man collapsed instantly as all of the air was forced out of his lungs. In a matter of seconds, the potbellied man had gone from a dangerous aggressor to a quivering mass, grasping his head with one hand and holding his arm across his large belly with the other. It was over. He wasn't going anywhere. Only one problem: how to get him up and back to the car with Jill?

As luck would have it, Jill showed up at just that moment. She'd been running along the trail ever since she got out of the car and rushed into the park. However, after about fifty yards of straight sprinting, she got completely winded and, in spite of her worry for her partner's safety, could manage little more than a trot. Almost completely out of breath, Jill stopped and put her hands on her knees when she saw Sarah. Quickly assessing the situation with her partner standing over the beaten-up suspect, she mustered out through panted breaths, "Oh… Sarah…thank…God…"

Sarah could not help but be mildly amused by Jill's exhaustion. Plus, it was not lost on her that her partner cared for her so much. It was good to know that someone so dedicated and loyal had her back.

She cracked a wry smile at Jill and said, "Hi, Jill. Glad you made it. I'm definitely going to need some help with this one."

Jill sighed as Sarah walked over to the incapacitated potbellied man lying on the ground and put the cuffs on him. Together, the two women got the man to his feet and slowly walked him back up the path toward the park gate.

CHAPTER 3

SEYMOUR ROSS LOVED cop shows and movies growing up. He especially liked the "buddy movie" subgenre. The friendship, loyalty, love, commitment, and admiration that two police officers had for each other on the shows—even if they were total opposites—was the pinnacle of human interaction to Seymour. He and his friends used to play cops and robbers around their quiet, suburban middle-class neighborhood using squirt guns. The kids who were the "good guys"—and Seymour always insisted on being one—pretended that they were motorcycle cops as they rode their bikes around to stop robberies in progress. These "robberies" usually involved Matchbox cars or bags of Army men, things of that nature, but to the kids they belonged to they were their most valued possessions.

The problem for sweet Seymour was that he did not have a cop's temperament. By necessity, the police of River City had to be hard, cynical, and untrusting. They need to look a perp in the eye and tell right away if they're lying. They couldn't be afraid to get a little rough when anyone was giving them trouble. Seymour's heart was in the right place with his idealistic "protect and serve" mentality. He exemplified all of the virtues of an honest, courageous, and upstanding police officer. What he lacked, however, was the street smarts, and in River City that could mean life or death.

This did not deter Seymour from applying to the police academy when he was old enough. He did very well in physical fitness, was a good marksman with his sidearm, and scored well on all tests. This was because Seymour was not only an intelligent young man, he also had the passion and love of the job to be the best he could be. His fellow trainees at the academy all liked him for his positive attitude and optimistic approach. The proudest, happiest day of Seymour's life was graduating with honors from the academy. Everyone in attendance was thrilled for him. They knew what such an honor meant to Seymour.

All of the higher-ups in the River City Police Department could tell a mile away that Seymour was too pleasant and kindhearted for the tougher police work. The streets would eat this rookie alive. Still, they couldn't deny that he was a genuine great guy. The trick was to give Seymour an assignment that was in line with his aptitude. Nothing too dangerous, but nothing too mundane either. They decided that traffic patrol was the best thing for the young officer. It's not a desk job, but he wouldn't be chasing after drug dealers either.

It's not what Seymour wanted. His whole life he dreamed of having a partner, a buddy—someone with whom to banter and bicker and bond. Traffic patrol was a solo gig. It meant that he'd be alone in a squad car for hours on end checking for speeders along some of the lesser-traveled roads where fewer cars meant drivers with a heavy foot put the pedal to the metal.

Nevertheless, and ever the team player, Seymour accepted his assignment and did his part to stop speeding as well as bring in some revenue to River City though the issuing of fines for speeding violations. Drivers caught speeding through work zones got fined double. *Just as well*, he thought, *they're menaces who deserved to be punished extra.* Seymour hit every quota for every month and was commended on several occasions for his above average service in the line of duty.

This went on for five years. Seymour did his job and did it well. Then one stiflingly humid July day, he caught a beat-up, four-door sedan going fifty miles per hour in a twenty-miles-per-hour zone. Seymour's car was cool inside, and he really didn't want to have to get out and walk in the heat, but this violation was too good to pass up. Plus, as an honorable officer of the law, he knew it was his duty to take charge with drivers as reckless as this one.

No other cars were coming, so Seymour was able to pull out immediately and flash his sirens. The driver of the beat-up sedan pulled over right away and parked to the side of the road. Seymour took a deep breath of cool air and stepped out into the summer heat.

As he approached the car, he could see the driver—a man in his midtwenties with his dark hair in a greasy ponytail and wearing a ragged T-shirt—was nervous and fidgety. Seymour put his fingers on the butt of his gun. He had never shot anyone before. He'd never even drawn his gun. But he kept a hand on his sidearm just in case. As Seymour approached the driver, the greasy-haired man rolled down his window. It was a crank window that took some effort to get down. Immediately the smell of stale cigarettes assaulted Seymour's nostrils. The smell was made worse by the heat of the day. In spite of his revulsion, Seymour leaned in toward the driver.

"Do you have any idea how fast you were going?" he said, politely yet firmly.

"No, sorry—I don't," replied the greasy-haired man. He was on edge. Seymour suspected he was on some kind of narcotic. An "upper" to be sure. The man pointed to his dashboard. "See, my speedometer is broken. It doesn't tell me how fast I go."

Seymour looked at the dash and felt a tinge of sympathy for the guy, but the law was the law. He looked back at the man, betraying no softness—a skill he had to learn. "Be that as it may, I still have to give you a ticket. License, insurance, and registration please."

"Okay…" The man's hands shook as he reached into his glove compartment. Seymour leaned over to see if he could catch a glimpse of what was inside, but the man's greasy head obstructed his view. The man closed the glove compartment and handed Seymour the insurance and registration with a sheepish, "Here you go." Seymour straightened up as the man put the papers in his hand. The man then reached into his pocket to retrieve his license. Just as he pulled it out of his wallet the glove compartment, which had a broken catch and didn't close properly, flew open and two baggies with white powder tumbled out.

Hearing the noise and thinking the man was incredibly suspicious, Seymour lowered his head and saw the two baggies sitting on top of the opened dash door. Before he could say a word, the greasy-haired man scraped what Seymour thought was a license against Seymour's throat. Except it wasn't a license; it was another card from the man's wallet. This was also no mere scrape with the edge of a plastic card. The man had affixed a box cutter blade to the edge of the card. It cut Seymour from behind his ear to right by his Adam's apple.

It took a split second for the pain to register and Seymour immediately put his hand on his neck. He felt a hot wetness, but knew immediately that it wasn't sweat. Seymour backed away from the car and looked at his hand. It was covered in blood. He put his hand back on his neck and, completely in shock, walked to his squad car. He could hear the greasy-haired man's car peel off as he entered the car and radioed for help.

Seymour waited in the cool car for ten minutes until an ambulance arrived. All the while he fought to keep from passing out by thinking of his fiancée—he was set to get married that Autumn— and hoped that the blade didn't hit an artery. He knew he was done for if an artery was nicked.

It was close, but no cigar. The blade missed his carotid artery by two millimeters. Seymour did get married that Autumn, and around the same time came the trial of the greasy-haired man. He wasn't hard to track down since in spite of his shock, Seymour managed to hold on to the man's insurance and registration documents. Turns out he was a low-level cocaine dealer who was late to a meeting because he was too busy getting high on his own supply, hence the speeding.

Seymour gladly testified against the man, who was indicted on charges of drug trafficking, attempted murder, and assaulting an officer. The judge all but literally threw the book at him. Seymour was happy to get such a villain off the streets, but couldn't find his way back on to them. The experience had soured him on being on patrol. Even traffic duty is deadly in River City. He decided, for the sake of himself and the sanity of his new wife—a lovely brunette whose name happened to be Autumn—that he would settle into something behind a desk. With his pleasant smile and upbeat attitude, the higher-ups in the River City Police Department determined that he would make the perfect desk sergeant. Who better to greet the public as they entered the building? Besides, they needed to replace the surly Sergeant McAllister, who should have retired years ago. This was a perfect chance to get McAllister out and for River City to reconnect with the public in a more positive way.

*****

It was exactly this smiling face and positive attitude that greeted Sarah and Jill as they walked in with the potbellied man. It had been a little over twenty-five years since Seymour's incident, and every once in a while the scar on his neck itched, usually when the weather changed with the seasons. He grinned at the two ladies as they dragged the unwilling perp to his desk, gently scratching his scar as Sarah pulled and Jill pushed the bloodied, haggard, unwilling, large-framed man.

"We got him!" said Jill, looking at Sergeant Ross for approval.

"Got who?" Seymour knew who she was talking about but wanted to have a little fun. He enjoyed busting Sarah's chops. He knew she could take it.

Sarah wasn't sure if he was kidding or not, though. Seymour was so busy sometimes that he couldn't commit to memory everything that was happening. He was forgetful at times too. After she got to know him well, Sarah used to tease Seymour that the cut on his neck drained too much blood from his brain and it did permanent damage. She quickly stopped this practice, though, as she could tell that Seymour didn't like it and she didn't want to hurt his feelings.

A bit exasperated, Sarah responded, "Who do you think? The guy I've been doing undercover work trying to nab for the past three nights."

"This is him?" Seymour could hardly believe it.

"It's him," Sarah quickly replied.

"It better be him," interjected Jill.

Sarah shot Jill one of those "Not you too" kind of looks. "It's him. He fits the description, plus he attacked me. Big mistake on his part though."

"So I see." Seymour raised an eyebrow, legitimately impressed. "Congratulations."

"Thanks, Sarge." Sarah and Seymour were on a first-name basis, but she enjoyed calling him "Sarge."

Seymour got serious. "Sarah. When you're done with the booking, Lieutenant Busby wants to see you."

"Okay, I'll see him after I'm done with this big lug."

Sarah grabbed the potbellied man by the collar and made a step toward booking. As if suddenly filled with a burst of energy, Jill perked up.

"No worries, Sarah. I got this. You go see Buzz."

"All right." Sarah let go of the collar. "All yours, Jill. Thanks."

Jill fake-smiled at her. "Nothing to it."

Jill took control of the collar. The potbellied man said nothing and offered no resistance. He knew he was beat, and there was nothing he could do. Jill led him away as Sarah headed in the opposite direction toward Lieutenant Busby's office.

CHAPTER 4

LIEUTENANT BUSBY'S OFFICE was a mess. Ever the since the budget cuts by the rat bastard mayor of River City, who Busby hated with a passion, it had been too much work and too little time. Less police meant less patrols. Less patrols meant less police presence. Less police presence meant more crime. More crime meant more complaints. More complaints meant that all of the officers he did have were stretched so thin they were barely three dimensional. Every day was a twelve-hour day to stay on top of it all. And weekends—what are those? It was true that crime doesn't sleep—it was wide awake in River City.

Busby long ago gave up on any kind of filing system. He piled up papers everywhere he could and hoped he could find them whenever needed. He usually could. Luckily, the River City Rapist case was relatively new, so it was on top. He was able to move it over to his "perp arrested" pile. But there was another case, right under it, that he needed to talk to her about. He grabbed the file and put it on his desk so it would be ready for Sarah when she came knocking. Busby perused the file to freshen his memory on the details.

The file held the photo and arrest record of one Vincent DiGrazio. His friends called him Vinny. He was a low-level hoodlum involved mostly in illegal gambling and petty theft. Nothing too major until yesterday afternoon.

The day started off for Vinny like any other. He got up at 10:00 a.m. since he was out late the night before and, as usual, drank way too much. This didn't really matter since his day job—delivering pizzas for a local pizzeria called Paisano's—didn't start until noon.

Besides his day didn't really pick up until around 1:00 p.m. after all of the orders started pouring in.

Vinny was in his midtwenties and lived with his mother in a two-bedroom apartment. She worked a lot of double shifts as a nurse, so they barely saw each other. Vinny couldn't afford his own place on his pizzeria-delivery salary—at least not one he cared to live in—and he was fine with his living situation since his mother was hardly ever there, and when she was there, she was too tired to give him any trouble. He had a roof over his head and food in the fridge. There was no reason to rock this boat. Vinny got himself together and drove his car to Paisano's. It was a short drive. Paisano's was Vinny's local pizzeria when he was growing up.

*****

The famous River City pizzeria was founded in 1951 by an immigrant couple from Naples who were looking for a better life in America after World War II. They found it and turned Paisano's into a neighborhood staple. Lines were around the block on Friday and Saturday nights just to get takeout.

Inevitably, the original owners retired. The couple's three children all moved far away and had no interest in the pizza business. Their niece, who was their only local relative, agreed to take over operation of Paisano's. She also grew up on the pizza and loved the business, but she cared more about the money than the quality. She switched suppliers for everything from sauce to cheese to paper plates. The prices to the customers all stayed the same so the profit margins improved, but the food quality dipped. Within a few years the word got around that Paisano's wasn't what it used to be. The lines around the block on Fridays and Saturdays disappeared. They were lucky to get fifty customers on those nights, when they used to get hundreds. Paisano's became the place that people went to when they needed something quick, or didn't feel like hiking across town to get better pizza.

Eventually the business lost so much money that the niece had no choice: she had to sell. A pair of college roommates, who enjoyed making pizzas for their friends while in school, bought the business. Neither was Italian—one was German Irish and the other was Puerto

Rican—but they made some great pies with quality ingredients. Slowly but surely, Paisano's got its reputation back.

This also, however, could not last. The two young men dated their college sweethearts while they ran the business. Pretty soon their girlfriends turned into fiancées and their fiancées turned into wives. Having children and starting a family was next for the two friends, but the pizzeria took up all of their time. They loved making pizzas and owning a business, but their attentions were increasingly becoming more focused elsewhere.

The decision was hard, but they mutually agreed to sell Paisano's. Right around that same time an up-and-coming entrepreneur named Leo Manetti was looking around the neighborhood for a business. He'd heard of Paisano's and thought that purchasing it would be a good way to get it back into Italian hands. Coming from a wealthy family, he could afford what the young men were asking and didn't even feel the need to haggle. He also vowed to maintain the quality by using nothing but the freshest and finest ingredients.

The real money for Leo wouldn't be in pizzas, though. It would be in the drugs that he secretly sold and delivered. All anyone had to do was order a spinach calzone with extra anchovies and no marinara sauce—something no one in their right mind ever did—and that would open the door to further discussions using code words. Extra ricotta was cocaine. Extra mozzarella was heroin. Extra basil was marijuana. He had a good assortment of "extras," and everything had a code name. To keep things simple, he only offered one size bag, which gave the user about a gram of their drug of choice. If anyone wanted more than that, they'd have to order two or three bags by saying something like, "Two extra of basil and three extra ricotta."

It was a good system that worked for years. Even after the FBI started surveillance on Paisano's because of Leo being the son of notorious mobster Mike "the Hammer" Manetti, it all sounded plausible. Strange, but not strange enough to raise suspicion.

While the FBI was interested in the dealings of Leo's father, River City Vice was interested in Leo. They set up some surveillance of their own, and they weren't so easily fooled by the code. Eventually they got confident enough to place an order of their own. A Vice Squad cop called Paisano's from a safe house and asked for a delivery of a spinach calzone with extra anchovies and no marinara sauce, along with some extra mozzarella.

*****

This was Vinny's first delivery of the day. He was grateful for the call since it was almost 1:00 p.m., and he was getting bored folding boxes and pretending to enjoy Italian soccer on the dining room's flat-screen television.

Vinny grabbed the order and took it to his car. He knew what was inside the box. All of the "special" deliveries were marked with a small red dot on the side of the box by the chef. These always made Vinny happy to see since it usually meant a nice tip, especially if the customer was the nervous type. Nervous people always tip more as a way of bribing you to keep your mouth shut about them. But Vinny didn't care. He wouldn't say anything anyway. What they did once they took the package from him was their business.

Everything looked normal to Vinny when he arrived at the house. Just an average split-level house with a small porch and a two-car garage. Vinny rang the doorbell. A middle-aged man in a semiclosed bathrobe and disheveled hair answered the door. *Thank goodness he has shorts on*, thought Vinny.

Vinny gave the man the bag. The man promptly looked inside and said in a voice that was louder than necessary, "Looks good." He then reached into his robe pocket for what Vinny thought was money. Turned out it was badge. The man in the robe told Vinny to stay right where he was, and before he knew it Vinny was surrounded by dozens of River City cops. It seemed like they sprung up out of nowhere. Seconds later, he was lying facedown on the porch, and handcuffs were being put around his wrists.

Busby was reviewing Vinny's file and this recent arrest when he heard a knock on his door. "Come in."

The door opened. As expected, it was Sarah.

"You wanted to see me, Lieutenant?"

"Yeah, Kolchek. Come in and close the door."

Sarah did as she was told and took a seat across from Busby. "What can I help you with, Lieutenant?"

"If you have a cure for chronic ulcers and sleep apnea, I'll take it."

Sarah grinned. *Even with all of the stress, Busby still has his sense of humor*, she thought. *It's probably what keeps him sane.* "Sorry, but I'm afraid I can't help you there."

"Then can you help me by taking on some more undercover work?"

"Undercover? What kind of undercover?" Sarah was exasperated and a bit annoyed. The nerve of this man. "I just got done pretending I like to jog at night to bring in one scumbag, and I'm not really in the mood for that crap again."

Busby could see that she was on edge and knew to not push too hard. He asked gently, "You know the River Murders case that homicide has been working on?"

Sarah calmed down once she heard the tone in his voice. "Yeah. The bodies of two girls were pulled from the river—"

"Three. They found another one this morning."

The news hit Sarah hard. She followed the story on the local news and heard the buzz about it around the station, but nothing about it crossed her path directly. Now she was sitting in her lieutenant's office having a conversation about it. This was as real as police work gets. She looked away and whispered, "Jesus." It was all she could muster.

"No clothes, no witnesses, no ID, no fingerprints. No nothing until…"

Busby tossed Vinny's file in Sarah's lap. She picked it up and fingered through it as Busby continued.

"We picked up this less-than-upstanding citizen this afternoon. His name is Vinny DiGrazio. He works delivering pizzas for Paisano's downtown."

"They make a good Sicilian slice." Sarah couldn't resist the remark. She needed to break the tension somehow and snap herself back to life. Plus it was true. They did make a damn good Sicilian slice. A lot of folks don't like all of the dough and prefer a thinner, Neapolitan crust. However, if done right, the crust on the Sicilian was light and airy and you barely noticed the thickness since it was so melt-in-your-mouth delectable. This was how Paisano's made theirs, and it was a slice worth admiring. Sarah started to get a little craving for it after she said it. Between the exercise and the adrenaline of the evening, she'd worked up quite an appetite.

Busby took her comment in stride and plowed through. "But it turns out that pizzas aren't all he's delivering. Paisano's has been under surveillance by Vice for suspected drug dealing, and sure enough, one of Vinny's deliveries yesterday afternoon came with a side order of heroin."

"I always preferred the garlic knots myself." Now she really was hungry.

"So they bring him in, and not only does he spill his guts about the drug running, he also said that he could help with the bodies that have been turning up in our otherwise pristine waterway."

Sarah looked closer at the rap sheet. "All I see here are minor offenses and petty crimes. How is he mixed up in murder?"

Busby suddenly got very serious. He gave Sarah a look she came to know as his "serious face." The air suddenly felt drier after she noticed it. Now she was thirsty on top of being hungry. Busby laid it out for her.

"That's where we need you to go undercover and gather some concrete evidence. And this'll be deep cover too—no going home at night—for yours and Dale's protection, given the nature of the assignment. We'll set you up with a new ID and an apartment."

Sarah was intrigued. It was a major responsibility to be asked to take on such an assignment. It was also a dangerous one. She gave Busby her version of a serious face. "Okay, I get it. This is no joke. But why all the cloak and dagger?"

"DiGrazio says that Paisano's is a front for the drug operations of the Manetti crime family."

"Manetti? As in Mike 'the Hammer' Manetti?"

Busby nodded. "Right, but this operation is run by his son, Leo. He also says that Leo runs a Brazilian-themed nightclub uptown called Amazon Glory, and at night, in the back of this club, he runs an illegal casino. The main attraction of this casino is the fight ring."

called Amazon Glory, and at night, in the back of this club, he runs an illegal casino. The main attraction of this casino is the fight ring."

That perked Sarah right up. She started to get a feeling that she knew exactly where this conversation was going. "Fight ring?"

Busby nodded again. "Female fight ring."

She knew it. Before Busby could continue any further, she blurted out, "Oh no!"

Exactly the reaction Busby wanted to avoid. Too late now. He put his hands up and gestured for her to calm down. "This is why we need you." His voice was calm and his tone was even. This approach worked on Sarah a few minutes ago, but now she wasn't having any of it.

"Are you kidding me? You know why I quit professional MMA, and now you want me to step back into the octagon?"

At this point Busy knew he all but lost control. Still, he had to keep trying as best as he could. "I know it's a lot to ask." He thought the empathetic approach would work. He was wrong.

"You're damn right it's a lot!" Sarah was more nervous than angry, but it all looked the same to Busby until she followed up with "I don't know if I can do this."

He could see she was having her doubts. This was a voluntary assignment, so he couldn't order her to take it. At the same time, he knew she would be the key to cracking the case. He found that the soft approach was best with Sarah, so he continued. "Sarah, I'm not asking for a decision right now, but will you at least consider it? And think about these poor girls. Who knows when the next one is going to turn up. You could save her life."

Sarah calmed herself. "I need to think about it."

Busby was relieved. It was all he needed to hear for now. "Fine.

Go home, think about it, and let me know tomorrow morning after you've slept on it."

"I will, Lieutenant," Sarah said as she got up and left. Breathing out a sigh of relief, Busby grabbed the file from off the top of the desk and put it on top of a pile.

CHAPTER 5

SARAH WAITED FOR Jill to finish up with booking the perp they caught that evening. She wanted to get home as soon as possible, but she had to wait—Jill was her ride home. Sarah felt beat up. She was tired, stressed, hungry, and craving carbs. She thought about asking Jill if she wanted to grab a slice on the way home. Not necessarily Paisano's since that was further across town, but perhaps at one of the three pizzerias they pass on the way. One good thing about having a large Italian immigrant population: a quick slice was never too far away.

But as she stood there waiting, Sarah eventually talked herself out of it. She didn't want to impose on Jill. She knew that Jill wanted to get home right away too, and put the evening behind her. Besides, Sarah had some frozen pizza in the fridge that was close to getting freezer burn from sitting there so long. It probably was best to heat that up and eat it before it goes bad.

Sarah knew she made the right call when she saw Jill. The woman looked beat—as if she was the one who jogged for almost a mile before getting attacked from behind and having to fight off a potbellied rapist. Sarah mustered up as much happiness as she could, but she wasn't really in the mood.

"Are you ready?" Sarah said through a fake smile.

"Sure am. Let's go," Jill said, feeling relieved that the day was finally coming to a close.

The two women were silent as they walked out to Jill's car and got in. Neither one spoke until they were well into their drive to Sarah's house. It was Jill who broke the silence. She could tell that something was bothering Sarah, and that she was in no mood to talk, but her curiosity got the better of her.

"So what did Busby want?" Jill asked as casually as possible. Her voice was soft and in a well-measured tone, but it seemed loud to Sarah, who was enjoying the quiet and was deep in thought.

Startled, Sarah replied, "He has another undercover job for me—or I guess for us, as I would think that you'd be my point per- son on it."

"Really? What is it?" "It's for homicide."

"Homicide? That's not our department."

"Yeah, but you know how things are. With all of the budget cuts and everyone spread so thin, it's not too shocking that we'd be called on to help out."

Fair point, thought Jill. "What's the assignment." "It's the River Murders."

A flash of excitement shot across Jill's face. This was the big time. "The River Murders? That's huge. The case is all over the news. So far there are two bodies that—"

"Three. Another one was found this morning. It was probably on the news tonight. We would have known about it if we were home and not chasing down perverts in the park."

Too true, thought Jill. "What do they want you to do?" "Apparently, they nabbed a small-time dealer with some connec-tions to it, and they want me to go undercover in this underground, all-women fight ring that the Manetti family is running inside of some Brazilian-themed nightclub."

"Wow—this is serious." Jill was half thrilled and half worried. "What are you going to tell Dale?"

"I don't know. I don't even know if I'm going to take it."

Jill couldn't believe her ears. How could Sarah not jump at the opportunity? Busby was right—Sarah was perfect for this assign- ment. Trying to not seem too indignant, she blurted out, "You have to take it!"

Sarah was unfazed and unsurprised by Jill's response. But it wasn't Jill's neck on the line. She remained calm. "Listen, I know I should—but I have a history with that type of fighting and some old wounds I don't want to reopen. Plus, Dale was looking forward to me settling into more routine police work and being around more." "I understand all of that, Sarah. But not only is this a huge case, you could so some real good for this city—and the women in it. Think about it. If another anonymous young woman gets pulled from the river, you're going to hate yourself. You know it."

She wasn't wrong. Sarah's sense of duty and honor made her feel drawn toward doing what was right, even if it wasn't the most convenient thing for her at the time.

Before Sarah could formulate any type of response, the car pulled up in front of her house. She looked over at her friend and partner and simply said, "I know you're right, Jill. Have a good night."

This was not the most satisfactory or definitive answer for Jill, who was still unsure of Sarah's answer as she watched her get out of the car. But she knew to not press it. Neither one of them was in the mood to continue the conversation anyway. She was confident that her partner would make the right call. Jill gave Sarah a reassuring nod as she shut the door and walked to her house.

Jill pulled away and headed home herself, hoping that her husband made the pot roast that she thawed out that morning and that her little beagle, a three-year-old named Sniffer, didn't ruin it. That dog was a real rascal at times. Not that it was all his fault. Her hus- band, Peter, had a bad habit of leaving food uncovered on the table where Sniffer could get to it. *We shall see*, thought Jill, as she turned the corner and headed down the main road to get her home.

Sarah was still in her front yard. Looking through the bay window, she could see into the living room. Dale, a softly handsome man of thirty-one, was sitting at the computer. Looking at him click- ing around, she couldn't help but think that this is how they met— through a computer.

*****

"Time flies" may be a cliché expression, but that doesn't mean it isn't true. It had been almost four years since she first met Dale

Johnson. She was a rookie back then. Even before the budget cuts by the recent mayor, police were in short supply and the streets were crime ridden. Looking to shine up its image and encourage more women to join, the department assigned Sarah to plain clothes duty right after graduation. The bulk of her day was in dealing with domestic abuse and victims of assault and battery. The department thought it was important to have a woman's presence in a depart- ment where the majority of the complainants are women. Soon they found themselves with two— Sarah and Jill—who were naturally partnered together.

The daily grind of used, abused, and battered victims wore Sarah out. She felt more like a social worker than a cop. This gave her a lot of respect for social workers; plus, she thought, she at least had the power to do something about it as part of the police force. But when all someone witnessed day after day was the worst of human- ity— husbands punching their wives and wives attacking their hus- bands— it was easy to think that no relationship was ever any good or worth any time or effort. It put Sarah in a major funk.

Then one Sunday while visiting her parents, she was sitting at the kitchen table while they cooked a big meal. Her parents had always enjoyed cooking together. They were listening to her rattle on about some of her worst most recent cases while her father pre- pared some steaks and her mother put a salad together. Then in the middle of telling a tale about an awful woman who threatened her live-in boyfriend with battery acid in front of their four-year-old- daughter, she stopped. She took a good look at her parents. They were listening to her as she talked and nodded along to let her know they were listening, but neither one said a word—either to her or to each other.

Then it hit Sarah: they didn't speak because they didn't have to. After thirty-two years of marriage, they had their routine down pat. One did not have to constantly tell the other one what they were doing. They just knew. It was instinct, or an ingrained habit. All of the years of not just living together but *being* together had made them into one functional unit. They could go about the business of making dinner while focusing their attention on their daughter and not worrying at all about what the other one was doing. Her mother knew what her father was going to do before he did it, and vice versa. This revelation was quickly followed by another revelation: that relationships can be good. They can last. They can be worthwhile. Moreover, this was what she wanted too. She wanted to find that special someone to spend the next decades of her life with and get to a point with him where they know each other this well. It could be done.

When her parents asked her why she had stopped telling the story, she didn't reveal any of these thoughts. They came up too quickly and were too fresh in her head. She needed time to mull them over a bit more. Sarah just vaguely stated that she just thought of something and proceeded to conclude the story. Her parents rolled with it, as they were genuinely intrigued on what happened with the acid. Turned out that no one was hurt, but a rug and a wall got a lit- tle messed up. The woman was arrested for risk of injury to a minor and ordered to stay away from her daughter and boyfriend until her trial. Sarah figured that the woman would most likely get slapped on the wrist with some anger-management classes and/or community service, then that would be it.

Dinner with her parents was great, but Sarah couldn't wait to get home that evening. Her revelation about her parents made her feel like she had a new lease on life. On her car ride home, she was able to think clearly and decided to go on to a dating website to see who was out there. She heard of a couple of different ones but didn't want to spend too much money and wanted a site with a large database.

Sarah was living in a one-floor walk-up at the time. As soon as she got inside, she threw her keys and her purse on a nearby couch and immediately went to the corner of the living room where she kept her computer on a small desk. She fired it up, connected to the Internet, and started her search.

After looking into a few dating sites, she decided that the first one that came up in the search was the best one. It was called Spark and offered a new subscriber deal of a three-month subscription for thirty bucks—half the normal cost. *It's number one for a reason,* Sarah thought as she entered in her credit card information.

Her profile was a little harder to create. Sarah had never been much for English class and had a hard time describing herself. She decided to keep things basic in the word department and let her photos do the talking instead. Sarah dusted off a CD of old photos from her MMA days and uploaded a few, along with a few more recent ones. The newest one was a photo of her at the finish line of the police department's annual 5K run from a month ago. She was sweaty but looked good.

With that out of the way, it was time for Sarah to browse. She wasn't sure exactly what she was looking for, but she was sure that she would know it when she saw it. Her previous relationships, if they could be called that, as a teenager were superficial and short- lived. Her martial arts training always came first. Now Sarah wanted to find something deeper, more meaningful, and hopefully more permanent.

She spent the next three months dodging the men who were just looking for a hookup and concentrating on the more serious ones. She got into some messaging back and forth with some of them. Others went as far as a date or two. But the spark she was looking for—that the website touted—wasn't there with any of them.

Not one to give up so easily, Sarah reupped for another three months, this time paying full price. The very next day she found him. She had never seen him before, but his smile caught her attention right away. There was a sweet, borderline nerdy quality to him that she found appealing. The name next to the photo was just "Dale," and his profile seemed interesting enough. She thought they would click, so she sent him a "nudge" to show him she was interested while leaving some mystery.

The next morning when she checked her e-mail, she was noti- fied by the Spark website that she had a message waiting for her. Dale had responded to her nudge with one of his, and he wrote her a message complimenting her on one of her MMA photographs.

She wrote him back and the two hit it off via the Spark website messaging system. After about two weeks they decided to meet for drinks at a local watering hole that they both knew. Sarah walked in nervous and saw Dale was already there sitting at the corner of the bar. In spite of his cool, calm, and collected manner and easy smile, she could tell that he was nervous too. Her years of police work had given her a sixth sense about these things. He invited her to sit, and the next four hours, which went by as if it was four minutes, were and always will be one of the fondest memories of her entire life. When he worked up his courage to kiss her at the end of the night, she knew he was a keeper.

Standing in her front yard, looking into the window at Dale, Sarah thought back to their first encounter this night. She thought about all of the great times they have had since then, like their first Christmas together, celebrating birthdays, meeting each other's fam- ilies, getting Chinese when a downed power line left them with no electricity on an especially muggy night, and going to baseball games. They were both fans of the River Rats, the River City minor-league baseball team. The team was terrible and came in last place almost every year, but they always enjoyed the night out.

Things were serious with Dale. This was the man she planned to marry. Along with that, she was going to play it safer and not take on the riskier assignments if she could avoid it. Dale knew it was a police officer's duty to be in harm's way to some degree, but as he fig- ured it, she already risked herself enough for River City and someone else could take it from here.

*****

Sarah took a deep breath and walked through the door. Dale was so engrossed in what he was doing that he didn't hear the door open and close. Feeling flirty, Sarah snuck up behind him, put her arms gently around his shoulders, and kissed him on the cheek.

"Hey," she said playfully, "what are you looking at?"

Dale was soft and sweet, but he could be very serious. His focus was laser-like when he was deep in thought about something, and this was one of those times. He was very matter-of-fact in his reply. "Checking the schedule for the veterinary conferences coming to the area. It's been a while since I've attended one, and I like to stay current." Then, realizing that he was being a bit rigid, he looked at Sarah sympathetically and asked, "How was your night?"

Sarah could be matter-of-fact too, when she wanted to be. "We caught him."

Dale was hit with a jolt of enthusiasm. "You did? That's amazing! I'm happy to hear it!" He got up and gave her a big kiss. She could tell he wasn't feigning this enthusiasm or just being polite—he really meant it. Dale continued, "I worry about you so much when you do things like that."

Sarah appreciated the concern, but she hated the feeling that Dale was worrying about her every day. "It's my job," she stated coldly. That was the best tone to have, given the direction that this conversation was about to take.

Dale could sense something was off by her curt yet accurate response, but played along as if his hopes of her being done with dangerous assignments were coming to fruition. "I know it's your job, but I still worry. Does this mean you're done?"

"I don't know." She knew it wasn't the answer Dale wanted to hear. *Here we go*, she thought.

She was right. Dale did not want to hear such a wishy-washy answer. "You don't know? What do you mean you don't know? We talked about this." His disappointment was clear.

There was nothing for Sarah to do except give it to him right between the eyes. "Yeah, I know. But I caught another case. It's the River Murders case that's been on the news. It'll be deep cover so that means I'll need to be away for a little while."

Dale couldn't believe what he was hearing. "You're kidding, right? We're going to get married, start a family."

"We still can, Dale," Sarah replied as reassuringly as possible. "We can once you've settled into more routine detective work.

This undercover stuff is too dangerous. I can't take the thought of you surrounded by thugs and lowlifes day in and day out. People who would kill you if they ever found out—"

"That's not going to happen." Sarah cut him off. She didn't like where he was headed. Still, Dale couldn't let it go and he persisted.

"But it can happen!" He started to get excited but caught himself.

He continued more calmly, "You know it, and you know I hate it." Sarah wasn't taking this lying down. She refused to be guilt-tripped and made out to be the bad guy. "Well, what about you?" Dale was equal parts confused and taken aback by the question.

"What about me?"

"You say you want to be a family man, but we can't even get a dog." This wasn't the most brazen recrimination, but with Dale she knew it would strike a nerve, and it did.

"Oh Jesus, Sarah! Not this again."

"You're a veterinarian for Christ's sake! Why are you so against having a pet?"

"Because you're not around to help! I deal with animals all day, and I love it, but the last thing I want to do when I get home is take care of another animal all by myself. It'll burn me out. I need you here to help me, but you won't be if you're gone all the time. What kind of mother are you going to be if you're not even here?"

Dale was capable of recriminating jabs too. That last comment crawled right under Sarah's skin. She got defensive. "I'll be a good mother! I'll be good because I care. I care about you, and I care about us as a family."

"I need to see that," Dale said coolly. He knew he scored his point, and there was no reason to spike the ball.

"You know what else I care about?" "What?" Dale was genuinely interested.

"I care about this city. I care about the people in it. I care about the three girls who have turned up dead in the past two weeks. I care enough to go undercover and bring their killers to justice." Her voice was sure and steady as she spoke these words.

All she needs now is a cape and cowl, Dale thought to himself. "So that's it then? You're going to do this?"

"I have to."

"But you don't. You're not the only one—"

"I am. I am the only one." Sarah cut him off for the second time in the conversation. *Better not make this a habit,* she thought. Then she continued, "I'm sorry you don't like it. I'm sorry I have to leave for a bit. And I promise this will be the last time."

"I've heard that before."

"I promise," said Sarah, and she meant it. "I want to believe you."

"Then believe me—it's true."

Dale could see the sincerity in Sarah's expression. Still, he couldn't help but have at least some reservations. "I believe you mean it now. It's later I'm worried about."

"Don't be."

Dale knew she was being honest with him. He also knew that there was nothing he could do to talk her out of what she set her mind to doing. Sure, he knew he was being a bit selfish by ask- ing her to not take the assignment, but in his mind, she had done enough already. A little selfishness was justified. There was nothing further to say, so Dale didn't say anything. He just smiled and nod- ded, then turned around and went back to his computer. He put in some earbuds too and played music while he continued browsing where he left off.

Sarah felt dejected. As she turned around and walked upstairs, she replayed the conversation in her mind and thought about how it could have gone better, especially since she knew what his reaction would be. She could have stayed calmer or presented her reasons better. *Oh well,* she thought, *it's in the past now. All we can do is move forward and be better next time.*

CHAPTER 6

SARAH WENT TO her and Dale's room, sat on the bed, and untied her shoes. Her feet were throbbing since the shoes were still new and not completely broken in yet. A feeling of great relief bordering on euphoria washed over her as she took off one shoe, and then the other. Sarah casually tossed them in the closet. She'd move them to the back later since who knew when she'd need them again.

Pools of sweat had collected under the arms of her polyester shirt. The tank top and running tights were another story. Those were drenched, and she had to peel them off her body. The cool air of the room prodded her moist, exposed skin and gave her a chill. Sarah darted over to her closet and grabbed a bathrobe. More than anything else in the world, she wanted to feel clean.

She also wanted to feel warm. Sarah let the water run in the shower for two minutes before checking the temperature. She wanted it to be hot. Not only did she feel cleaner after a hot shower, she found the hot water relaxing for both her muscles and her mood. When the heat was where she wanted it to be and she couldn't see herself in the mirror because of it being completely fogged over, she knew it was time to get in. Sarah disrobed and hung the robe on a hook attached to the door. She removed her sports bra and thong panties, placing them in a small pile on the floor.

The feeling of comfort immediately swooped through Sarah as the hot water caressed her arm, then her shoulders, then her breasts, until finally she was completely under the spout. This was better than a soak in a hot tub for her. There were no more cares or worries for Sarah at that moment. No creeps stalking the streets, no murder- ers dumping bodies, no arguments with her fiancé—just Sarah and the calm, heavenly bliss of this much-needed shower.

Once she was sufficiently soaked, it was time to lather up. Sarah took her mesh bath sponge on a stick from off its hook on the shower caddy and grabbed a bottle of moisturizing bodywash. She squeezed the tube and poured out a bit more than necessary. This wasn't because she needed extra to clean herself. It was because she loved the scent so much. It was a new one she recently tried called coconut lime verbena that she was head over heels about. A mere whiff of the fragrance made her feel like she was relaxing on the beach on a trop- ical island—a place where she really wished she was right then. But short of that, the bodywash would have to do.

As Sarah was lathering up the sponge and lingering her nose over it to breathe in the sweet-citrus scent, she started to feel tension in her forehead. Then it got worse. Her temples started throbbing. It really hit hard when a sharp pain felt like it was splitting her head in two down the middle. Sarah was yanked out of her private ethereal plane and slammed back into the real world. The massive headache made Sarah drop the sponge. It was all over her cranium, down to the base of her skull, and into her neck.

Barely able to stand because of the agony, Sarah stumbled out of the shower. She made her way to the medicine cabinet with the fogged-up mirror and swung the door open. Among the perfumes, creams, and razors was a bottle of prescription pain medication. Her name was on the label along with instructions to take one pill as needed. Sarah popped the top and poured the pills into her hand. It was a generous pour—five came out. Sarah stared at them for a couple of seconds through pain-filled, squinting eyes. She considered popping them all. She hadn't had one of these headaches in a while, and the last time she had one it wasn't this bad.

Coming to her senses about taking so many pain pills, she put three back in the bottle. Two was still one more than the recom- mended dose, but she needed the extra. This pain was too much. Sarah popped the pills in her mouth with one hand and turned on the faucet with the other. She cupped her hands under the spout, slurped the water she collected, and swallowed the pills. After about thirty seconds she started to feel good again.

As the pain dissipated, Sarah thought about what could have possibly triggered the headache. Was it the bodywash? Sometimes fragrances can cause reactions. But she immediately dismissed the idea. She never had issues with fragrances before. Besides, she loved that scent too much to give it up without incontrovertible proof that it was the cause. It had to be the stress. After all, Sarah had a long night. She got into a fight, got pressure put on her by her lieutenant to take on a dangerous, stressful assignment, and to top it all off she had a blowup with her fiancé. The tension had gotten to her, simple as that, and the coconut lime verbena was not able to rescue her in time.

When Sarah felt good enough, she put her robe back on, grabbed her small pile of clothes from off the floor, and went back into the bedroom. She tossed her sweaty underwear into the hamper and chose some clean, fresh garments to relax and go to sleep in. The next best thing after a nice, hot shower after an evening like this was a good night's sleep.

As she finished putting her nightclothes on, she looked over at the bookcase in her room. It was mostly filled with Dale's veteri- nary manual and technical books. Sarah wasn't much of a reader, and Dale regarded fiction as a waste of time. But it wasn't the books that caught Sarah's eye; it was the three trophies sitting on top of the case, flanked on either side by pictures of their respective parents.

Sarah walked over to the case and read the engravings on the trophies. They all had her name on them and marked the year and tournament she had won during her time on a small, local mixed martial arts circuit. The trophy figures were of a woman mixed martial artist in full gear. They were nicely done and changed every year. The trophy from eight years ago had the figure in a fighting stance, the one from seven years ago had her delivering a roundhouse kick, and the one from six years ago had her ready to grapple. Sarah found a song her father used to play for her to psyche her up, "Undefeated" by Def

Leppard, blaring in her brain. She was subtly moving her body to the music, thinking of all of the good times with her dad— and the reluctant support of her mom who hated the violence of the sport but was still proud of her—when she heard a voice behind her say, "Reminiscing?"

Sarah whirled around, startled. She didn't hear anyone come up behind her. This fact was even more disturbing to her since her police training and years as a cop had given her an acute, eyes in the back of her head level of situational awareness. But her guard was down. Plus, it was only Dale, not some ax murderer.

"A little bit. Yeah." Sarah's rapid heartbeat got slower as Dale smiled at her and walked into the room. It was almost back to nor- mal rhythm by the time he got to the bed and sat down.

He looked at her sympathetically. "Listen, Sarah—about what I said earlier…"

"Just forget it." Sarah really didn't want to go at it again.

"No, I can't forget it. I know you'll make a great mother. I'm sorry I said that."

That was sweet. Sarah decided to volley back in kind. "I'm sorry about what I said too. I understand about the dog. Really, I do."

Dale appreciated the sentiment, but there were some things he had to get off his chest. "It's terrible that these girls are turning up dead. I know you can help. I just hate all of this undercover stuff. It's too dangerous, and it makes me anxious. There are other ways to track down whoever is responsible."

"But having me go undercover is the best way. And I swear, I'm done after this." Sarah sat down next to Dale on the bed. She gently took his hand in hers. She wanted to comfort him.

"Just be safe, okay?" he pleaded in a whisper. "I will," Sarah reassured him.

They kissed. As their lips first touched, it was soft and gentle. As the kiss continued it escalated into something deep, hot, wet, and passionate. Partially aroused, Dale broke off the kiss and put his lips next to Sarah's ear. He whispered, "I better make the most out of tonight if you're going to be gone for a while."

Sarah, herself aroused from the kiss, had her lips next to Dale's ear and whispered back, "Me too."

Dale was still in his clothes from the office. He unbuttoned his shirt and flung it off as Sarah unbuckled his belt and unzipped his pants. She could see the bulge in his boxer shorts. It was a sight she was familiar with and she knew he was only about halfway to full mast. Sarah knew just the thing to get him the rest of the way.

Dale removed his pants as Sarah removed her nightclothes, which comprised of a pair of shorts and a T-shirt. Since Sarah didn't wear a bra to bed, all that was left on her were the panties that she had only moments ago put on. Dale, getting even further excited, whipped off his undershirt and kicked off his boxers with reckless abandon. Completely naked and with his animal nature taking con- trol, this usually reserved man rushed at Sarah like a predator toward its prey.

Dale felt his favorite body part get harder as he ferociously kissed Sarah and played with her breasts. Sarah didn't have any complaints about him doing it either. It revved her engine too. Leaving one hand on her breast, Dale took the other and grabbed Sarah's ass. It was firm with just the right amount of flesh to grab and squeeze. He found it to be a major turn on. By this point, Dale was hard enough to enter Sarah—and she was ready too—but Dale preferred to take his time and do what he called "priming the pump."

Pressing her against him so she could feel how hard he was, Dale took his hand off Sarah's breast and moved it lower. He reached into her panties. His fingers sent rays of pleasure coursing through Sarah as he touched her clitoris. He then stuck his middle finger into Sarah's dripping wet and waiting vagina. Seconds later, he added his forefinger. He moved his fingers back and forth in unison, sending Sarah into the throes of ecstasy.

Dale could tell by Sarah's moaning that she was close to orgasm, so he finished the job. The sound of her moans of pleasure coupled with the thought of what a capable and fantastic job he was doing gave Dale a thrill. He was ready to pop off himself from all the excite- ment.

Sarah's panties almost ripped at the seam as Dale quickly and forcefully lowered them down her legs. Dale felt the warm wet spot that Sarah left on them just a moment before as he crumpled them up and tossed them away. By coincidence, they landed on top of the trophy with the roundhouse kicking figure.

The room felt like it was 120 degrees even though Dale and Sarah were both completely naked. The body heat each of them was giving off was intense. Sarah was red and still flushed from the orgasm she just had. But Dale didn't have his yet, and he wasn't about to show Sarah any mercy. Plus, he knew that she could take it. He climbed back on Sarah through her spread apart legs and entered her with his visibly throbbing penis. His thrusts were quick and deter- mined. There was still some aggression toward her that he had to let out. Sarah welcomed it as she moaned even louder than she did before.

After several good pumps, Dale came. Sarah felt the hot, sticky explosion inside of her. She could also feel him getting limper, but he kept pumping away. His orgasm may have been achieved, but he still wasn't done giving it to her. After ten or so extra pumps, Dale's member had all the consistency of a wet noodle. He wanted very much to make a woman orgasm twice in one lovemaking session—a goal he had been trying to achieve since sophomore year at college— and tried his best with Sarah. Not this time, though. He made her orgasm once, plus he gave her further pleasure on the way to achiev- ing his own orgasm, which was close, but no cigar. Sarah had heard of women who had never orgasmed—with a man anyway—and she thought of how terrible that must be. She felt sorry for those women. They were missing something wonderful.

Dale eventually gave up trying to get Sarah off again, and he rolled off her. Both were sweaty and exhausted. Dale all of a sud- den felt a chill. He got up and grabbed his T-shirt and boxer shorts. Sarah felt like she could use another shower, but she didn't feel like getting up. As she looked over at Dale putting his underclothes on, she saw her panties hanging from her trophy. Sarah smiled at this as she pulled the covers over herself and turned over on her side. She was ready for sleep.

Sleep came quickly, and Sarah slept deeply. Her dreams were vivid when her body was this relaxed. Normally this was a good thing. She mostly had happy dreams. But the stress and the pressure of her upcoming assignment gave her a dream that was most unwelcome.

In her dream, it was five years ago and Sarah was at her last mixed martial arts tournament. Her opponent was brute of a woman named Melinda Gomez. Everyone called her "Big Mel," and with her imposing frame and near-masculine musculature, it was easy to see why.

*****

Melinda was by all accounts a normal-looking baby girl. However, even as a child of elementary-school age, she was a noted tomboy who enjoyed roughhousing and competition more than she enjoyed playing with dolls or having pretend tea parties like her female peers.

The real change with Melinda came when she was twelve and hit puberty. That's when her body kicked up the release of testoster- one. She developed denser bones as well as bigger and stronger mus- cles than her female classmates. She also started getting peach fuzz on her lip and chin. Her parents took her to their family doctor since they were worried about her acne getting too severe. The doctor was less worried about the acne and more worried about Melinda's physical development. He thought that Melinda might have ovar- ian tumors that were blocking the production of female hormones, but tests and images came back negative. He couldn't explain it. Somehow a flip was switched in her body, and the testosterone was flowing through her.

The doctor gave her a benzoyl peroxide face wash and a topical cream for the problem spots. That, along with a strict moisturizing routine, got rid of the acne and kept her skin looking healthy. He also prescribed hormone-replacement therapy for Melinda. She had estrogen and progesterone pills to take daily. After a few months of taking the pills, the facial hair receded. Melinda also started getting her periods—a side of womanhood she could have lived without, but at least they were a reassuring sign that the pills were working.

No pills, creams, or washes could change Melinda's personality though. She still enjoyed sparring at her local boxing gym. She added to her skills by getting into judo. Then once Melinda learned that testosterone was the key to building muscle, she cut back on the pills by taking them every other day, then once every three days, while hitting the weights as hard as she could. By the time Melinda was eighteen years old, she was tough, buff, and had won multiple junior-league competitions in judo.

That was the age that she decided to turn professional and made herself known on the local MMA circuit—the same one as Sarah. Sarah, a champion herself for three years running, had heard the rumors of "Big Mel." She went to a fight of Melinda's to scope her out and was impressed at Melinda's skill and athleticism. She also couldn't help but be at least a little intimidated by Melinda's size. Still, she saw where the holes were in Melinda's game—the hun- gry eighteen-year-old fighter still had some skills that she needed to hone—and formulated a way to beat her at the championship where they would inevitably meet.

*****

Sarah's dream always started in the middle of that championship fight—Sarah's last MMA fight—with Melinda. It wasn't pleasant. Sarah was backed up to the fence, and Melinda was mercilessly pummeling her. Sarah had her guard up, but there wasn't much more she could take. Melinda stopped. Sarah thought it was a good opportunity to push Melinda away. She was wrong. Melinda popped her in the jaw with a left hook. Sarah tumbled to the ground and rolled on her back.

Melinda felt confident. She knelt behind Sarah and put her in a choke hold. She squeezed her sweaty, meaty right bicep along Sarah's throat and locked in the hold with her left arm. Sarah strug- gled for air. She knew that if she passed out then she would be done, and the championship would go to Melinda. She thought back to all of the stretching and warming up she did when taking karate. Sarah used to grow impatient at the warm-up and just wanted to get straight to the lesson. Right then, though, she was grateful for the stretching. It gave her enough flexibility to swing her right leg back with all of her might and kick Melinda in the nose with the bottom of her toes. Melinda relinquished her grip and cupped her nose in agony. When she looked at her hand, her palm was coated with blood.

The crowd couldn't believe what they just saw. They thought it was all over for Sarah. The arena erupted when Sarah delivered her surprise kick. Everyone was on their feet, cheering her on.

Sarah felt energized by the crowd's cheers. She recovered from the choke hold while Melinda was startled and nursing her nose. Both women got themselves together and stood up at the same time. Every eyeball in the audience was focused on them, in the octagon, staring each other down. The roar of the crowd was deafening. The excitement was so palpable it felt like it could be cut with a knife. Everyone was eagerly anticipating what was going to happen next.

Sarah charged at Melinda and delivered a dropkick. Melinda got forced back from the middle of the mat all the way to the fence. The entire cage rattled from the impact, and she collapsed to the mat. Wasting no time, Sarah rushed to her opponent and put her in an arm bar—a submission move that Sarah trained to perfection. Using it, she could cause excruciating pain. Opponents typically gave up in mere seconds after being caught in it.

Melinda, however, was no typical opponent. She was deter- mined to continue the fight and find a way to win. Yet all she could do was shriek and struggle. Sarah had no mercy—she tightened the arm bar and applied more pressure.

"Give up!" Sarah would never allow herself to take pity on an opponent, but she didn't want to torture anyone either.

Ever defiant and determined, Melinda screamed back, "Never!" Sarah could see tears starting to well in Melinda's eyes. She gave Melinda credit—she was tough. But this had to end. Sarah applied more pressure. There was an audible pop as Melinda's elbow joint dislocated. Melinda howled in excruciating pain. Sensing something was wrong, and more than a little disturbed himself, the referee broke them apart. He took Melinda off to one side to talk to her. Sensing it was over—there was no way Melinda could continue to fight with that injury—Sarah faced the crowd. She held up her arms in victory as the crowd gave their approval.

Big mistake. Melinda looked past the referee, who was asking her questions about her fitness to continue. She saw Sarah celebrate as if she won, but it wasn't over yet. The piercing discomfort of her injury melted away and was replaced by a white-hot rage. It bubbled inside of her, uncontrollable and relentless. With her good arm, she shoved the referee out of her way and charged at Sarah full speed. She was at Sarah in seconds, and Sarah was completely oblivious to what was happening behind her. As Melinda got to Sarah, she arched her good arm back and used her momentum to punch Sarah as hard as she could.

The punch landed on Sarah's neck, at the point where it meets the base of the skull. Sarah went flying headfirst into the fence, slam- ming into it with her forehead. Then she fell to the floor. After she hit the mat, she rolled over on to her side. By this point, the cheers of the crowd had turned to boos at Melinda and the cheap shot she gave to Sarah. All she could hear above the hissing and jeers of the crowd was the referee, understandably furious, admonishing Melinda. The last thing Sarah saw before she passed out was the look of smug sat- isfaction on Melinda's face.

Back in the bedroom, Sarah awoke from her dream. She was dripping with sweat, as if she was actually in the fight and not just dreaming about it. Looking over at Dale, who was on his side facing out, she could tell that he was still sound asleep. Relieved that her sweaty, terrible dream didn't bother her fiancé, Sarah rolled over to her side and stared at the green glow coming from the numbers on her alarm clock.

CHAPTER 7

THE NEXT MORNING, Sarah didn't even want to move. She went in and out of sleep for the remaining half of the night and did not again fall into the deep, restful sleep she so badly needed. She stayed in bed until her alarm went off. When it finally did, she was so annoyed that she slammed her hand down on the button. For a moment, she thought she broke it. A small part of her wished that she had.

Sarah packed a small bag to take with her while undercover. She was careful to only bring a few clothes and some necessities. No personal items and certainly nothing that could identify her as a cop. On assignments like these, she knew she'd have a per diem that she could tap into to buy food and whatever other items she needed.

Dale was halfway through with his breakfast—black coffee and oatmeal with blueberries and agave syrup—by the time Sarah got to the kitchen. She wasn't hungry. She just wanted the coffee, which smelled heavenly to her. Her brief moment of pleasure at the scent of the coffee wafting through the air was quickly derailed by Dale, who took one look at her and said, "Jesus, Sarah. You look like you got run over and dragged along a gravel road."

Not the most tactful statement a man has ever made to the woman he loves, but Sarah couldn't argue. She had a lousy night's sleep, and she knew that she must have looked like something the cat dragged in, chewed on for a bit, swallowed, and then spit out. In an attempt to keep the proceedings as polite as possible, she replied with a somewhat sarcastic "Good morning to you too."

"I mean it. Are you okay? Are you sure you're up for what you have to do?" Dale wasn't trying to be a jerk. He was legitimately concerned about her.

Sarah put on her best happy face. She didn't want him getting anxious on their last morning together for a while. "Yeah, I am. I just need some coffee and I'm good to go. It was just a bad dream."

Dale was relieved but still interested. "Bad dream? About what?"

"My last fight."

"I remember you told me about that. The one with a woman called Big Mel, right?'

"I turned my back on her for one second."

"It's not your fault she cheap-shotted you. If I remember correctly, you said she was banned for life for that."

"She was. That still doesn't change the fact that she gave me a concussion that left me with a head injury that gives me massive headaches."

Dale paused for a moment in thought. Then very seriously, he asked, "Sarah, does this dream have anything to do with your undercover assignment?" He was fishing, but he had a hunch.

"Well…" Sarah started hesitantly, "the lieutenant believes that the dead girls are linked to some kind of underground fight ring. He wants me to pose as a fighter to infiltrate the ring, and gather evidence on a case against Leo Manetti, who we think is responsible for their deaths."

Dale wasn't expecting to reel in anything at all, and now he hooked a big fish. "Manetti? As in the mob family?" He suddenly understood why this is the first he was hearing of this little detail. Dale had heard the stories all of his life—some true, some partially true, and some completely made up—about the Manetti family's notorious dealings in River City. The only thing that helped him determine fact from fiction was the notion that the more horrific the story was, the more likely it was to be true.

There was no point in Sarah trying to hide or sugarcoat the truth. She gave Dale a nod. Before he could say anything else, she reached out and grabbed his cheek. It was soft and smooth. He just shaved that morning and she caught the faint, fading scent of his aftershave as she moved in closer to him. She looked at him lovingly. As they locked eyes, she whispered, "I know this is dangerous, but as long as I know I have you here, I know I'll be all right. You don't have to worry about me at all. Rest easy. You'll see me again before you know it." Sarah kissed him softly on the lips. She wasn't just saying things to make him feel good. She meant it. "Then after this is over, I am done."

Dale could feel anxiety start to swell in him. He looked away. Sarah sensed it. "Look at me." Her voice was forceful and commanding. Dale complied. He'd never seen his fiancée so serious. Sarah caressed his other cheek with her other hand. With his head held gently in her hands and using the same forceful tone of voice, she reiterated: "I am done."

The police station was busier than usual when Sarah reported for duty at 8:30 a.m. Perhaps her arrest of the River City Rapist inspired other officers to get more serious and make more arrests. She stroked her ego with the thought for a few seconds, then let it go. It was probably just a coincidence.

Sarah's first stop was over to where she and Jill shared a desk. She knew she left Jill hanging the previous night and felt bad about it. On Sarah's way in there was a delicatessen that made terrific bagels. There was nothing better than getting them while they were fresh and hot. Sarah stopped there for breakfast for herself. She kept it simple, just an everything bagel with butter. Sarah loved the way the butter melted into the air pockets of the hot bagel. While there she got Jill's favorite—a pumpernickel bagel with cream cheese, lettuce, tomato, and extra Nova lox. It was expensive but worth it. After all, she didn't want any bad feelings with her partner, especially since Jill would be her only contact with her normal life.

As expected, Jill was at her desk and staring blankly at her screen. Sarah approached from the side, and Jill didn't even notice her until Sarah was right next to her and plopped the bag with the bagel on her desk. Sarah had sometimes seriously wondered about Jill's peripheral vision, but she didn't feel like busting her chops about it.

Jill's trance was broken the instant the bag hit her desk. She knew what it was. She could smell it. She also knew why it was being given to her. "Taking the undercover assignment, huh?"

Jill's a top detective for a reason, Sarah thought sardonically. It was time to be serious, though. "Yup. I'm going to Busby's office after seeing you to let him know. I'm ready to go if you are."

Half of Jill's excitement in that moment was from hearing the good news. The other half was from the bagel. She removed it from the bag and unwrapped it ritualistically. Holding the bagel up with both hands and examining it, she spouted off, "I am" before taking a bite. Her eyes never moved to Sarah. They stayed fixated on the bagel. This did not mean she wasn't interested in her friend, partner, and bagel bringer though. "How did Dale handle the news?" she politely inquired between bites.

"He hates it but understands why I have to do it." Sarah was equal parts amused and dismayed at how such a long, complicated, and difficult conversation with her fiancé could be so accurately boiled down into one simple sentence.

This was finally enough to get Jill to move her concentration away from her bagel and on to Sarah. "He'll be fine Sarah, don't worry." She would have been more reassuring if she didn't have a spot of cream cheese on her upper lip, but Sarah appreciated the gesture. "Are you okay handling things on your own with that fat idiot and whatever mouth breather they give him from the Public Defender's office?" This was more than a much-needed change of subject. Sarah truly wanted to make sure that her partner was okay holding down the fort while she was away.

Jill pointed to her screen. "I was actually just rereading the report before submitting. It's due on Busby's desk by 9:00 a.m. You want to look it over?"

Sarah shook he head. "Nah, I'm good. Thank you."

Jill grinned. She knew what the answer was going to be. Sarah was more a woman of action than of letters and words.

Sarah continued, "Speaking of Buzz, I'm heading over right now to let him know that it's a go." She took a few steps back and, just before turning to walk away, said jovially, "Enjoy your breakfast." She couldn't resist.

"You bet I will." As her partner walked off, Jill turned her attention back to the bagel and took another big bite.

Sarah stepped softly when approaching Busby's office and gave the door a gentle rap. She knew she had a fifty-fifty shot of him being in a good mood this early in the morning and didn't want to do anything to aggravate him. "Come in" came the reply to her knock. Relieved that he sounded like he was in a good mood, Sarah turned the knob and entered.

The office looked the same as it did yesterday, even with all of the hullabaloo happening in the station. She thought that more arrests would have made the case files in his office go down at least a bit. Then she thought better. She'd been around long enough to know that the wheels of justice turned slowly in River City, if they turned at all—and when they weren't turning in reverse. In spite of how he sounded a moment ago, Busby looked like he could use some good news. So she gave it to him.

"Just came in to tell you I'm accepting the undercover assignment." Sarah said it all in one breath, as if she had to get the words out fast or they wouldn't come out at all.

Busby betrayed no emotion, then said, "Great, I figured you would."

I guess I didn't leave him in as much suspense as I thought, Sarah mused to herself.

Busby opened the top drawer of his desk, grabbed what was on top, and tossed it toward Sarah. It was a license with Sarah's picture on it, but nothing else was accurate to her personal information.

He continued, "Here's your new ID, and requisitions can give you the car and the address of the apartment we rented for you. I'll hold your badge until this is all over."

Sarah plopped down her River City PD badge and ID, then picked up the license. She gave it a look over. The picture they used wasn't her best one. Busby clearly pulled it from a police-league bowl- ing night from a year and a half ago when Sarah had a little bit too much to drink. She bowled a 190 that night, though—the closest she had ever come to breaking 200—so there might have been some- thing to it. When she was studying martial arts, Sarah had heard of drunken fighting. Why not drunken bowling?

The only thing that really bothered her was the name. "Sarah Connor. Really, Chief?"

Busby threw his hands up in the air. He clearly wasn't in the mood for any grief, and she was in danger of pushing his buttons. "It was all I could think of at the time, and I just blurted it out, okay? If anyone asks, tell them your parents were big *Terminator* fans."

"All right, will do." Sarah knew better than to press any further. She needed to save her strength for the day ahead anyway. Then she decided to look on the bright side. "At least my first name is still Sarah."

"That's a very positive attitude—I like it," Busby said while nodding his head. "I figured it's easier for you to remember." He paused for a few seconds, searching for anything else he needed to say. After arriving at nothing, he broke the silence. "DiGrazio is wait- ing for you in Interrogation Room A. Now go…and good luck."

"Thanks, Lieutenant." Sarah pocketed her new license and left her boss to his piles of paper.

Interrogation Room A was one of three interrogation rooms at the station. While all of the rooms were the same, lined up one after the other, Sarah liked Interrogation Room A the least. There was a creepy vibe to it that gave her the chills. Perhaps because it was the room where a local maternity-ward nurse once confessed to mur- dering newborn infants in her care and blaming it on sudden infant death syndrome. Or perhaps it was because it was the room where a white-collar criminal— brought in to answer some routine questions about an embezzlement investigation at his firm—tried to commit suicide by grabbing a pen from the interviewing office and stabbing himself in the neck with it. Rumor has it that while he missed his carotid artery, he did hit the bone and almost paralyzed himself. Or maybe it was because this same room was where a twenty-year-old street punk, suspected of a murder in his neighborhood, attacked the veteran cop conducting the interview and in a frenzy of rage, started gnawing on the officer's face. Whatever the reason, she hated the angry vibes in that room and hated having to go in there. Still, it was her job and Vinny DiGrazio was waiting.

Sarah was a bit taken aback when she entered the room, but it wasn't from the room itself and its past history. It was from Vinny. He was not at all what she expected. He was a scrawny, pale, greasy-looking guy in his midtwenties with mussed-up hair. "Vinny DiGrazio?" she asked, wanting to make sure they put the right guy in the room.

Vinny looked up at her, relieved that someone had finally come into the room to talk to him. He had been sitting there only ten minutes, but it felt like an hour. "That's me." His throat was dry, and he could barely get the words out.

Time for introductions then, Sarah thought. "I'm Officer Sarah Kolchek. I hear you want to cooperate with us in our investigation of the River Murders. Is that right?"

Vinny shrunk in his seat. He looked like he was trying to get physically smaller, as if he could disappear from the room and Sarah wouldn't see him anymore. "Yeah, about that. I…don't know."

Sarah was in no mood for games. This had to move forward regardless if this little weasel wanted it to or not. "Well, it was your tip-off under questioning yesterday that's the reason I'm here. It's also the reason you are here in an interrogation room talking to me right now and not sitting in a jail cell, where, frankly, I think you belong."

"It's just that if Mr. Manetti ever finds out—"

"Which Manetti? Mike, or his son Leo?" Vinny just said the magic word "Manetti," and Sarah didn't care about letting him finish his sentence.

"Either one! Listen, I could be in some major trouble here!"

"You're already in some major trouble, Vinny! So you better get real friendly real fast and start talking, or the trouble you're in is going to get a whole hell of a lot worse. Capisce?"

At that moment, Sarah realized that she had not yet sat down. She was bearing down hard on Vinny, and he was clamming up. This was no good. She needed his cooperation for her assignment to go anywhere. It was hard playing both good cop and bad cop, but she'd have to give it a try. She took a deep breath and sat down slowly. Looking over at Vinny, she almost felt sorry for him and the predicament he was in. Then she remembered why he was there. That helped.

Trying a new approach, Sarah looked Vinny square in the eye and asked, "What's the connection between the Manetti Crime Family and these girls?"

Not a question Vinny wanted to answer. He hunched over and looked down. This was not the response Sarah wanted. She tried coaxing him out of his silence with the same soft touch she used to get women to open up about the abuse they'd been through. "Don't stare at your shoes, Vinny. The answer isn't down there. Look at me."

As if he didn't hear her—or worse, was ignoring her—Vinny kept staring down. Sarah found this intolerable. This wasn't like dealing with a battered woman who was afraid to talk; this was like dealing with an obstinate child who refused to talk. It was time to get more forceful.

"Look at me!" Sarah slammed her hand on the table as she yelled.

Vinny risked getting whiplash from picking his head up so fast. "All right. Jesus. I'm looking at you!"

"Good! Now tell me about the connection between the Manettis and the three dead girls."

"Okay, okay—" Vinny was starting to realize he had no choice.

Sarah wasn't going to let him off easy. He had to help her.

Sarah pressed the point. "Part of your deal is that you help me, Vinny."

"Right, right, okay!" Vinny held his hands up defensively. His instincts from past similar experiences told him that Sarah was on the brink of slugging him. He wasn't wrong, but Sarah was a better cop than to do something like that.

"Now talk," Sarah said. She was no nonsense, and she meant it so he knew he better do it.

"It's this club uptown. Leo Manetti owns it. It's called Amazon Glory." Vinny started to hesitate.

"Go on," said Sarah. Her voice was encouraging. She needed to get him to want to tell his story. She certainly wanted to hear it.

Vinny started spilling the beans. "The front part of it is a bar and nightclub, it's all Amazon rain forest themed. But in the back is where the VIPs go. There's gambling back there, but the main attrac- tion is the fight ring—the octagon."

"Who fights in this octagon?"

"Girls," came the matter-of-fact, one-word reply from Vinny. "Just girls?" inquired Sarah.

"Yeah. It's all girls—like the Amazons, get it? It's part of the theme. Leo has this thing for really toned, athletic women…and he likes watching them pummel the crap out of each other, I guess."

"How long has this been going on?"

"About three months. Girls fight for a cut of profit with Leo. They get paid based on how well they do in a bracket. Then Leo says he will pay one hundred thousand dollars to anyone who can beat Claudia—"

"Claudia?"

"Yeah, she's Leo's girlfriend and she kind of comanages the place with him." Vinny leaned in close to Sarah. "She's the one who's been killing the girls in the fights. She's brutal, takes things too far." He whispered as if they weren't in a police interrogation room and had to worry about eavesdroppers. But it felt good. Vinny felt like a load had been lifted from his shoulders. It was done and that was that. No taking it back now. He was in this for the long haul.

Sarah was now in it for the long haul too. More than that, she was officially intrigued. "Sounds like someone I want to meet. Can you take me there?"

Vinny had nothing to lose anymore. He shrugged his narrow shoulders and said, "Sure. When?"

Sarah was quick and blunt with her response. "Now."

CHAPTER 8

CLAUDIA SZABO WAS the one-and-only daughter of Karol and Adele Szabo, immigrants from Slovakia. Karol and Adele used to joke that Claudia was multinational, since she was conceived in late 1992 in what was then Czechoslovakia. She developed in her mother's womb in the country of Slovakia, then on July 3, 1993, she was born. As the American adults used to tell Claudia while growing up, she was "almost a firecracker."

Karole and Adele settled in a largely Eastern European community in River City. The neighborhood was full of ethnic Slavs, Poles, Czechs, Hungarians, Romanians, Croatians, and Russians. All were welcome, and it gave these new Americans a sense of familiarity in this strange new land they chose to call home. Early enough in the morning, the smell of paczki from the Polish baker filled the air. The Hungarian butcher became so well known around the city that there was a two-hour line around the block just for his *szalonna*. It got to be so crowded that Mr. Meszaros, the head butcher who always seemed underdressed unless he was wearing a bloody apron, decided to take preorders only. Call a day in advance, and he would have your order ready for pickup after noon the next day.

Karol and Adele very quickly discovered that while America was the land of opportunity, you had to work for it. There were no free handouts here. But put in the time, do the work, and the rewards will come. That's what they believed.

Young Claudia got a different message growing up. She saw her father work twelve-hour days at the local furniture factory for just enough pay to barely scrape by, even after he was promoted to shift supervisor. She watched as her mother ran herself ragged working at a dry cleaner's, preparing dinner, and spending what little time she had with her family until it was time to go to bed and do it all over again. Claudia's parents barely had any time for her growing up. She was left on her own a lot after school because her parents couldn't afford daycare. When Claudia was younger, she would stay indoors and watch TV. But as she got older, she became more interested in what was happening outside of the walls of the two-bedroom apart- ment she lived in with her parents.

Starting at age fourteen, she ventured out more after school. It was a strange time to be out and about. All of the responsible adults were at work. Most of the kids were either doing after-school activities—none of which interested Claudia—or were in their homes. Only certain types of kids—street kids with no supervision, like her—were out on the streets.

It was on these streets growing up that Claudia soon discovered a new way of living, and a lifestyle that set her on track to avoid the daily grind that ensnared her parents. One day she bravely ventured to the Italian neighborhood five blocks away. She was famished by the time she got there. Her lunch was light that day—just a salad and some water—and the walk worked up an appetite. Her parents would occasionally pick up pizza from Paisano's in this neighbor- hood. She decided to stop by there for a slice.

It wasn't just the pizza that she was there for. She liked the two guys behind the counter—she overheard once that they were college roommates who bought the business together—and enjoyed flirting with them. Of course, she was too young for them, plus they were both engaged, but she did it anyway. At the very least, it was good practice. She became a regular at Paisano's, which delighted the two proprietors but irritated Maria and Tina, two girls from the neigh- borhood who were the same age as Claudia.

Maria and Tina never said anything to Claudia, finding it better to passive-aggressively scoff at her from afar. Claudia's parents were scraping by, so Claudia was never dressed in the most fashionable clothes or had expensive jewelry, something the comparatively middle-class girls teased her about endlessly to themselves.

This went on for two years with Claudia venturing to the Italian neighborhood at least twice a week for an after-school slice and Maria and Tina making fun of her. As time went on, Maria and Tina got bolder, ridiculing Claudia while sitting at a table right next to her. They thought Claudia couldn't hear them, but she could. As shallow and stupid as the girls' comments were, they filled Claudia with a white-hot rage she had never felt before. The unfairness of it all bothered her the most. It wasn't her fault that her parents couldn't afford fashionable clothes or fancy jewelry. They worked hard and did their best.

One day, instead of heading straight home after her slice, Claudia waited outside Paisano's for Maria and Tina. Her rage bub- bling inside of her from head to toe, Claudia stepped in front of Maria and Tina as they exited Paisano's, blocking their path down the sidewalk.

"I heard what you two were saying about me in there." Claudia was barely keeping herself composed by the time she got these words out.

"You shouldn't eavesdrop," said Maria defiantly.

"Yeah. Nosy bitch," said Tina snootily as she forced her way by Claudia, knocking into her shoulder.

That lit the fuse. Claudia turned around and jumped on Tina's back, taking her to the ground. Maria immediately grabbed Claudia and pulled her off. Claudia stomped on Maria's foot as hard as she could. Maria let go of Claudia to attend to her throbbing foot, but by then Tina had gotten up off the sidewalk. She grabbed Claudia's hair. Tina had been in situations like this before, and at most she expected Claudia to scratch at her arms or kick at her shins. What she didn't know was that Claudia was no ordinary girl. She fought through the pain of getting her hair pulled, reared her right arm back, and socked Tina in the jaw with a right hook.

Tina had never felt anything like it in her life. She'd been scratched and bitten and had her own hair pulled—but she'd never been punched.

It stung for an instant and then settled into a dull pain. As if the punch wasn't rough enough, Claudia aimed higher with her kick. It didn't land on Tina's shin; it caught her between the legs. Tina's Catholic schoolgirl skirt and white tights offered no pro- tection from such a devastating blow. A streak of pain shot through her, from her groin to her throat. She would not have been surprised if she coughed up an ovary right there on the sidewalk.

Seeing her opponent as a quivering mass of pain in a plaid skirt did little to satisfy Claudia. She was on fire, and as far as she was concerned, she was just getting started. Claudia delivered two kicks to Tina's ribs before Maria's foot felt well enough so she could stand on it. Maria dove toward Claudia, trying to tackle her to the ground. It didn't work. Claudia was too powerful and too angry. Maria might as well have tried to tackle a telephone pole. Instead of going down, Claudia stood up as stubborn as can be, wailing on the Maria's back and head with her fists. It was between the fourth and fifth blow that Maria let go and hit the ground. Seeing a great opportunity to dole out some more punishment—and not feeling the least bit tired— Claudia got on her knees and was about to continue her assault when she heard a voice call out, "Oh! What are ya doin'?"

Claudia looked up and saw a well-tanned young man, no more than a few years older than her, with slicked back hair and wearing a freshly pressed, perfectly tailored suit, get out of a black Cadillac and walk toward her. He was followed close behind by a large, well-dressed, gorilla-looking man. Claudia stopped herself with the sound of his voice. It took her by surprise—she didn't see the car pull up. Maria and Tina took notice as well. They stood up as best as they could while nursing their respective injuries.

When the man got close, he towered over the three girls. The gorilla-looking man stayed about five feet back, looking around for any nosy passersby. "What the hell is going on here?" demanded the man.

Before Claudia could say anything, Tina interjected, "She jumped us!"

The man shot a glance at Claudia. His stare was cold. It felt as if it pierced through her. She could barely talk. All she could do was shake her head no.

The man looked over to Maria, who was doubled over in pain, taking deep breaths. "Maria, what happened here?"

"Nothing," Maria barely eked out.

"Nothing?" said the man. "This doesn't look like nothing to me. Come on, Maria. I knew your brother until he got sent away. Be honest. What happened?"

"I don't know," said Maria. "It all happened so fast."

The man looked at Tina. "What about you, Tina? I remember your sister. She's married now, right?"

"She just had her first kid—a boy," Tina said respectfully. "Well, what would she say right now if she saw you fighting

in the street? What kind of example is that for an aunt to set for her little nephew?"

"I don't know," said Tina sheepishly.

"You don't know. Neither one of you seem to know anything. Here's what I know though…" He squared up to Claudia and looked at her. Claudia thought her eyes were deceiving her. It looked like he was beaming. He continued, gesturing to Claudia with his hands, "I know that this girl just kicked the ever-loving crap out of the two of you." He paused, smiling, then carried on, "And I know that you two are no pushovers. Look at Bruno back there," he said, pointing to the gorilla-looking man. "He's scared to go near you two for fear of getting his head cracked open with one wrong word." Bruno knew he was kidding, so he took the man's verbal jab with a smirk and a nod. The man continued on about Claudia. "You got backbone, kid. What's your name?"

Claudia, relieved that she was getting complimented instead of a dose of her own medicine, answered quickly, "Claudia."

"Claudia." That's a sweet name. "You're pretty tough, Claudia, you know that?"

"Thanks" came the reply. Claudia had never thought about her toughness one way or the other.

"I like it. You come here often?"

"A couple times a week. I like to get a slice after school now and then. It's all I can afford with the allowance from my parents."

This piqued the man's interest. "How would you like to make some real money?

"Sure."

"Come back on Monday, I'll have a job for you. You see, I'm buying Paisano's from these guys, and I'm sure I could use an extra hand in the kitchen or with the tables. Sound good?"

Claudia was thrilled. This was her chance to earn her own money and to let her parents keep what they earn. "Yeah, this sounds great to me. Thank you."

"You're welcome." The man turned to Maria and Tina. "I want you girls working for me too. You two clearly need to be off the streets." He gave all three girls a look once over and concluded with "And I want the three of you to all get along." Then he smiled and focused on Claudia. "Or at the very least, you gotta respect Claudia here. She's the toughest and strongest out of the three of you. Don't mess with her. She can handle herself, that's for damn sure."

Claudia smiled back. She was speechless. The man pointed to Maria and Tina. "All right you two, get outta here." They turned around and left the instant he said it. He then pointed to Claudia. "And you, I'll see you on Monday."

"Okay." Claudia turned and started to talk away, then stopped herself. "Wait! When I come back on Monday, who should I ask for?"

The man pointed to himself and said coolly, "Ask for me." "And who are you?"

The man betrayed a slight hint of disappointment as his smug, self-satisfied smile dipped a little bit, then he let her know, "I'm Leo. Leo Manetti."

"Okay, thank you." Claudia waved goodbye and walked away

as Leo and Bruno entered Paisano's. On her way home she thought about how she'd miss flirting with the guys behind the counter. Then she remembered that she had a job—her own money—lined up for Monday. The thought of earning her own paycheck made the disappointment of not seeing the guys again melt away.

Claudia worked hard at Paisano's. She had just enough time between the end of school and the start of her shift to get her homework done, but she always felt like she was rushing through it because she couldn't wait to get to work. Her studies were a distraction. What she really cared about was making money, and she was good at it. She waited tables, prepared salads and desserts, and made good tips. Leo was in and out a lot. When he was there, he spent most of his time in a private back room that only he—and a few trusted associates, like Bruno—were allowed into.

One night after closing, Claudia's curiosity got the better of her. She'd worked there part-time for over a year. She was planning on staying there and going full-time after she graduated high school in the coming spring. She knew that Leo liked her, and it wouldn't be a problem. The only thing that bothered her about the idea of staying on was that back room. If she was going to feel comfortable working there, she needed to know what was in it. The problem was getting in—the door was locked at all times.

Locked though it may be, it was just a simple wooden door with a simple knob. She saw in a movie once that locks like that could be picked with a credit card. This was actually Claudia's motivation to get her first credit card when she turned eighteen. Secondary factors were that she was earning her own money and wanted to increase her buying power. Her primary motivation was that she wanted to get through that door.

One night after closing, Claudia locked the front door to the restaurant and turned off all of the lights except for one in the kitchen. This allowed her just enough light to see what she was doing. She had just received the credit card in the mail the day before, and it was still in the envelope in her purse. She took the envelope out, ripped it open, and removed the brand-new credit card. After pick- ing bits of gunked-up glue from off the back of the card, she slid it into the side of the door and jiggled it around like she saw in the movie. It didn't work. She tried again, this time pushing more forcefully on the card. She could see it bending under the pressure, but she didn't care, she wanted in. It still didn't work. She tried one more time, forcing the card in with all of her might while giving the door a shove with her other arm. She put all of her strength into the endeavor. Then *bam!*—the door flew open and Claudia tumbled in after it.

After Claudia got up and dusted herself off, she found a light switch and flipped it. The room was small, and all she noticed at first was a round table with two chairs parked under it. Then she looked across the room and focused on the shelves in the back. Her jaw dropped when she realized what she was looking at. It was the stockroom of a drug store—only the illegal kind, not the local pharmacy. She moved in closer and examined the contents of the shelves. Marijuana, cocaine, heroin, crystal meth, LSD, and PCP— anything you could think of, it was all here. Claudia had never done drugs and wasn't interested in them, but she knew the seriousness of what she stumbled upon and knew she had to get out of there. She rushed to the light switch, turned it off, and then headed for the exit. She backed out of the room and carefully closed the door behind her, making sure it was shut all the way. She tested the knob to make sure it locked properly. It did—thank goodness. Relieved, Sarah turned around and bumped her head right into Bruno's big, broad, barrel chest.

Bruno did not look happy. He grabbed Claudia by the shoul- ders and dragged her over to a table. Never one to appreciate being manhandled, the thought crossed her mind to knee him in the nuts and make a run for it. Then her better senses come through and she realized that Bruno knew who she was, where she worked, and where she—and her parents—lived. It would only slow him down, not pre- vent her from getting caught. Plus, it struck her that he was the kind of guy who would just get angrier if she tried something like that, though it was hard to imagine him being any angrier than he already was. His face was red and his eyes were bloodshot. He wanted to kill her, but he didn't. Instead, when they got to the table, Bruno pointed to a chair and growled, "Sit!"

Claudia complied. He leaned over and got in her face. "Don't move!" Claudia could smell the traces of whiskey on his breath. Not only was he angry and wanted to kill her, he was drunk. Claudia knew better than to push her luck. She sat quietly as Bruno walked away and went to the phone on the wall. She knew he was calling Leo, which meant she was in big trouble. When Bruno was done with the call, he sat in a chair across the restaurant, by the front door. He just stared at her, not saying a word. Claudia knew better than to even try to make conversation. Instead, she stared down at the credit card in her hand. Her forced entry into the room had bent the edge pretty good. *I hope I can still swipe it like this,* she thought to herself.

After about ten minutes that seemed like thirty, Leo arrived. He didn't look happy, but he certainly looked less furious than Bruno. He walked over to the table with Claudia and sat down. Bruno stayed put, still staring at her.

"So you've had a busy evening," Leo said casually. Claudia was mildly relieved that his breath didn't have a trace of whiskey on it.

Claudia figured the best strategy was to humble herself and throw herself at his mercy. Maybe she'd just get off with a beating. She could take a beating if she had to take one. She started, "Mr. Manetti—"

"Leo. You know you can call me Leo. Please." His charming smile when he said this shot a streak of bone-chilling fear up Claudia's spine. It seemed out of place, and she didn't like it.

Barely managing to keep her composure, Claudia carried on, "Leo…I am so, so, so sorry. I have no idea what I was thinking. It was really stupid of me. Please, just let me go and I promise I'll forget everything I saw and this will never happen again."

"Let you go? I *should* kill you, you know that?" Leo's smile was gone. Claudia felt like all of the blood was being drained out her body. She felt weak, like she was going to faint. Her breathing started to get heavy as her head got lighter and lighter.

Leo saw that she wasn't handling this well. He called over to Bruno. "Hey, Bruno, quick—get her something will ya? Maybe grab a bottle of water and some garlic knots. This girl is about to pass out on us."

Bruno moved as fast he could to the kitchen. He came back seconds later with a tray of the requested items. Leo grabbed the water bottle and opened it for Claudia as she sat up and grabbed a garlic knot. She devoured it greedily and swiped the water form Leo's hand to wash it down.

"Feel better?" Leo at least looked like he was legitimately concerned.

"Yeah," came the reply, partially muffled by a mouthful of garlic knot.

"Good," said Leo, pausing for a brief moment and then continuing, "I think you missed the operative word in my sentence. I said I should kill you. I didn't say I was gonna do it."

"Are you?" asked Claudia nervously. If this was it, she wanted to know already. The suspense was too much to bear.

Leo thought for a couple of seconds, then finally said, "No." Waves of relief poured over Claudia. Then he carried on, "Killing you would be a waste. You're pretty, you're tough, you're good with the customers...and I like you. I liked you ever since the day I saw you kicking the crap out of Tina and Maria."

Claudia didn't know what to say. She looked up at him and smiled.

Leo smiled back, then he laid it on her. "Listen, how about we forget this whole thing. As a matter of fact, to show that there are no hard feelings, how about I take you out to dinner tomorrow."

The invitation made Claudia feel a combination of nervous and flattered. She wasn't sure if she should take him up on it. She was also smart enough to know that even though Leo phrased it like a question, he wasn't really asking. Then it occurred to her. "I have to work tomorrow. It's Friday, and I have the dinner shift. We're open for an extra two hours, and the tips make a difference for me." She looked at him pleadingly while she spoke, hoping he'd understand.

Leo did understand. He just didn't care. He'd dreamed about working his way into Claudia's panties since he first laid eyes on her, and he wasn't letting this excuse fly—not in a restaurant that he owned. "That's not a problem, Claudia. Everyone works on Friday, and we have enough coverage. Maria and Tina and everyone else will manage. And I'll give you double the tips you'd earn plus I'll pay you for the shift even though you didn't work it." It's like he had the answer ready and waiting for her.

Claudia's eyes lit up at the money she'd earn. "You can do that?" "Sure, I can do anything. I own the place, remember?" Claudia thought about it. It was only one dinner, one night.

What was the harm?

Never a patient man, Leo pressed her. "So how 'bout it?"

Claudia finished weighing the pluses and minuses in her head and finally said, "Okay. Let's do it."

The next evening, Claudia was nervous about letting her parents know who she was having dinner with that night. They'd never met Leo, but they knew he was a member of the Manetti crime family, and they were already apprehensive about her working at Paisano's. She told them she was just seeing some friends from school and hav- ing a much-deserved Friday night out after working so hard on so many of them. She gave them both a kiss before she put on her jacket and went outside. Leo said he would pick her up at six, and it was almost time.

The car was already waiting for her when she got outside. Leo had a reputation for punctuality and did not disappoint. He was seated in the back seat of his black Cadillac. Standing on the sidewalk and opening the door for her was Bruno, who made no effort to hide his contempt for her as she made her way to the car. Feeling brave and deciding to not let him get to her, she smiled as she got in the car and gave him a "Thanks, big guy." She was barely seated when he slammed the door behind her.

The ride to the restaurant was full of the usual mundane first- date chitchat. Leo complimented Claudia on how great she looked, then spent the rest of the ride nervously cracking jokes to put her at ease. She returned the favor by nervously laughing at everything he said.

Bruno was ready to shoot the both of them by the time they got to the restaurant. There was only so much he could take. He thanked God for His mercy as he pulled up to the restaurant and got out to open the door. Normal etiquette was to offer the lady a hand getting out, but he extended no such courtesy to Claudia, instead pretending to look around to see if anyone dangerous was coming.

There was a line to get to the restaurant, which was a quiet, upscale Italian eatery with fine linens on the table. The maître d' waved Leo past the line, and Claudia followed him in. The entire dining room was almost entirely lit by votive candles on the tables. It created a great, romantic ambience but made it a bit difficult for Claudia to see where she was going. She breathed a sigh of relief after she was seated. The menu she was promptly handed was only one page—much different than the four-page menus they had at Paisano's. She wondered how good the place could be with a menu so short, then she saw the prices. If a plate of pasta bolognaise was going for thirty bucks, they must be doing something right.

Leo ordered a Manhattan and a bottle of champagne. The champagne toast that Leo insisted upon to kick off the evening was the only alcohol Claudia had that night, preferring to mostly stick with ice water. She was, after all, under legal drinking age and didn't want to rouse any of her parents' suspicions when she got home. Leo was a different story. Over the course of the evening, he sin- gle-handedly polished off the rest of the champagne and had two more Manhattans.

Except for the fine restaurant and above-average food—the best eggplant parmigiana Claudia ever had, including what they serve at Paisano's—the date was nothing special. Leo got progressively drunk, at one point accidentally opening his mouth before he swallowed a sip of Manhattan and drooling on his chin. He talked mostly about himself, and about how one day he would take over from his dad and be king of the city. Try as he might to impress his date, she wasn't having it. Claudia played along as best as she could, but by the end of the evening she was exhausted from acting entertained and just wanted to go home.

Two hours after she found her way to the table in the dark, it was time to go. Claudia was relieved that it was over. When they got outside, the fresh air gave her a wake-up call. She suddenly felt invigorated. Her senses were more heightened. Perhaps this is why she was the one who noticed two men in ski masks walking toward them with their hands inside their jackets as they waited for Bruno to pull the car around.

She was about to point them out and say something to Leo when the car pulled up. Leo tugged at her arm to go toward the car as Bruno got out. That was when Claudia saw Bruno's back explode as what sounded like the *pop-pop* of firecrackers rang out in the otherwise still and quiet evening. Bruno hit the pavement hard. Instinctively, Leo grabbed Claudia and shielded her from the two assailants by placing his body between them and her as they made their way to the car.

Unfortunately for Claudia, what Leo didn't notice was a third gunman approaching from the opposite side of the two that just took Bruno down. The gunman fired at Leo, but she was in the way. A bullet caught her in the shoulder as they made it to the car. The back door offered some protection as she dove inside.

"Stay down!" Leo called out to her, drawing his gun.

The door offered Leo some protection as he fired at the man bearing down on him. He fired a three shots, but he was so drunk that all he managed to do was put one in a lamppost and two in a trash can. This sent the assailant ducking for cover in an alley, which gave Leo enough time to get in the front and slide over to the driver's seat.

Before he could put the car in gear, the assailant moved out of the alley and started firing. All of the cars that carry the Manetti family had bulletproof glass, but this didn't change the fact that Leo ducked instinctually, even in his drunken stupor. Shots rang out next to Leo, outside of the driver's side car door. The assailant took two slugs to the chest and went down instantly. Leo looked through his door window and saw Bruno on his knees, holding his gun and barely able to keep himself upright.

Not that it mattered. In the instant that Leo saw Bruno, the back of his head erupted in a geyser of dark red. The two men had finished the job on Bruno and killed him. Leo looked in his rearview to get a bead on them, threw the car in reverse, then jammed on the gas as hard as he could. Claudia shrieked in horror as the car hit both men. One spun off to the side and another tumbled completely over the car, landing in front of it. Leo put the car in drive and hit the gas once again. The man in front of the car didn't have a chance. The pop sound that the man's head made when it got squashed by the car haunted Claudia for months afterward.

Leo checked his side-view mirror as the car darted away. Witnesses were left in shock and horror. Two masked men were left dead, and another was badly injured in the legs and pelvis. Also lying there was Bruno, his dear friend and trusted bodyguard. "Pissed off" barely covered the feelings of free-flowing rage Leo was feeling at the moment, which were intensified by the amount of alcohol running through his system. Worst of all, his date was injured, nursing her shoulder with the bullet lodged in it.

"We'll get 'em, Claudia! I swear it to you!" Leo was seething. His voice was deeper than normal. He looked and sounded like a man possessed by a demon who just wanted to kill. "Hang in there. I'm taking you to get that bullet out."

"The hospital?" Claudia wanted to take the question back as soon as she asked it. So naïve.

"No! No hospital! I got a doctor on the Manetti payroll who handles these situations. We'll get you fixed."

Claudia sat back in her seat with her hand on her shoulder. She watched the lights of the city at night whiz by as Leo sped down roads and skidded around corners. After ten minutes of harrowing, drunken driving, the car stopped. Leo got out and rushed to the back to get Claudia. As she got out, she noticed where they were. It was a kind of a hospital at least.

"Leo, are we in the right place?" "Yeah. Come on."

"But this is the River City *Animal* Hospital…"

"I know. This is where the doctor is. Now come on."

Claudia could see that he was getting impatient. Plus, he was drunk—and had a gun. She pushed the issue no further and followed him. Instead of going through the front door, they went through the service entrance and into a storage room. Boxes of animal food and medical supplies were piled up all around. Leo pointed to a stur- dy-looking box off to the side and commanded, "Sit. I'll be right back."

Claudia did as he said. Within three minutes, Leo returned with a doctor dressed in scrubs and wearing a medical mask. Leo carried a small plastic bag, and the doctor carried with him a bottle of rubbing alcohol, some cotton, a syringe, a scalpel, a pair of very long forceps, and a metal tray. Claudia got a bit nervous as she saw the doctor walking toward her but calmed down once she heard his low, whispery, soothing voice say, "Relax. I'm here to help. Let me take a look."

Claudia removed her hand from covering the wound on her shoulder and let the doctor look it over. As he did this, Leo arranged a series of same-size boxes together. The doctor turned to Leo. "You're right. It's still in there. Let's get her moved over."

Proud of himself for being able to spot a wound with a lodged bullet versus a through and through, Leo smiled as he walked over to Claudia. He took her by her good arm as the doctor moved into position. He led her over to where he had arranged the boxes and told her to lie down. Claudia pieced it together quickly. It was time for an operation to extract the bullet.

Once she was on her back on top of the boxes, the doctor rubbed the wound with the rubbing alcohol and injected her shoulder with the syringe. "That was a local anesthetic. It may take a minute or two to feel numb. Let me know when it does."

The three all sat in silence for a minute and waited. Finally, Claudia said, "It's numb." Then, feeling a burst of toughness she added, "Do what you gotta do."

The doctor immediately got to work with the scalpel, slicing away at Claudia's flesh to get to the bullet. Once he carved a path, he dug in further with the forceps. Claudia winced and clenched her teeth to handle the burden of the pain. The cutting wasn't too bad, but the rooting around in her shoulder with the forceps was excruci- ating. She thought about how thankful she was that she got an anes- thetic before the doctor started cutting and poking around. *If I didn't get that anesthetic, she thought, then how would this feel?*

Claudia was on the verge of screaming, when all of a sudden, she felt relief in the pressure in her arm. Then she heard a clinking sound in the metal tray. She breathed in slow and deep as the doctor tilted the tray to show her the small piece of blood-covered metal that caused her so much pain and discomfort. The doctor then looked at Leo and said, "I'll take the bag."

Leo picked up the plastic bag that he carried in from off the floor and handed it to the doctor, who removed what looked like a needle and thread from the bag, but bigger and shaped differently. The doctor cleaned and dried Claudia's shoulder, then stitched it up. Once done, he pulled a cloth sling out of the bag and fitted it over

Claudia's head and around her arm. "I'm sure this goes without say- ing," said the doctor, "but don't use this arm. It needs to heal. You'll need a least two months, maybe more."

"Maybe we should get you one of those cones so you don't pick at it," chuckled Leo. He was back to his old jokey self now that the worst was over. There was something charming about him to Claudia this time, though. Perhaps it was the fact that he tried to protect her while the bullets were flying, or that he cared for her after she got shot, or the whole ordeal in general, but she felt a connection to him. It's one that she didn't feel after dinner and probably would not have felt if they didn't go through that hellish nightmare together. She found the quip oddly charming and started giggling herself. The doctor, however, was having none of it.

"Looks like I'm done here," the doctor stated, getting up. He reached into his pocket and pulled out a bottle of pills. He handed them to Claudia and continued, "The pain will come back for a few days after the anesthetic wears off. Take one—just *one*—of these when you feel the pain. It will gradually feel better as you start to recover. Good night to you both." With that, the doctor turned and walked back through the door.

Leo walked over to Claudia. "Congratulations." "For what?" Claudia was legitimately confused.

"You were tough the way you took that bullet. I've seen guys get hit with less than that and they're crying for their mommy. You are one tough cookie, kid."

Claudia swelled with pride and smiled. "Thanks." The way she saw it this was praise from Caesar. This guy would know.

Leo offered her his hand. "Let's go." She took it and the two exited the storage room.

The ride on the way home was quiet. Claudia thought about what to say to her parents. She decided to keep it simple and tell them that she and her friends went clubbing and she slipped on the dance floor. As long as they didn't see her wounded shoulder and just saw her arm in a sling, they'd buy it. Even if they did notice her shoulder, she could just tell them that she fell on a broken glass when she slipped.

Vet though he was, the doctor was right in his estimate. Claudia's arm took about two months to heal. In that time she continued working at Paisano's but did light duty like answer the phone and fold pizza boxes—an especially challenging endeavor to undertake with one arm in a sling. Leo and Claudia had gone out a few more times, and he'd really grown on her. Leo had always liked Claudia, so it was easy for him to become involved with her. The two were now a couple.

When it was time for the stitches to come out, Leo did the honors himself one night after closing. While he snipped away at the stitches, he delivered some exciting news to Claudia.

"Guess who we found?"

"Who?" Claudia kept the query simple for fear that Leo couldn't cut the stitches and carry on a conversation at the same time. She liked the guy—and her feelings were starting to get deeper than that—but still knew he had limits on how many things he could do at once.

"The last guy," came the self-satisfied reply from Leo.

"What last guy?" Claudia had an inclination of who he was talking about, but she wanted to hear him say it.

"The last guy from that night. When you got this." Leo pointed at her shoulder wound with the scissors. He only had a few more left and Claudia wanted to know more.

"Really? How?" she asked enthusiastically.

Leo finished cutting the final stitch and put the scissors down.

He was now able to focus his full attention to Claudia.

"Our heroin comes in through Chinatown. It arrives packed in with bags of rice and packets of soy sauce. My guys went there for a pick up a few days ago, and one of the Chinese guys was walking with a limp. My guy asked him what was wrong, and he said he fell down some stairs."

"Maybe he did." Claudia wanted to make sure this wasn't a wild-goose chase.

"True," replied Leo, sounding uncharacteristically reasonable. "It could have been a coincidence that this guy, who has always been at the exchange in the past, fell down some stairs on the same night that we got shot at and Bruno got killed, and just recovered and is coming back now. It's possible."

Claudia couldn't help but notice a devilish grin creep on to Leo's face. It was bait, and she bit. "So?"

"So yesterday I had some of my boys track him down and pick him up. We questioned him." Leo paused, waiting for Claudia to react. He enjoyed keeping her in suspense and playing this little mind game.

"And?" Claudia was starting to lose her patience.

"After some, let's say, extreme interrogation, he confessed. He said that he was with those other two guys that night. He was the one I hit with the car when I backed up. The one whose head I didn't crush, obviously."

"Why was he trying to kill us?" Claudia's frustration was turn- ing into a simmering rage.

Leo couldn't resist pushing her buttons. He quipped, "Actually, they were trying to kill me. You just happened to be there."

"Leo!" Claudia shouted so loud that Leo felt a quick piercing in his ear drum.

"All right. Relax, Claudia. Just sayin'. Anyway, this hit wasn't sanctioned by any of the Chinese bosses. These guys had it in their heads to take over complete control of the heroin in River City by eliminating their number one rival—me. You just happened to be with me that night, and they took out Bruno because they knew he was good with a gun and sworn to protect me. One of them found out the hard way how right that was."

"Where is he now?" Claudia was practically jumping out of her seat.

"I got him chained up at an abandoned shoe factory downtown. As far as the Chinese are concerned, this guy is a dishonor and they turned their back on him. He's all ours—if you're interested."

"Hell yes, I'm interested." Claudia got up and headed out with- out looking at Leo. "Let's go. Now!"

The abandoned shoe factory was in an old industrial part of town that had since been partially built up as the dining and enter- tainment district of River City. It had been years since River City had any industry, and many factories like this sat dormant in the area. Some were purchased and converted into theaters, concert venues, restaurants, bars, and nightclubs. It was a good way for some com- merce to come back to the city, and it gave the people of River City a place to go to let off some steam and have some fun.

Leo pulled up to the shambles of a factory at the end of a road, away from the noise, lights, and excitement of the next block over. He barely put it in park and Claudia was already out of the car and headed in. Leo quickly followed and caught up to her at the door. He took some keys from his pocket and opened the padlock on the door.

The musky odor of mold and mildew slammed Claudia's nose as soon as she entered. She wasn't taken aback for long, though. As soon as Leo flipped on the floodlights that his boys set up, she saw, chained to a chair in the middle of the factory floor, the swollen, bloody husk of one of the men who shot at her that evening. The other two were dead. She knew this would be her last chance to get any payback on her own, and did she ever want it.

"Unchain him," she demanded of Leo.

Leo took another key out of his pocket and walked behind the man in the chair. With a click the chains were undone. The echo of them falling onto the concrete floor rattled throughout the big, empty factory. The Chinese man sitting on the chair didn't react at all.

"Aww, look at this," Leo said tauntingly as he walked in front of the man. "He barely has the strength to move his head. There's no way he's going to be able to stand up to whatever you have in mind." Leo leaned in closer to the man. "Isn't that right?" Leo asked, their faces now inches apart.

In a flash, the Chinese man's bloody, sweaty forehead connected with Leo's nose. It broke instantly. Leo scurried away, grasping his nose in pain and screaming, trying to stop the gush of blood flowing out of his nostrils. The man got up from the chair and darted for the exit.

Claudia reacted quickly. She thought he might have been play- ing possum and was ready. The man's limp was apparent in his run, but it didn't slow him down too much. He was almost at the door by the time Claudia dive tackled him, sending them both flying into the wall. She was taking no chances. She immediately started knee- ing him in the small of the back. This hurt him especially bad since his back and pelvis were also injured when he got hit and were just starting to feel better.

Once the Chinese man was on the ground, Claudia turned him over and began striking him with her fists. Her blows were fierce and merciless. One after the other, after the other, after the other— left, right, left, right—rained down on the man's face and neck. She worked herself into a frenzy, uncontrollable. She couldn't stop punching if she wanted. By the time Leo was seeing straight enough to rush over and pull her off him, the damage from her berserk pum- meling had already been done. When Claudia looked down, she saw what she'd done. The Chinese man's face was completely caved in and unrecognizable. She looked at her hands. They were bruised and hurt badly. She was sure she fractured fingers on both hands.

"Let's go," Leo said, gently. "I'll get some boys to take care of this mess. You got him."

Claudia didn't say a word. She just got up and followed him out. The car ride back was dead quiet. Even though neither one spoke a word, there was a tension in the air. It wasn't an angry tension though. It was a lustful one. Neither one would admit it to the other one out loud, but they were both turned on by what just happened. Leo looked at Claudia's bruised and battered knuckles like they were badges of honor. Claudia was still on an adrenaline high. The beating she gave the Chinese man had gotten her fired up in other ways that she'd never felt before. Looking over at Leo, she thought he looked sexy with the busted nose. She wanted him right then and there.

Leo's house—a two-story, gated minimansion on the outskirts of town that overlooked the river—was closest, so he drove there. Leo went right to the kitchen and got an ice pack for Claudia's hand. He'd been there before when he'd punched someone too hard and his fist landed on the other guy's forehead instead of his temple. As he handed the ice pack to Claudia, he noticed the way she was looking at him. He had experience in this area too. He knew when a girl was horny and didn't just want it but needed it.

Claudia threw the ice pack to the floor. She forgot about her hands. Leo forgot about his nose. If anything, the pain added to the passion. He grabbed her roughly and kissed her as hard as he could. She kissed him back with equal ferocity. Before either of them knew it, they were naked in the middle of Leo's kitchen. He picked Claudia up and sat her down on the island in the middle of the kitchen. The cold of the marble sent shivers streaking up her spine. She squealed from the surprise and tilted her head up. By the time she got used to the cold sensation and put her head back down, Leo was already inside of her, thrusting away. Suddenly for Claudia, there was no more cold, nor was there any pain. There were only the throes of ecstasy.

Three major happenings occurred that night. It was the first time Claudia killed someone—and she liked it. It was the first time Claudia has sex, not just with Leo, but with anyone—and she liked it even more. Last but not least, it gave Leo the inspiration for an idea that had been gestating in his brain for a while. He liked to see women fight, and he needed a place to make it happen. He'd buy the shoe factory and convert it into a nightclub, but that was only a front. In the back would be gambling as well as the crowning centerpiece—an MMA-style octagon where women could fight and anyone watching could bet. With Claudia as his champion, he could make a fortune. He even thought of the name for it: Amazon Glory.

CHAPTER 9

A MAZON GLORY TOOK longer than Leo liked to get up and running. This was mostly because he wanted to keep it from his father and be a surprise, to prove to his old man that he could do things on his own. It was also a matter of pride for Leo. He hated the idea of having everything handed down to him. He hated even more the idea that people were sneering behind his back that he didn't have any juice and couldn't make anything on his own, that he was spoiled. This would prove them wrong.

After almost ten full years of sneaking around and having contractors he could trust go in and out of the place to do what needed to be done, he was ready to open. The establishment had an Amazon rain forest theme for the nightclub in the front. The back, with the gambling and the fighting, was what he really cared about. Now that he was ready for fighting, he had a major problem: finding fighters.

He first turned to his prostitution racket, offering the ladies extra cash to fight. This didn't last long. Most of the women were out- of-shape drug addicts who could barely throw a punch. They could barely fight each other and were no match at all for Claudia, who was training in the Brazilian martial art of capoeira, as if she wasn't vicious and deadly enough already. Claudia took these other women down without breaking a sweat. The derisive bet on the casino floor was on how few kicks it would take Claudia to knock out a hooker.

Desperate to give Claudia some kind of a challenge, he moved Maria and Tina from Paisano's to Amazon Glory. He also wanted them to take capoeira in keeping with his Amazon theme, but they instead opted for Krav Maga, an especially aggressive style of Israeli hand-to-hand combat. This actually worked out fairly well since it mixed things up a bit, and after Maria and Tina had enough training Claudia was sufficiently challenged, but it was getting tiresome to watch the same fights over and over again.

Then one day with a few strokes of the keys on his laptop Leo found his answer. Desperate, he Googled "martial arts women." What he discovered were several websites dedicated to Eastern European female martial artists. The disciplines ranged from kickboxing to judo to karate, and they were all from the area of the world where Claudia had her ancestry. It was perfect—he would get these young women from Eastern Europe to come here and fight Claudia. He just needed her help to lure them over.

Leo wanted her to contact the women through their websites and tell them that he was holding a competition in River City that offered a one-hundred-thousand-dollar prize to anyone who could beat his champion, Claudia. Those who were interested could click a link to a website showing Claudia and her skills and sign up. To sweeten the deal, Leo even offered to cover airfare and living arrange- ments in River City. He also developed a bracket system in which the women would fight each other, and the champion of all of them would then win the right to challenge Claudia. How well they did in the bracket would determine what percentage of the gambling profits they got paid on top of the added bonus of potentially win- ning one hundred thousand dollars. The women could stay as long as they wanted—Leo knew a high-ranking immigration official on the Manetti payroll who could extend their visas for as long as needed.

Claudia was reluctant to help at first. She didn't like the pressure of such a high-stakes competition. But after a while, so many women had arrived that she felt like a queen bee. Claudia liked this feeling. She was the champion, the one on top of the proverbial food chain, and it was up to her to defend her title.

Defend it she did—a little too well. The first death in the octa- gon was at the first championship. Claudia had been dormant for five days as the fights went on night after night. She trained every day to stay sharp, but it wasn't the same as actual competition. She was itching to get in and fight. Claudia wanted to see blood. She wanted to taste it. She got both wishes when she pounded in the face of a Slovenian girl named Karolina. Claudia was surprised at what she'd done when it was all over. The frenzy she'd experienced before with the Chinese man had taken her over once again. When she came back to reality, all she could hear were the cheers erupting from the audience. This was death sport, and they loved it. If Claudia was being honest with herself, she loved it too.

The next couple of championship rounds went off without as much excitement. Claudia won, but no one got killed. The opponent who lost went back into the tournament bracket and was able to try again. Then one night while fighting a Romanian kickboxer named Anya, Claudia landed a spin kick to the side of her head. Anya was dazed but refused to fall. Angered at such insolence, Claudia aimed a kick at her upper chest. Unfortunately, in her rage Claudia's aim was off, and she kicked the defenseless Anya in the throat, crushing her windpipe. Claudia threw up her arms in victory as Anya collapsed to the mat and choked to death on her own blood.

There were some rumblings among the women now that two of them were accidentally killed in the octagon. They looked at Claudia with a combination of admiration for her skill and ferocity as well as fear at what she might do. It is for this reason that none of them dared to say anything to her or to Leo, and none of them tried to back out or run away. They knew that in the octagon they at least had a fighting chance to stay alive. If they tried to quit, no such chance would be given. Plus, their portion of the profit from the casino was enough to keep them quiet and allow them to buy some nice clothes and jewelry, with the added benefit of incentivizing them to keep fighting.

The third and latest death was less of an accident. By some stroke of luck, a Ukrainian named Katia won the bracket. She was a judo expert, well-versed in grapples and throws, and it was a miracle that she beat a taller opponent who was trained in kung fu. None of this mattered when it came to her fight with Claudia. Katia had never seen capoeira before and was dazzled by the elegance of it right up until the time she was kicked in the jaw. From there, she didn't have a chance. Claudia immediately had the upper hand and took full advantage. She enjoyed toying with her much-shorter opponent. Katia scratched at Claudia's arms as the champion put her in a choke- hold. Claudia held Katia in so little regard that she thought nothing of snapping her neck to end the fight. To Claudia, it was just another fight. To Katia, it was the end of her life.

To Leo it was a problem. This was the third death in seven weeks. None of the other combatants had defected yet, but it was getting to be a bit much. He also had a body disposal problem. It was winter and the ground was frozen, so burial was out. The only thing he could think to do—without telling his dad—was to have Maria and Tina throw the bodies in the river. Of course, he would rather have his boys do it, but he'd been distancing himself from them since they really worked for his father, and he knew word would get back to him. He had to play the hand he was dealt. The problem with Maria and Tina was that they weren't as skilled—and perhaps didn't care—about weighing the bodies down so they didn't come up later. So far, they were zero for three in keeping bodies weighed down. This was what led Sarah and Vinny into Amazon Glory one morning.

*****

As Sarah walked in, she was struck by the dedication to the Amazon theme. There were Brazilian rain forest trees everywhere. A giant rubber anaconda was wrapped around the biggest one. There was a "Little Amazon River"—according to the sign—that flowed through the floor. There were several bridges where people could cross over. Last but not least, there was a giant fish tank behind the bar with live piranhas in it. In front of the tank were glass shelves showcasing the usual bottles of booze.

Claudia was behind the bar, cleaning glasses with a cloth. Maria and Tina were both roaming around with rags and spray bottles, wiping down tables. The place was empty except for the three of them. Sarah and Vinny were immediately noticed as soon as they walked in. Claudia was especially surprised to see Vinny.

"Vinny DiGrazio? I thought you got pinched," Claudia said with an equal mixture of surprise and suspicion. She didn't bother to acknowledge Sarah.

Vinny was shit scared of Claudia. He knew what she could do, even to him. Still, he recovered quickly and regained his composure before he replied, "I did. They didn't have much on me. I made bail." Claudia was skeptical but willing to play along. "Is that right? And who's this?"

"I got a new girl for Leo to see…for the fights."

This was Sarah's one-and-only way in. She silently hoped that Claudia would take the bait. Claudia, however, said nothing. Instead, she pushed a button under the fish tank. The tank slowly descended so that the open top was accessible. It's right around then that Sarah noticed a plate of meat resting on the bar. Claudia picked up a piece of meat and grinned. "You know what happens to fresh meat around here…" She tossed the meat in the tank. A wild, effervescent feeding frenzy ensued.

The intent of this move by Claudia was to unnerve Vinny, but he kept his cool. "Yeah, I know, Claudia. Can we see Leo or not? Is he in?"

Claudia was mildly impressed that Vinny didn't get rattled at the piranha feeding, but she was having too much fun trying. "He's in. But what makes you think he wants to see this…girl you just found on the street?"

"She can fight," Vinny said confidently, in spite of the fact that he had never actually seen Sarah fight.

"Oh, can she?" It wasn't that Claudia doubted Sarah so much as it was that she didn't trust Vinny and wasn't sure what he was up to. "That's right." Vinny was insistent—not one of his usual traits.

Something seemed off to Claudia. Something seemed off to Maria and Tina too. They both walked over to the bar.

Tina spoke first. "Everything okay, Claudia?"

Claudia was done fooling around. "Yeah. These two were just leaving," she replied.

Maria grabbed Sarah's arm and said, "You heard her. Let's go."

Big mistake. Before Maria knew it, Sarah grabbed her hand and twisted it back. Maria collapsed to her knees in pain. Tina grabbed Sarah by the scruff of her neck. Sarah back kicked Tina in the crotch, spun around, and flung her over the bar. A grinning Claudia casually sidestepped as Tina landed with a thud.

By the time that all went down with Tina, Maria was back on her feet. She threw a punch at Sarah. Sarah blocked it and hit her with a jab of her own. Maria was stunned. Sarah took the opportu- nity to drop-kick her. Maria flew back and hit the anaconda tree. The snake shook from the impact.

Sarah rose just in time to see Tina standing behind the bar and holding a lemon wedge. She squeezed it into Sarah's eyes. Tina laughed sadistically. She was about to take advantage and pounce on Sarah when out of nowhere she got a fist in the jaw. At first Tina wondered how Vinny got the nerve to jump in the fight. Then she realized that during the whole fight, he was standing in the corner. The punch came from Claudia.

"No! That's not the way we do things here. We fight fair and square, using our fists, and our legs, and our bodies." Claudia was seething at Tina. "No"—Claudia punched Tina again, even harder, right in the temple. Tina fell so hard and so fast that she made a sack of rocks look like a bag of feathers. She looked down at Tina and finished her sentence—"cheating!"

Claudia then turned her attention to Sarah, who was squinting through red, stung eyes. As she threw a towel into Sarah's chest, she gave her the good news, "Come on. You passed the test. Let's go see Leo." Sarah gave her eyes a rough wipe to clean away the tears and what was left of the lemon juice. As Claudia led her through a back door toward Leo's office, she saw well enough to catch a glimpse of

Tina lying unconscious on the floor. *Serves her right*, Sarah thought to herself as they left the bar with Vinny, now out from cowering in his corner, following close behind.

Sarah was impressed by Leo. He had handsomer, more chiseled features and a more athletic physique than she was expecting. He clearly took care of himself better than most men in his line of work. Leo was so wrapped up in his paperwork, that he didn't even notice Claudia come in with Sarah and Vinny. She started off with a simple "Hey, Leo."

Leo knew the voice all too well and didn't care about the company, so he didn't bother to look up. This was one cool customer. "Hey" came the reply from Leo as he carried on with his work.

"I've got some new blood for you. Meet Sarah."

Now he was interested. Things were getting stale with the same women fighting over and over again, and it was hard to get new recruits with Claudia's reputation. He needed some replacements badly, and was in no position to be choosy. But one look at Sarah and he could tell that she could hold her own. No need to be choosy about her. Still, not wanting to tip his hand, Leo continued to play it cool. "She can fight?" he asked casually.

"She just kicked the hell out of Maria and Tina, if that's what you mean." Claudia grinned with satisfaction. These words—and the events of mere moments ago that inspired them—brought Claudia more pleasure than she expected.

"Interesting," said Leo as he rose from his desk and walked over to Sarah. He gave her a good look up and down. She looked even better to him up close. He was breathing her in, literally and figura- tively. Sarah was starting to get mildly uncomfortable when, out of the corner of his eye, Leo spotted Vinny.

"You! I never thought I'd see you again you little prick! Where's the ten grand?" Sarah's inspection was over. Leo's attention was com- pletely on Vinny.

Vinny shrugged. "I don't have it."

Leo pushed himself between Sarah and Claudia and got up close to Vinny. Leo towered over Vinny by around six inches and literally looked down on him. The effect was made even more noticeable with Vinny's hunched shoulders and "hangdog eyes to the ground" expression. "What do you mean you don't have it?"

"I mean I don't…I don't have it. The cops took it. And the drugs. They confiscated everything."

"I want that money. I'm in it deep with my dad over this screwup."

Vinny stirred up some courage from inside himself and looked up at Leo. He couldn't quite look him in the eye. He got to about nose level, which was as high up as Vinny wanted to get. He was afraid that if he went any higher, Leo would perceive himself as being threatened. That was the last thing Vinny wanted. "I know you are, and I want to make it right. That's why I'm here," he sput- tered out.

"Huh? How's that?" Leo was legitimately perplexed.

"Sarah over here is a really good fighter. I've seen what she can do on the streets. She'll make you that money back."

"Is that so?" Leo was testing Vinny, pushing him to see if he'd back down at all—an indication that he was trying to put one over on Leo.

Vinny held his ground and stayed true. "Yeah. That's so," he replied with confidence.

Sarah had enough of these two verbally jabbing each other. "And what do I get out of the deal?"

Leo turned his attention back to Sarah. "You? You, my newest warrior princess, get 1 percent of the night's gross just for showing up and 5 percent if you win your match." He then pointed at Vinny. "Same goes for Vinny here. He can pay me back with his 10 percent finder's fee—if you win it all against her." Leo redirected his point toward Claudia.

Sarah pretended to think it over for a few seconds and then responded with, "So I better win."

Leo walked behind his desk and stood in front of a big curtain.

"Yeah, you better. For Vinny's sake—and for yours. But to win, you need to survive in here."

Leo pulled the rope to the side of the curtain and it slid open to reveal a window. Sarah walked to the window and peered through. She was immediately stuck by the fenced-in octagon that served as the centerpiece to the converted shoe factory floor. It was standing-room only all around the octagon. On the mezzanine were casino tables for blackjack and poker. In the left corner was the roulette wheel, and in the right corner was the craps table. All that was missing were the slot machines.

Leo looked over at Sarah and grinned. He could see that she was a bit awestruck and clearly impressed with his operation. He walked next to her and joined her in looking out at the old factory floor. It was quiet now, but come that evening it would be bustling with gamblers and fight lovers from all over the city.

Leo licked his lips and asked, "You like it? This place used to be a shoe factory back in the day. It was abandoned for a while, till I bought it. Up front we have the Amazon Club, open to the pub- lic. But back here, on the old factory floor, we have the VIP area. Any type of gambling you want plus, my favorite, the fights. Women only. It's my thing. What can I say? I like seeing strong women fight each other. Any questions?"

Sarah shook her head. She saw all she needed to see to give her a good idea of what was happening. "Nope. Seems pretty straight-forward to me."

"Good. Come back tonight. Ten o'clock. That's when I like to start the show."

"You got it." Sarah gave Leo a quick nod before she turned to leave.

This initial meeting went better than expected. Sarah proved what she could do, didn't ask too many questions, kept her state- ments short and simple, and showed deference as she was leaving. The only wild card was Vinny. Between Sarah and Vinny, it was Vinny that Leo was most focused on. Not one to let such things as a confiscated ten thousand dollars go easily, Leo shouted after Vinny as Claudia showed him and Sarah the way out: "And Vinny—she better be every bit as good as you say she is!"

Leo closed the curtain and sat back down at his desk. He just stared at his paperwork. He didn't feel like getting back into it. They were just orders for the liquor suppliers and could wait. Something about the whole situation with Vinny and Sarah had really stirred him up. He knew Claudia would be back to talk to him. A minute later, she walked through the door.

"What do you think?" Leo wanted an honest appraisal now that they were alone.

Claudia quickly assessed what she saw earlier and rendered an honest opinion. "I think she's good, but not that good. I got a girl in mind who I think can take care of her tonight."

This was exactly what Leo needed to hear. Claudia made his way to his desk and was standing by him. An enthusiastic Leo grabbed her by the waist and pulled her in close. "Good," he said as his hand traveled down to give Claudia's firm left butt cheek a tight squeeze with his right hand. He then continued, "I'll put my money on her to beat this…Sarah."

"Do it," Claudia replied, leaning down and returning Leo's grope with a gentle, over-the-pants fondling. She could feel that he was at around three quarters of the way to completely hard already. A tinge of jealousy rose up in Claudia that some of it might be because of Sarah. This caused her to briefly tighten her grip a bit harder than she should have, pinching Leo's left testicle. The jealousy went away as quick as it came and she eased off.

Far from hurting Leo, the pinch got him up the rest of the way. He just had to continue one final thought, which of course, was about the focus of his ire earlier. "That little weasel Vinny can find some other way to pay me back."

Claudia was done hearing about Vinny. She didn't like the little maggot either, and it was killing her mood. She tilted her head and kissed Leo hard on the mouth. Leo tightened his grip on Claudia's ass while he slid his other hand up her shirt. All of the working out and training had made Claudia lose a little in the chest over the years. This disappointed Leo, but he didn't say anything. Claudia's breasts were still his favorite part of her, and he knew that things like that would inevitably happen to lean, fit women. He accepted it.

While Leo was amusing himself with his favorite areas on Claudia's front and back, Claudia was gaining access to her favor- ite part of him. She undid his belt and very carefully unzipped his pants. She didn't want a repeat of the incident on New Year's Eve five years ago when, unbeknownst to her, Leo's erect penis had protruded through the fly in his boxer shorts and was rubbing up against his zipper. She unzipped too quickly and it caught some of the skin on Leo's shaft. The black eye she carried around with her for two weeks was lesson enough to make sure that she went slowly and didn't repeat the same mistake. She made sure his penis was clear of the zipper and safe before pulling it down.

Once she had his now pulsating protrusion staring straight at her, she gave Leo a nice surprise. He thought for sure that she would remove her panties and straddle him over his chair. Instead, she slid her head down and inserted his member into her mouth. This wasn't her favorite thing to do, but she wasn't totally against it. Her biggest objection was that Leo overpowdered his scrotum after showering, and some of that powder inevitably got onto his dick, which got into her mouth. It dried out her tongue and tasted rancid, but every once in a while, she liked to remind her man what she could do for him. Leo's eyes lit up with delight. He leaned back in his chair and relaxed as Claudia went to work. Leo didn't need drugs. This was the best high he could get.

CHAPTER 10

SARAH DROPPED VINNY off at his mother's after they left the club and spent the whole day getting adjusted to her new apartment. It was lightly furnished with a sofa, a television, and a bed. Decorations were sparse and of the mass-produced variety easily purchased at department stores. Sarah bought herself some groceries for the week and stocked the pantry and refrigerator. She tested the electric stove to make sure it still worked. It did, but she was too nervous thinking about the evening ahead to cook anything, let alone eat.

What Sarah wanted to do more than anything was take a hot bath. The bathroom was just off the bedroom. After she unpacked her things, she grabbed her toiletries to put them away. Even though Sarah was delighted that she had running water in the tap and the toilet flushed and filled with no issue, she was disappointed that there was a shower stall only. She really wanted a bath. But having no choice, she slid the frosted glass door open, turned on the shower, finished unpacking, and grabbed a towel while she waited for the water to get hot. The old pipes in the apartment building made get- ting the water hot a painfully slow process. After five minutes it was just above warm, but Sarah didn't feel like waiting any longer. She stripped and got in.

The stink of Amazon Glory felt like it seeped into Sarah's pores, and she wanted to steam it out with hot water. As she grabbed the soap and sponge, she thought of what was to come. For the first time since she agreed to go undercover, Sarah felt nervous. This was no longer just an idea of a noble assignment. It was real. She was in it. She would have to stay in it for the long haul and see it through to the end. Sarah knew that. She did her best to get the thoughts of things to come out of her head as she gave herself a gentle scrubbing.

As Sarah started to scrub closer to her belly, her thoughts turned to Dale. As she got closer to her clitoris, the thoughts of Dale changed from those of happy times spent together at an amusement park or at her parents' house on Mothers' Day, and turned graphically sexual. She scrubbed her labia rougher and rougher as she thought of each part of him she liked from head to toe: his eyes, his chin, his chest, his butt, and of course, his most fun part of all. Her hand almost shattered the glass door of the shower as she braced herself for her orgasm.

After such an adventurous shower, a hot and exhausted Sarah needed a nap. It was early evening, and she had a few hours before she was due back to Amazon Glory. She quickly dried herself off, threw on her robe, and lay down on her bed. A spring on the right side of the mattress immediately poked her in the back. Sarah moved to the left, making a mental note to flip the mattress later. She was asleep within seconds.

Sarah's sleep was calm and restful. By the time she was awakened at eight forty-five to the sound of a car horn blaring at a reck- less pedestrian walking across the street near her window, she had recouped her strength and was ready to go. Sarah stumbled out of bed, went into the bathroom, and before turning the light on she splashed some very cold water on her face. It was invigorating. Now she was ready.

It was close to ten o'clock before Sarah knew it. On her way to Amazon Glory, she picked up Vinny at his mother's. They arrived with ten minutes to spare. Sarah parked the car and was about to go through the front when Vinny pointed her toward an alley and told her to follow him. Going with a strange man down a dark alley late at night was usually not a smart move for a woman, but her instincts told her that Vinny wouldn't try anything—plus she could take him if he did.

After walking to almost the end of the alley, Sarah and Vinny came to a door. Vinny knocked on it, and a burly bouncer opened the door. He smiled when he saw Vinny.

"Vinny DiGrazio! I can't believe you're still alive—and that you're showing your face here. Leo is super pissed about that ten grand you lost."

"Hey, Carmine. Yeah, that's why I'm here," Vinny replied with a nervous chuckle.

"How did you get out of that pinch anyway?" "Lack of evidence." "Huh?"

Carmine went from genuinely curious to genuinely confused. It's a good thing that during their car ride together Sarah coached him on what to say if he got asked. "What I mean is…" started Vinny, pausing to buy time so he could remember what he needed to say, "they pinched me for delivery and got the drugs. However, I kept my mouth shut about the operation, and they couldn't prove that I had any knowledge that I was delivering anything more than food, so they couldn't hold me for more than a day and the assistant DA—some punk do-gooder— had to let me go."

Carmine looked proud, the way a father would look at a son who just accomplished something. This was in spite of the fact that Carmine wasn't any more than five or so years older than Vinny. At long last, Carmine acknowledged Sarah, who was standing behind Vinny the entire time.

"Who is she?" He looked at Sarah while he asked Vinny this question.

"Oh, her? She's a new fighter I brought in for Leo. She's going to help me pay off the ten grand I owe him."

"Is that so?" Carmine raised an eyebrow and looked Sarah up and down.

"Yeah, that's so." Vinny liked Carmine and appreciated that Carmine was one of the few people at Amazon Glory who liked him, but his eyeballing of Sarah was a bit disconcerting. He needed to end the conversation quickly and get inside, so he rapidly followed up with "She's on the list."

Carmine held up the clipboard he was holding and looked over the sheet of paper on it. "All right. What's her name?"

"Sarah," replied Vinny.

"Sarah Connor," chimed in Sarah.

Carmine looked at her and smiled. "Just like the chick from the *Terminator* movies."

Sarah felt her insides drop. Of all the names! But she just smiled and nodded. "Yeah—that's me."

Carmine spotted her name on the bottom of the list. "Ah. Here she is. Okay, you two can go in." Vinny stepped inside. Sarah hiked her gym bag over her shoulder and moved past Carmine. He quickly put his arm across the door, blocking her access inside. "After I check your bag." Sarah had no choice. She handed the bag over. Carmine unzipped it and checked inside. There wasn't much. Just a towel and the clothes she'd wear during the fight. Carmine inspected Sarah's sports bra a little too closely and carefully for her taste, but she let it go. She didn't want to say or do anything to rock the boat.

With a zip, Carmine resecured Sarah's bag and handed it back to her. She grabbed it and was on her way. Vinny led her to the fight- er's entrance to the locker room. Sarah was unimpressed. As nice as the rest of the club and the casino looked, the locker room was just the opposite. The lockers were creaky and old. The benches were worn out and dirty. Sarah peeked over to the plumbing area and saw tiles covered in water damage from years of leaky pipes and neglect. She didn't even want to see how the toilets looked. Whatever Leo's budget was for renovating the place, it stopped at the locker room.

The locker room was bustling with a dozen or so women in various stages of dress. They all spoke either in heavily accented English or in languages that sounded Eastern European to Sarah's ears. Vinny's presence in the locker room didn't faze them at all. Their Eastern European way of life in regard to nudity was a sharp contrast to Sarah's more modest view. But there was no way she was changing with him in there. She tapped Vinny on the shoulder and asked, "Can you go and find out when I'll be fighting, and who?"

Vinny looked a little disappointed. It was a bit like getting kicked out of heaven. "Okay, I'll go find Tina or Maria and get a copy of the bracket tonight." She waited for Vinny to exit the doors leading out to the casino floor before she started changing. She switched clothes quickly and without drawing attention to herself.

Sarah was done changing clothes by the time Vinny returned. She was pacing back and forth, getting herself psyched up for the fight. She stopped and looked at the piece of paper Vinny held in his hand, which showed Sarah at the bottom of the bracket facing off against a karate fighter called Lenka. It was perfect. Sarah was well trained in karate, and this would be a good fight.

The evening went by slowly as ladies got announced, went out, then come back in. It was almost midnight by the time Sarah was due in the octagon. A toilet flushed in the back of the locker room. Vinny stepped out of a stall, wiping drips of vomit off his chin with one hand, and spraying Country Fresh Scent deodorizer with the other.

As Sarah looked away in disgust, she saw a blond-haired young woman in the corner of the locker room practicing some kicks. She was the only other one besides Sarah who had not gone to fight. Sarah didn't need her detective skills to figure out that this was Lenka. Sarah caught Lenka's eye as she threw some jabs. She gave Sarah a slight head nod. Sarah returned the nod, noting that Lenka looked very serious. This fight was going to be no joke.

The fight before Sarah's and Lenka's was done, and the two women who fought returned to the locker room. Sarah could tell immediately who won—it was the one without the busted nose and blood all down her front. The victor went to her locker and grabbed a towel before heading to the showers. The bloody one went straight for the sink and tried to clean herself up as best as she could.

Vinny watched in horror as the bloodied woman stormed past him. Sarah was pacing in front of him and staying loose while Vinny sat on the bench. He looked up at Sarah. "You ready for this?"

Sarah was trying to focus on the fight ahead. She was a big believer in visualizing. Vinny's question was an annoying interrup- tion, but she knew he was nervous. She thought it better to politely answer his question and be as positive as possible in an effort to keep him from throwing up again. "Do I have a choice?"

"No. And we're both screwed if you lose tonight," said the visibly shaking Vinny.

"I won't lose." Her visualizing was starting to work. Making the statement out loud made her believe it even more.

"Yeah, but if you do…"

Now he was starting to piss her off. Sarah wasn't about to let Vinny bring her down and make her visualizing go all to waste. She was done being polite. She stopped pacing and looked at him sternly. "Vinny, damn it, if you say that one more time I'll shove my—"

A voice from behind interrupted her before Sarah could let Vinny know what she would shove where. It was Maria at the entrance to the casino, saying, "Hey! Are you two ready to go?"

Sarah gave Vinny the dirtiest look she could muster before turning around and facing Maria. "Yeah, I'm ready." Lenka didn't say anything. Once again, she nodded slightly. This was an indication to Maria that she too was ready to go.

Sarah and Lenka lined up behind Maria, who was standing in front of the door. "All right then. Let's go!" Maria flung open the door as Lenka and then Sarah walked down the path from the locker room to the octagon. The crowd was super drunk and extra rowdy. The stench of sweat and booze was suffocating. Sarah was happy to get inside the octagon to some relatively fresh air.

Vinny stayed by the door. He bit his fingernails, a nervous habit that he had once grown out of but had come back recently. There was nothing more he could do. He looked on as Claudia climbed into the octagon to do her duties as ring announcer. There was no microphone, but she didn't need one.

"Ladies and gentlemen, this is our final bout for this evening. It's a matchup of karate versus karate. To my left is a newcomer here at Amazon Glory. Give it up for Sarah!" Claudia pointed to Sarah with her left arm, and the crowd cheered politely. Until Sarah proved herself and they saw what she could do, this was to be expected. Claudia then gestured to her right with her arm and continued, "And you saw last week what this quick little fox can do. Back again, the amazing karate fighter Lenka!" The roar of the crowd got noticeably louder for Lenka. Sarah had no idea what she did last week that left such an impression, but it must have made quite a stir.

Maria and Tina moved about the crowd, taking bets. Vinny had almost completely chewed through the nails on the index and middle fingers of his left hand. Claudia called Sarah and Lenka to the center of the octagon and spoke in a low voice to both of them. "Okay, ladies. No ref, no rules—except one: just keep it clean and have a fair fight. You both know what the means, right?" Both women nodded without breaking eye contact with one another. Satisfied, Claudia wrapped up what she had to say with "Good. I'm going to exit now, and as soon as the gate closes behind me, begin. Fight is over when one of you submits or is knocked out."

Claudia turned and walked to the gate. Soon after, Sarah turned to walk to the side of the octagon. As soon as she did—bam! Rabbit punch by Lenka. She followed it up with a leg sweep. Before she knew it, Sarah was on the ground.

Lenka was fast. She swiftly jumped on Sarah and started pounding on her mercilessly. Sarah put up her arms and did all she could to deflect the blows. Seizing an opportunity at just the right moment, she raked Lenka's face with her fingers. Lenka sprung up. She grasped her face in pain.

Sarah carefully got to her feet. She was a bit wobbly but doing okay. Sarah crossed over to Lenka and started working the body. The moment Lenka took her hands off her face and put her arms down to protect her body, pop! Sarah gave her a roundhouse kick to the side of the head. Lenka was lifted into the air and did some spins before landing on a pretty unforgiving mat.

Sarah bent down and grabbed Lenka by the hair, lifting her head up. She could tell instantly that Lenka was out cold. Sarah threw her arms up in victory. The crowd went nuts, cheering for her. Vinny spit out the nail from his pinky finger that he was working on and jumped for joy. Sarah had proven herself and, more importantly, made it so Leo would get off his back.

Vinny waited outside the locker room while Sarah showered and changed. Lenka was taken to the vet to check on her concussion, and all of the other ladies were done for the evening, so Sarah had the place to herself. Once she was done, she joined Vinny as they both headed to Leo's office.

Sarah walked in with Vinny just as Leo finished transferring money from a large safe into a duffel bag. Leo zipped the duffel and looked up. He wasn't too thrilled to see them and barely managed to mutter "Congratulations" in Sarah's general direction.

Sarah shrugged and tried to control the smirk on her face from getting too big. She simply replied, "Thanks."

"I suppose you want your cut."

Sarah was feeling bold and was getting a little more than fed up with Leo's cold rudeness. She gave him a dose of his own wise guy medicine. "I didn't come up her to admire the wallpaper. Yeah, I want my money."

Leo had to control a smirk of his own. Sarah had moxie. He liked that. He reached into the safe and pulled out a stack of bills. He threw it to Sarah with a curt "Here you go."

Vinny's eyes got wide as he looked at the money Sarah was holding. "Does this mean we're square?" he asked Leo excitedly.

"No. It doesn't mean we're square, Vinny. I'll let you know when we're square," Leo replied to Vinny in a firm and forceful tone. He then turned to Sarah and spoke more calmly. "You know, I bet against you tonight. Claudia said you didn't have what it takes, but it looks like you do."

Sarah shrugged again and suppressed another smirk. "Now you know."

"Yeah, now I do. Lucky for you and this pip-squeak over here, everyone else bet against you too, so while I may have lost personally, the house actually made some good money tonight. I want you back here again tomorrow night for another fight. Okay?"

"Yeah. Okay."

"And if you can do again what you did tonight…" Leo walked over to the window overlooking the casino and motioned for Sarah to follow him. "You'll get a shot at one hundred grand, by challeng- ing her…"

Sarah looked out the window at the near empty casino. The gambling tended to die down after the fights ended. The fighting was, after all, a hard act to follow. In the middle of the octagon, Claudia was sparring with another woman. Sarah recognized this woman as Priscilla, a large, muscular woman who had lost the first fight of the evening. Priscilla was a brawler who was beaten by a kick- boxer who was faster and taller than her. The other woman's height and speed advantage kept Priscilla at a distance until she couldn't take anymore and had to give up.

This didn't matter to Claudia, who was using Priscilla as a human punching bag. Priscilla's face was a mangled mess of blood and flesh. After staying on her feet for way longer than anyone would think humanly possible, Priscilla finally fell. This didn't matter one bit to Claudia. She was in one of her frenzied states. Mind blank and with fire in her eyes, she jumped on top of Priscilla and continued to pummel her in her already unconscious head.

Sarah watched this all unfold in abject horror. She'd never seen such relentless brutality in all of her years fighting. Without saying a word to either Leo or Vinny, she stormed out of the office and ran as fast as she could to the casino floor. Priscilla was barely breathing and in danger of choking on her own blood by the time Sarah got into the octagon. As Claudia reared her arm back for a blow—what more than likely would have been a lethal one—Sarah grabbed her wrist. With the deadly blow stopped before it could land, Sarah used her other arm to push Claudia off Priscilla.

"Stop! She's had enough!" Sarah screamed.

"I say when she's had enough!" Claudia growled back. "She dares to come in here and fight for the right to challenge me. Now she has, and she gets what she deserves. But okay, I'm done. Just remember this: you keep it up and I'll give this to you some day. And when I do, there's gonna be no one there to stop me." Claudia got up and stormed away in disgust, giving Priscilla's limp and defense- less leg a kick on her way out of the octagon. Sarah rushed over to Priscilla, picked her head up, and slapped her cheek gently in an attempt to revive her.

Leo and Vinny were standing in the middle of the path to the octagon as Claudia approached. Leo didn't say anything. He didn't have to—the dirty look he gave Claudia said it all. Claudia, still fired up, stopped. "What?" she said indignantly.

"We'll talk after you shower," replied Leo. His voice was extra deep, and he spoke with authority.

"Fine—whatever." Claudia continued on and pushed Vinny out of the way, saying, "Get out of my way you little maggot" for good measure.

By the time Leo and Vinny got to the octagon, Sarah had successfully revived Priscilla. Even though Priscilla's face was totally swollen and she couldn't talk, at least she was breathing—even if barely—and it looked like she would live. Leo turned to Vinny. "Go get Carmine." Vinny scurried away.

Leo squatted down and looked at Priscilla. He winced when he saw the extent of the damage to her face. "You'll be okay, kid," he said reassuringly.

Sarah was less reassured. "What the hell was that?" she demanded.

Leo stood up. Sarah stayed bent down, holding Priscilla. "Sorry you had to see that. I've talked to Claudia about it before, and it looks like I'll have to have another discussion with her tonight. She goes crazy—literally. She gets into these frenzies where she just can't control herself. She takes things too far. Then things like this happen. It's a good thing you stopped her."

"She would have killed this girl!" insisted Sarah. Leo's casual attitude toward Claudia's extreme violence was mind-numbing. Then she quickly thought about it. If he got off on women fighters, then she must have been like some kind of ultimate prize—a woman who would fight, batter, and kill without compunction. Not that Leo was a man of high morals himself. These two were a match made in hell. Leo just nodded in agreement. "I'm glad you stopped her." Sarah was skeptical at this statement. She figured that Leo liked the killing. It got him hot for Claudia. The only problem for him was that she was doing it too much and too often. Disposing of the bod-ies was becoming a real hassle that he simply did not need.

Vinny returned with Carmine. Leo put a hand on Carmine's shoulder and whispered, "Take her to the vet" in his ear.

Carmine turned to Vinny. "Can you help me take her to the car?"

Vinny agreed and he, Carmine, and Sarah helped Priscilla stand up and walk out of the octagon as Leo looked on. He watched the four of them disappear from the casino. He stayed inside the octagon for a minute, looking at the lights and imagining the crowd. His father was a boxer and taught Leo some techniques when he was younger. Those memories of youth coursing through his head, Leo ducked, rolled, jabbed, and threw a roundhouse and an uppercut in the middle of the octagon, a champ in his own mind.

It was 7:15 a.m., and Jill was already sitting in a booth at the Good Eats Diner, located in the dining and entertainment district, waiting for Sarah. The expected meeting wasn't until seven thirty, but Jill decided to get there early to secure a corner booth in the back of the diner that was not next to a window. The diner itself was a River City classic. Established in 1953 and well known for the eggs over easy and corned beef hash special, there was no better place for a home-cooked breakfast and a cup of weak coffee. Jill sipped coffee and pretended to read the local newspaper, the *River City Gazette* as she waited. She couldn't really concentrate on the paper though. Not when she got a text from Sarah at 2:00 a.m. to meet her here. It sounded urgent. The *Gazette* was a rag anyway. The editor in chief's mayor-supporting, antipolice stance sickened her. She stared at the banner on the front page with its hideous font and wondered how this paper was still in business.

Lost in thought, she did not notice a completely disheveled and haggard-looking woman plop down in the seat across from her. When she looked up and saw that it was Sarah, she was aghast. "Whoa! What the hell happened to you?" Not the most sensitive of statements, but an honest one.

Sarah was in no mood to explain all that went on the previous evening. "Let's just say I had a rough night last night and leave it at that."

"Fair enough," Jill shrugged while sipping her tepid coffee. Sarah, meanwhile, took the pill bottle out of her pocket and plunked it on the table. "What are those?" Jill questioned most curiously. She had no idea Sarah was taking any prescription medication.

"I get awful headaches in high-stress situations. Trust me when I tell you, this definitely counts." Sarah then popped a couple of pills and looked around for her water. It suddenly dawned on her that she just arrived, and the waitress hadn't come over yet. Ever the pragma- tist, Sarah washed the pills down with a big gulp of Jill's water.

Jill didn't really care since all she wanted was her coffee. Still, she couldn't let this one slide so easily. "Thank goodness I wasn't drink- ing that," she stated sarcastically.

"It's water. They have more." Sarah's sarcasm matched Jill's in tone and bite. Then she got serious and asked, "How is Vice's case against Manetti going? Any progress?"

Jill knew the banter was over, and it was time to get down to the shoptalk. "None. If that place was a front for the Manetti drug operation, there's no way to tie it back to them. They managed to keep their hands very clean with Paisano's. All we have are recordings of a bunch of strange orders and one unreliable witness—your pal Vinny—pointing the finger at them. Vice thinks it's too flimsy. With nothing concrete, they can just say that Paisano's was running its own operation, and they knew nothing about it."

Sarah thought for a moment. "Well, someone obviously had to supply them if that were true."

"They'd blame the Chinese. Vice says they can see this coming a mile away if they act on what they have right now, which isn't much." "Damn." Sarah was hoping for an out to her situation. No such luck.

Jill continued, "That's why we need you to get what you can at that Amazon club. What do you have so far?"

"It's quite an operation. We could bust him right now for the illegal casino he's running," Sarah said excitedly, hoping for another out. No such luck again. Jill had to shoot her down. "Yeah, but the lieutenant wants more than that. He wants to link these murders to the Hammer. Any leads on those?"

"Nothing solid, but I'm pretty sure they were all beaten to death by the same woman."

Jill's eyes widened. This was huge news to hear. "Really? Who?" she asked, barely able to keep her voice down.

Sarah was less excited. Her closeness to the situation caused her to be more measured and matter-of-fact in her response. "Her name's Claudia. She's Leo Manetti's girlfriend—and right-hand goon."

"Interesting," Jill said calmly, trying her best to emulate Sarah's more straightforward view of the situation. All three of the bodies did suffer massive blunt force trauma, as if they were beaten to death."

Jill was referencing the coroner's reports. Sarah recalled what she'd seen too. "I remember something else from the coroner's reports too: that one of the victims had traces of skin under her fingernails." "Right," said Jill, a bit confused. She could see the wheels turn-ing in Sarah's head but wasn't sure where they were going. "What are you thinking?"

Sarah filled her in on the plan that just formulated from their discussion. "I think that if I get in the ring with Claudia, I can scratch her and get some skin under my nails. If it matches the DNA from the skin under the victim's nails, we know we have our killer."

Jill understood the plan all too well. This would require Sarah to be in the ring with a woman who might beat her to death. She admired Sarah's bravery but was concerned. "All right, but be careful. She's killed three already—that we know of."

Sarah nodded. She knew even better than Jill that a lot of care was going to be needed to make it out alive. "I will. She's tough but not invincible."

"After that, we can implicate Leo Manetti, then all we have to do is trace it back to his father."

"Speaking of—you bring it?" Sarah's text had asked Jill to bring a special little something with her—a small tracking device that could adhere to any surface. Jill swung by the precinct to pick it up on her way to the diner.

"Yup, I got it." Jill took the tracker out of her pocket. When she opened her fist, it was in the palm of her hand, no bigger than a dime. Jill put it on a napkin and casually slid it to Sarah while taking another sip of now room temperature coffee.

"You think you can get this tracker into the bag you told me about?"

"Yeah, I do. I may need Vinny to help with a little distraction, but I think I can do it."

"I hope so," said Jill, letting out a small giggle. She couldn't believe that Vinny was being—and would be—so helpful. She was also amazed at Sarah's level of trust in him. "Where is the little rat anyway?" she asked.

"Who knows?" she said with indifference. "He's not going any- where with that ankle bracelet on. He better do what I say, or else."

Jill smiled. This was exactly what she needed to hear. It gave her confidence that Sarah was still in control in the situation. "That's right. And don't let him forget it."

"I won't. I have to go. I need to rest up for tonight. See you soon."

"See you soon," Jill said, thinking to herself that her coffee cup was almost empty and the waitress was nowhere to be seen. Was she on break? She then had the thought that she better say something more encouraging to Sarah, so she followed it up with "And, Sarah… good luck."

CHAPTER 11

MIKE "THE HAMMER" Manetti—a slender, very well-groomed and finely tailored fifty-eight-year-old man with olive skin and fine dark hair with streaks of gray on the sides—sat at the desk in his home office. The house itself was opulent and well-decorated with a warm, homey feel. There was a lot of dark mahogany and leather in the decor. The Hammer's life was stressful, and it helped him to relax. His wife, Catarina, didn't complain. He took good care of his family—especially her—and she got what she wanted in other ways like fine jewelry, fashionable clothes, and fancy dinners at high-end restaurants.

The local football team, the River City Mongeese, were playing that day. The Hammer was watching it on the sixty-inch 4K television affixed to the wall across from his desk. The team was named after the woodland creatures that used to live in the lowland forest near the river that gave River City its name. This was before the industrial revolution. Over the decades between the city's found- ing in 1799 to the early 1850s, the mongoose population of River City was completely driven away. The team mascot was a memory of times long since gone. Still, the Hammer thought it was a stupid mascot. Or at the very least they could have named the team the Mongooses, which was the more accepted plural. Mongeese sounded terrible to him.

Nevertheless, he rooted for his home team. He enjoyed sit- ting back in the afternoon on his high-backed, leather-bound desk chair, sipping a cognac, smoking a cigar, and watching a game. Sports were a major part of the Hammer's life—even before he took a cut of the bookie action in the city as the head of the Manetti crime family.

*****

The Hammer's sport of choice wasn't football, however. He preferred individual competition over team sport. His favorite was the sweet science: boxing. Growing up in the Italian neighborhood in River City, his best option to make something of himself was to either get really good grades, become a successful athlete, or join a gang. While he didn't exactly find the life of crime unappealing, he figured the honest options were the best ones. Since he had undiagnosed dyslexia until the age of twelve, Michael found school a frustrating experience. He was put in all remedial classes and even his own parents thought he was slow. The experience put a bitter taste in young Michael's mouth for school. He wanted out as soon as he could get out. This left him only one option: athletics. For him, it was just a matter of choosing a sport and exceling at it.

By a happy coincidence the local boxing gym, called Marco's, was on the corner of the street he grew up on. After middle school every day, starting at age thirteen, Michael came home, kissed his mother, threw his books in his room, grabbed a snack, and headed off to the gym. His mother didn't mind him going out and didn't ask too many questions. Michael was always home in time for supper, and he did his homework later at night.

At first Michael went to the gym just to watch the boxers train and see what it was like. After a month, he would stand in the corner of the gym, copying what he saw—sticking, moving, and shadowboxing with the men in the gym. One day the owner of the gym, a husky, retired ex-prizefighter named Marco Di Ventura, noticed young Michael. He was impressed with what the kid was picking up just by watching the boxers. He walked up behind Michael one day when he was shadowboxing and gave him a friendly "You got some moves, kid."

Michael froze in midpunch. He put his arm down and turned around slowly to face Marco. To his relief, Marco didn't look upset.

Regardless, he was at a loss for words. He clearly wasn't a member of the gym and figured he'd might get called out eventually. He was hoping it wouldn't happen, though—at least not this soon. It's not his fault that the guy at the front desk didn't check memberships. The guy barely looked up from his daily crossword puzzle as Michael snuck by.

Marco could see that Michael was frazzled. He continued. "How old are you?"

Michael swallowed before he spoke. "Thirteen, sir."

"You can call me Marco. I work for a living." Marco smiled at Michael, hoping the tension with the kid would be broken. It wasn't, but he pressed on. "If you're thirteen, then you're not supposed to be in here. No one can legally train here until they're at least sixteen."

Michael hung his head in shame. Now he was thinking that Marco was going to call his parents. He was in for a beating if Marco did that. But after a deep breath, Marco said something that would change Michael Manetti's life. "However, if you work here, then you can be in here."

Michael's face betrayed his confusion. Marco saw it and explained further. "Unofficially, of course. You're too young to be hired outright, but if you come here after school every day like you've been doing and clean the locker rooms, help with the laundry, and run and errand here and there for me, I'll let you stay around. Any downtime and you can watch the boxers train like you've been doing. I'll pay you under the table, and no one has to know except for us. Deal?"

It took Michael a second to absorb all that he had just heard. Once he did, he excitedly said, "Deal!" Marco stuck out his meaty hand. Michael took it, and they shook on the deal.

The next three years were the happiest Michael had ever been. He loved working at the gym. The boxers appreciated having the kid around to bring them a water bottle, or a towel, or when nec- essary, a spit bucket, and he liked them too. Michael managed to get friendly with a few of the boxers, and they would occasionally give him a pointer or two when they saw him working out in the corner.

Then came the big day. Michael turned sixteen years old. This meant that he was officially able to join the gym and be trained. Marco knew that Michael was looking forward to this day—it was all he'd talked about for the past six weeks—and as a gift on his six- teenth birthday, Marco presented him with a membership card. The dues were paid in full for the entire year. Marco was a bit sad that the cheap help he'd had around the gym was going away—Michael's ability to run with a spit bucket and not spill a drop was uncanny and spoke to his incredible balance—but he was gaining a very promising young boxer.

The River City Boxing Association, in accordance with state guidelines, allowed young men to be trained to box starting at age sixteen; however, they were not legally allowed to fight until they were eighteen. Michael spent the two years between his sixteenth and eighteenth birthdays training as hard as he could. He conditioned himself to have the best stamina, best strength, and best technique of anyone in the gym. By the time Michael reached the eighteen-year milestone, he was pumped, primed, and ready for action.

Michael quickly burned off what little belly fat he carried with him shortly after he started training. He followed a strict diet and exercise regimen. Even though Michael missed his mother's capellini carbonara and sometimes had to force himself out of bed at five in the morning to go for a three-mile run to start the day, he knew the sacrifices would pay off. As a result, Michael became lean and wiry, with superb muscle definition. Marco went with Michael to the RCBA headquarters in midtown to officially register to box. He came in at a lean, mean 144.8 pounds and was pronounced a welterweight. Six months later, Michael was in his first welter- weight bout.

The fight was at the Riverside Arena. Michael and his Puerto Rican opponent, twenty-one-year-old Federico, "Zoom Zoom" Espinoza, were one of three fights on the undercard that evening with the main event being a light heavyweight bout. Michael felt tense that evening and was a bit worried about Espinoza. This was Espinoza's sixth fight with a three-win, two-loss record and one knockout. Espinoza was called Zoom Zoom because of his ability to move around the ring so quickly every round and never tire out. Michael and Marco had been studying video footage of Espinoza as part of training. The strategy was to bring Espinoza in close—corner him if Michael could—and pound on him until he hit the mat and the referee sent Michael to his corner.

The strategy worked, but not until Espinoza had gotten in a few good licks. For the first three rounds, he danced around Michael, making the rookie boxer's head spin. Then it was a jab here and a hook there, scoring points on Michael. One surprise uppercut in round three even sent Michael to the mat for a nine count.

Michael was shrewd, though. He watched Espinoza closely and saw that he had a tell. Whenever Espinoza would scurry left, he twisted his wrist on his left hand to the left. When moving right, he twisted his right wrist to the right. Michael caught on to this pat- tern early in round two. It was something that neither he nor Marco picked up on in the video they watched. It was consistent enough where Michael felt that he could exploit it in round four.

After the bell rang for round four, Espinoza came out light- footed, practically dancing as he hopped. He was as confident as ever. That changed quickly. Espinoza threw a couple of jabs at Michael that he blocked. Then Michael saw it. As Espinoza brought his left arm back from a jab, he twisted his wrist to the left. Before Espinoza could make his move, Michael wound up his right hook and let it fly. Espinoza's head ran right into Michael's fist. Espinoza thought his head might fly off from the impact of the punch, which was assisted by his own momentum moving into it. The lights in the arena got blurry for Espinoza, then went dark. Round four was over within twenty seconds. Michael had won by knockout.

The crowd erupted in cheers. They didn't know Michael, but they knew a good fight when they saw one. Local sports reporters, gamblers, bookies, and everyone at the RCBA took notice of Michael. The new kid in the ring officially made a name for himself when Espinoza, after he recovered, was interviewed by a reporter about getting knocked out by the hot newcomer and said, "It wasn't like getting punched by a fist.

It was like getting hit by a hammer." From then on, the name stuck. He was Mike "the Hammer" Manetti.

Michael liked the moniker and adopted it. All promotional materials for him called him the Hammer for all his fights. For the next five years, Mike "the Hammer" Manetti made a name for him- self as a force to be reckoned with. It wasn't just Espinoza who talked about the impact of his punches. Other opponents did as well. By the time he was high enough in the rankings to earn a shot at the welterweight title, Michael was ten and zero with seven knockouts. He was clearly doing something right and was riding high on the thought of being champ.

One afternoon, while Michael was walking home from train- ing, two burly men exited a car and blocked his path. They didn't give their names, but they knew who Michael was, and they asked to speak to him. Michael got a bad vibe from the men and told them he didn't have time, then tried to move past them. The men moved to block his path again. This time the second man opened up his jacket and flashed Michael his revolver. He very quietly but insistently said to Michael, "Make time."

The first man opened the rear car door. The second man with the gun walked with Michael and had him get in first. The first man stayed outside and stood watch while the man with the gun talked to Michael in the back seat of the car.

"You're Mike 'the Hammer' Manetti, right?" the man said, squinting at Michael as he looked over his face. Michael nodded. The man continued, "Good. Then I need you to do me a favor."

Michael felt his stomach get queasy. He'd heard the rumors of the Bianchi crime family taking an interest in boxing and fixing some matches. Before the man with the gun even said it, Michael knew what was coming.

The man paid no attention to Michael's noticeable shift in demeanor and discomfort. He carried on. "You're fighting Jack 'Ironhead' Morris for the title this Saturday, right?"

"Right," Michael replied weakly. He was feeling intimidated and exactly where he didn't want to be in spite of knowing it could happen.

The man smiled a sly smile at Michael. "Good. The person that I represent…let's just say he's very powerful and has a lot of money riding on that fight. In the fifth round, if you should happen to go down and not get back up again, he would make it worth your while."

"How worth my while?" Even Michael was stunned that he had the courage to ask that question. Before he knew it, the words were falling out of his mouth.

The man wasn't taken aback at all. He expected the question and was prepared with the answer. "Fifty Gs' worth it. How is that?" Michael couldn't lie to himself. It was a big number and double what he would earn for winning the fight. However, his honor, his record, his reputation, and most importantly, the title was at stake.

As tempting as it was, he had a hard time saying yes. "Let me think about it," he said nervously.

The man leaned back in his seat. He admired the kid's tough- ness for not caving in, though it was the last thing he expected. "Okay, think it over," he said, "but don't take too long. We'll be back tomorrow for your answer."

The man opened the car door and got out. Michael got out after him. As he exited the car, the two men stood close to him. The man with the gun said, "Have a good evening. We'll see you tomor- row" as the other man glared at Michael.

Saying nothing and wanting to escape the situation as fast as possible, Michael started to head home. After walking for about fifty yards, he looked behind him and saw that the two men were sitting in the car watching him. Not wanting to tip off where he lived— the last thing he wanted was to put his parents in danger—Michael turned around and headed back to the gym.

The driver's side window was down and the first man was smoking a cigarette as he watched Michael while the man with the gun looked through the pages of a small notebook. Michael walked on the other side of the street from the car. He did his best to keep his head down and move past them as quickly as possible. The man in the driver's seat ashed his cigarette as Michael passed by the car. For a moment, Michael was afraid they might ask him where he was going. He quickly decided to tell them that he forgot something if they asked, but they didn't.

The car peeled away as Michael made it to the gym's front door. His heart was beating out of his chest. He'd been in enough boxing matches to give him the confidence to handle himself physically, but that was an intense psychological and emotional experience like he had never felt before.

His legs felt like gelatin as he walked up the stairs to Marco's office. Luckily for him, Marco was there late looking over receipts. Judging by the pile on his desk, business was good. Having a contender for the championship tended to do things like that for a gym. Marco shot up from his desk when he saw a perspiring, pale-looking Michael in his doorway. "Whoa! Michael, what hap- pened? Please, sit down." He took Michael by the arm and led him to the chair in front of his desk.

It felt good for Michael to get off his feet. He took a deep breath and explained. "Bianchi goons. One of them had a gun. He made me get into a car and told me that he'd pay me fifty thousand dollars if I took a dive during the championship fight on Saturday."

Marco looked somber and concerned. "What did you tell them?" he asked.

"I told them I'd think about it."

There was a long pause. Marco was expecting a more detailed answer. "And?" he prodded.

"And…that's it," said Michael. "They let me go to think about it and told me they'd be back tomorrow. I started walking home but got scared that they would follow me so I came back here."

Marco nodded. "Smart move. You don't want people like that knowing where you live."

"They pulled away as I came in here. Michael was starting to feel better and started to get up. "I should get home. My mom is probably worried about me by now."

Marco put his hand up. "Stop!" Michael froze still in the middle of getting up. "Sit back down," Marco commanded.

Confused, Michael did as he was told. "Why? What's up?" "Just because they pulled away, it doesn't mean they still aren't watching. I grew up with guys like that, the ones that get into crime. They have the patience of a chopping block. The odds are that they're still out there somewhere you can't see them, just waiting to follow you."

Now Michael was starting to feel rattled again. "What should I do?" he asked.

"Stay here. I have a cot that I can set up in the locker room." "What about my mom?"

"Call her. Tell her that I asked you to stay here with me for the next few days until the fight as a kind of last-minute boot camp to make sure that you're in top condition for the title bout."

Michael didn't like the idea of lying to his mother. Marco sensed this and advised, "It's better than telling her you're hiding out from gangsters, right?"

Michael saw the wisdom when Marco put it that way. Marco picked up the phone on his desk and put it in front of Michael. "Call her."

Michael picked up the receiver. He dialed his home number with trembling fingers. His mother answered after a ring and a half. As Michael predicted, she was worried about him and was hoping he would call. After he calmed her down and assured he that he was okay, he explained to her that he had to stay there exactly as Marco told him to do. When his mom asked if she could stop by the gym and see him or bring him anything, he shot her down by saying no—Marco wanted no outside disturbances. He apologized for the last-minute notice and let her know that he'd see her in three days, on Saturday night after the fight. Michael told his mom that he loved her and hung up.

Marco was impressed with how cool Michael acted under pressure in spite of being so nervous in the beginning. This was a good trait for a boxer.

Michael was decidedly less pleased with himself, but what was done was done. Since that was now over, Michael had bigger problems to worry about. He needed advice and guidance from his mentor. "Now, what should I do about these guys that asked me throw the fight?"

Marco looked sternly at Michael. The young man braced himself. He'd seen that look before and knew that whatever was coming next was going to be serious. "What do you want to do?"

This threw Michael off-kilter. Marco was not usually the "answer a question with a question" type. There was a long pause as Michael thought seriously, weighing the money he could make versus winning the championship. There was also the risk factor to consider. He knew what could happen if he refused.

Finally Michael made up his mind. "I don't want to do it. I want to be champ. But I know the consequences if I don't do this thing." He paused again, thinking some more, then came out with, "I gotta do it, don't I?"

"If you think you do," said Marco, his face betraying a combination of disappointment and relief. Marco had a friend who was a better boxer than him when he first started out. The friend was asked to take a dive—it wasn't even a championship fight, just an under- card bout—but refused. Two weeks later his arm was found stuck in a storm drain. The rest of him was never recovered. As much as it sickened Marco, he knew the wise move was to let the mobsters have their way and pray that the RCBA didn't catch on.

"I do," Michael replied definitively. He wasn't proud of his decision. However, he was still young and figured that someday it would be his turn if he did this favor now.

Michael tossed and turned all night, and not just because the cot was the most uncomfortable thing he had ever slept on. His choice to throw the fight ate away at his conscience. Whenever it really started to bother him, he tried to think of all the bad things that would happen if he didn't do it. It helped him get a few hours of intermittent sleep.

Being summer, and with nowhere else to be, Michael could spend all day at the gym. Even though the idea of a boot camp was just a ploy to ease the mind of Michael's mother, Marco turned it into fact, doing two training sessions with Michael per day—one in the morning and one in the afternoon.

Michael walked out of the gym the next day after the afternoon session, and as expected the two men from yesterday were waiting for him. Michael approached them slowly and carefully, but was less nervous now that he knew he was giving them what in their minds would be good news.

The man with the gun spoke first as soon as Michael was in earshot. "So have you made a decision?"

"Yeah," said Michael.

And?" the man asked impatiently. "I'll do it."

Both men smiled. "I knew you'd make the right decision," the man with the gun exclaimed. He reached into his coat pocket and pulled out a yellow envelope. He handed it to Michael. "Here's a taste," the man continued quietly. "It's ten thousand. Consider it a down payment on the remaining forty Gs you'll get after you come through on Saturday."

Michael frowned as he took the money and tucked it into his pants and under his shirt. The first man saw this and patted Michael on the shoulder. "Cheer up, kid. In two more days, you're gonna have more money than you or anyone in your family has ever seen in their lives. Just think about that." The man with the gun nodded in agreement.

After giving them both a nod of understanding and accordance, Michael turned and walked back to the gym. Marco cautioned that even if Michael agreed, they would still watch him until he came through, so no going home—it still wasn't safe. Plus, Marco really liked his boot camp idea and wanted to get in another two sessions with Michael the following day. Just because Michael was going to lose this fight, it was no reason to slack on training.

When Michael got back into the gym he threw the envelope on the cot. He stared at it, thinking about what it symbolized. On the one hand he sold out, cashed in, and agreed to cheat for the mob. On the other hand, he'd be dead if he didn't comply. He moved the envelope under his cot, both to get it out of his sight and also for safekeeping. Aggression was swelling up in Michael, and he needed a release. He left the locker room and did some bag work to let it out.

The night of the big fight was so humid, the air outside could be cut with a knife. Inside the air-conditioned River City Arena, the crowd was so jam-packed that all of the body heat increased the room temperature by at least five degrees. The only cool place in the whole big room was in the ring; that was where Michael was headed, with Marco behind him.

Shortly after Michael's entrance into the ring to a less-than-stellar reception from the crowd, the reigning welterweight champion, Jack "Ironhead" Morris, was announced. The crowd erupted with cheers for him. Morris made his way to the ring with an entourage of trainers, coaches, and assistants. He took his sweet time getting into the ring, so Michael looked around at the audience. That's where he spotted, in the front row on Morris's side, Giuseppe "the Boss" Bianchi. He was flanked on either side by the two men who talked to Michael. Bianchi was hard to miss. He was a large man. Plus, he'd had his picture in the paper quite a few times as Michael was grow- ing up. But that was not why Michael spotted him so easily. Michael spotted him because in an arena full of tens of thousands of people cheering and watching Morris enter the ring, Bianchi was the only one sitting with his arms folded, staring at Michael.

A chill went up Michael's spine, He looked away and headed to his corner. Marco was waiting for him. "Tune out all the noise, kid," Marco said as he helped Michael take off his robe, "It's just you and him now."

Michael nodded and hopped up and down to stay loose. The referee called both boxers to the middle of the ring. He gave them both the usual spiel about a fair fight, watch the low blows and rabbit punches, blah blah blah… Michael understood why it had to be said, but he could recite it in his sleep. What he preferred concentrating on was his opponent, looking him over and sizing him up. His assessment of Morris was unimpressive to say the least. Michael regarded him as slight of build for a welterweight. From the weigh-in he knew that Morris came in at 142.2 pounds. Michael couldn't help but think that the scales were tipped by about ten pounds. Morris was also at least four inches shorter than Michael. The only thing exceptional, perhaps, about Morris was his extra thick cranium, which gave him a Cro-Magnon-like appearance. This was how Morris developed his reputation and gained the nickname Ironhead. It was said that his opponents could tire themselves out punching Morris in the head, and he'd barely feel it.

Mike "the Hammer" Manetti and Jack "Ironhead" Morris did a pretty good dance for three rounds. Michael figured that Morris knew about the set up and was putting on a show to make it look believable, but each boxer barely touched the other one. Michael decided that in the fourth round, he'd better inject a little more excitement into the proceedings so it looked good.

The bell rang for the fourth round, and the two boxers did what they'd been doing—a jab here, a hook there, the occasional body blow. After about a minute Michael decided to spice things up, and after a series of body blows, just as Morris stopped protecting himself, Michael nailed him with an uppercut. It was nothing too powerful, at least by Michael's standards, but it caught Morris off guard, and he went down like a bag of rocks.

The referee rushed over and sent a completely bewildered Michael to his corner. Marco was waiting for him, looking equally perplexed. As soon as Michael got to the corner, Marco asked, "Did they tell you he had a glass jaw?"

"No!" exclaimed a very worried Michael. He turned around and looked at Morris lying on the canvas. He was out cold—breathing, but in no shape to get up.

"Son of a bitch!" said Marco as the referee counted. "The only way this bum ever became champ—and kept it—was if all of his fights were rigged. There's no way this guy ever won a legitimate fight."

"What about the iron head?" Michael asked, confused.

"That's all bull—something they made up to sound legit based on the way this guy looks. The sad truth though is that while his forehead may be thick, his jaw is not. You're about to become the champ, Michael."

Sure enough, as soon as Marco got done speaking those words, the referee counted to ten and pronounced Michael the winner via knockout. The referee called Michael to the center of the ring and held up his arm in victory as members of Morris's crew worked to resuscitate their boxer. As soon as the announcement was done and Michael was handed the welterweight championship belt, he went back to his corner. Now more than ever, Michael needed advice from his trainer, coach, and mentor. Marco had this advice, given to Michael in one short word: "Run."

Michael exited the ring and sprinted down the hall back to the locker room. Marco wasn't as fast as Michael but followed as closely behind as he could. As soon as he got in, Michael threw his newly earned championship belt to the ground and began tearing at the strings on his gloves with his teeth. His heart was racing with the thought of boss Bianchi and his goons hot on his tail. He felt like he swallowed his Adam's apple when the door burst open after a few seconds of gnawing. He was relieved to see it was Marco, who already had the scissors ready.

Without a word spoken, Marco expertly cut the gloves off both of Michael's hands in seconds. There was no time to fool around with knots. Once done, he looked at Michael, and Michael could see that Marco was gravely concerned. "Go!" Marco insisted. "Get out! Run— and go far away!" Dressed in nothing but his boxing shorts and boots, Michael made a mad dash for the back exit. He could hear the locker room door open far behind him as he rounded the corner. He knew that at that moment Marco was face to face with Bianchi and the two men who roughed him up. Marco was on his own. There was nothing Michael could do to help him. It was him they wanted anyway. He needed to flee.

Michael walked the fifty blocks from the arena in the dining and entertainment district to his home in the Italian neighborhood, unwrapping his hands along the way. He was paranoid the whole time, ducking into alleys and hiding behind garbage bins whenever he saw a pair of headlights he thought were driving just a bit too slow. Michael's parents had attended the fight that evening. He looked up and saw the light was on in the apartment, so he knew they were home. This made sense since they drove and weren't hiding from gangsters. Since they were early risers, Michael figured that they stayed up late just to congratulate him on his big win. He had no idea how he was going to break it to them that his plan was to pack a bag, leave town—possibly leave the country—and would not be sure if and when he'd ever see them again.

When Michael opened the door to the apartment, his blood ran cold. Sitting at the table were his mother, his father, and Boss Bianchi. Michael stood in the doorway in stunned silence for what felt like an eternity until Bianchi said in a cool voice, "Come in, kid. And close the door."

Michael did as he was told. "How did you find me?" he asked. Bianchi pointed toward the bathroom that was adjacent to the kitchen. "Take a look in there. We didn't want to get blood all over the place in here."

Michael crept to the bathroom. He didn't want to look, but knew he had to. *What blood is he talking about?* he thought to himself as he made his way. His question was soon answered when he saw Marco laying in the bathtub, bleeding out slowly from the multiple puncture wounds in his torso. Sitting next to him and holding the bloody pair of scissors that did the job—Michael recognized them as the same ones Marco used to cut off his gloves—was the man who a few days before held a gun on Michael and asked him to throw the fight. The man grimaced menacingly at Michael as he stroked the scissors back and forth with his index finger. Feeling sick, Michael turned away and headed back to the kitchen.

Within the few seconds that it took Michael to get back to the kitchen table, his whole body felt weak. His knees were about to give out. He had to sit down. Bianchi watched this all unfold with a surprising amount of sympathy. He tapped Michael on the forearm. "Don't be too mad at your trainer. He really put up a fight. You should see my other guy. He's around the block, waiting with the car, but you should see him. Your trainer knocked him out cold in one punch. That man packs a wallop. It took my other guy a lot of stabs with those scissors to get him to give you up. You have to understand, Michael—there is only so much a man can take before he wants it all to end. Your trainer hit his limit, so here we are."

The words "your trainer" infuriated Michael enough for him to get some strength back. *The man's name is Marco Di Ventura, and he is a good friend, trainer, and mentor,* thought Michael. *Now he's dying in my bathtub.* He kept these thoughts to himself, though. He already knew he was in enough hot water and didn't want to make things any worse for himself or for his parents.

Bianchi continued, "Now we need to talk about what hap- pened tonight. But first, I'm the kind of person who likes to make sure I have all of my facts right. There's already been enough blood- shed tonight, and I don't want any more on account of me acting rashly." Bianchi turned his head toward the bathroom and shouted, "Anthony—come out here now."

Anthony—the goon with the gun from earlier who also stabbed Marco—put the scissors on the bathroom counter top and stepped into the kitchen. Bianchi looked at him very seriously and asked, "Take a look at this young man. Do you see him?"

"I do," replied Anthony.

"This is the young man you made our arrangement with, correct?"

"That is correct."

"Okay, good. I need to be sure that you asked the right guy the right question. Did you ask this young man a question, Anthony?"

"Yes, I did.

"And what did you ask him?"

"I asked him if he'd throw the fight."

Michael's parents couldn't believe their ears. They reacted to this revelation with shock and disbelief. Bianchi didn't even look at them. He kept his gaze locked on to Anthony as he put up a hand to signal them to be silent. They immediately obliged. Michael saw how disappointed his parents were and it crushed him.

"Very good," Bianchi coolly stated. "And what did this young man reply?"

"Well, it took a day…he had to think it over…but he said yes." "I see." Bianchi fixed his serpentine sights on Michael. "Is this

correct, Michael? Or is Anthony a liar."

Finally, Michael felt like he had a chance to talk, to explain. "It's all true, Mr. Bianchi, but I swear what happened tonight was an accident. I didn't know that the other guy would go down so easy. Honestly, if I'd have known—"

Bianchi held up him hand, similar to the way he did to his parents, signaling Michael to be quiet. "My only concern is with what happened. The how and the why I leave up to you. The fact that a mistake was made is on you. You made an agreement with my associate here, which is by extension an agreement with me, and you broke it. Accident or not, you broke it. And in the process, you cost me a five-hundred-thousand dollar bet. Amends must be made. I will first try to conduct business in a gentlemanly way and ask you this ques- tion: do you have five hundred thousand dollars that you can give me right now, or anytime, say, within the next month, to pay me back?"

Michael was confused by the question. Bianchi obviously could see where Michael lived—and that he still lived with his parents. He couldn't afford to move out on his own yet, let alone make a five-hundred-thousand-dollar payment. So Michael did the only thing he could do and answered honestly, "No."

Bianchi grimaced and shook his head. "Too bad." Reaching down, he grabbed a small ball-peen hammer he had waiting by his side. Michael recognized it as the one from his dad's toolbox. Bianchi laid the hammer on the table and said to Michael in a flat tone, "If you can't pay me back, I can't let you box again."

Before Michael knew what was happening, Anthony was behind him. Anthony grabbed Michael's wrists and forced his hands flat on the table. Michael's parents looked away in horror as Bianchi raised the hammer over his head. All fake pretenses and faux sympathy were gone. Bianchi shouted, "You wanna be the hammer. Now you'll get the hammer!"

Michael's mother screamed as Bianchi slammed the ham- mer down. His father grabbed her and held her tight. Both shut their eyes in horror as Bianchi rained blow after blow down onto Michael's hands with the hammer. For his part, Michael gritted his teeth, scrunched up his face, and bore the blows. As a trained boxer, he knew how to deal with pain, though he'd never felt pain like this before. He watched as the hammer went down on each hand. He felt the blunt force trauma of the impact. After a few seconds, he could feel the sharp pain of the shattered bones of his hand moving under his skin.

It was over almost as quickly as it began. For a man as strong and as angry as Bianchi, it didn't take much to crush a pair of hands.

Anthony let go of Michael's wrists. Michael looked at his bloodied, mangled hands. An out-of-breath Bianchi threw the hammer down on the table and said, "Okay. Now we're through—and so are you." Michael's mother was sobbing and in hysterics. She was incon- solable, no matter how hard her father tried. Neither one said a word to Michael. Bianchi and Anthony went into the bathroom. He could hear them pulling down the shower curtain. He knew they were going to use it to wrap up Marco's body and dispose of it somehow. Michael said nothing. He barely moved. He just stared at his hands, smashed and crooked. He knew he'd never box again.

CHAPTER 12

MIKE "THE HAMMER" Manetti leaned back in his leather-bound chair and finished off his third cognac as the third quarter wound down in the River City Mongeese game. The buzz he felt from the cognac only encouraged him to act out on the agitation that he was feeling. He almost stood up from his chair as he shouted, "You call that pass protection! My eighty-year-old mother could block better than that right guard. How are these bums supposed to cover the spread if their QB keeps getting sacked like that?!"

Silvio Russo, a friend of Michael's for thirty-five years, looked over at his slightly drunk friend and shrugged. Silvio was never a man of many words, and that was part of what Michael liked about him. He knew that Silvio could be trusted to not blab any secrets. He also knew that Silvio wouldn't give him any back talk or any grief and just be there as a good friend.

*****

Michael and Silvio met after Michael had his tragic "accident" that crushed his hands and prevented him from boxing again. After the casts came off, Michael had to start a new chapter in his life. His hands healed decently, but some of his fingers were slightly crooked, his grip strength was not what it used to be, making a fist was a challenge, and he was prone to arthritic flare-ups. He thought about returning to the gym as a trainer, but after Marco's disappearance his wife declared him legally dead, which he was as far as Michael knew, so she sold the gym and moved out of town with her two young daughters.

All Michael thought about during his recovery was getting revenge on Bianchi. He knew it was an impossible task, but it was a dream that kept him going. The problem with his hands was that he couldn't hold a gun properly or pull a trigger. He could handle a knife, though. That's what he wanted to do to Bianchi—cut him up slow. Let him bleed out like he made Marco bleed out.

Eventually, Michael found work at the local butcher shop. The butcher, a kindly old man named Furio, was a fan of Michael's and felt bad that he landed on hard times so he gave Michael a job. The job was perfect for Michael. It's where he could exercise his hands and train them to handle a knife. He could also learn cutting skills— skills that he hoped to one day use to get revenge on Bianchi. This is also where he met two coworkers who would eventually become trusted allies and associates for years to come: Silvio and Bruno.

Bruno was always a large man with a stocky build. Silvio in comparison was more slightly built. He was even more slender than Michael, who used to joke that Silvio couldn't even make feather-weight. Both young men were in their early twenties, around the same age as Michael. They grew up friends in the Italian neighbor- hood and went into the Army together after graduating from River City High. Even though they were assigned to active combat duty and were deployed on a few missions, they never spoke of their time in the Army. "It's a part of my life I'm trying to forget," Bruno once told Michael. From that point on, Michael knew to not pry.

Aside from gaining a good friend, there was another benefit for Michael in getting to know Silvio: his sister, Catarina. She was two grades ahead of Michael, and he vaguely remembered seeing her around the halls at school. His interests were at Marco's gym back then; he barely paid attention to anything or anyone when he was in high school. She recently moved back in with her parents after she broke off an engagement with her fiancé. She caught him cheating on her with one of her bridesmaids. Silvio generously offered to kill them both with the .38 snub nose he kept in his bedside table, but she politely declined.

If Michael could go back and change one thing about his time in school, it was that he wished he'd paid attention to her. When she came in one day to pick up some lamb chops for the dinner she was cooking that evening, he was smitten. He couldn't believe this gorgeous woman with light brown hair and fair skin—clearly of northern Italian descent—was around him every day at school, and he'd never noticed her. He sure noticed her now, though. *Her fiancé must have been some kind of huge knucklehead to let this fabulous woman go*, he thought. What drove him even crazier was the fact that she remembered him.

"You're the boxer, right?" she shouted after Michael as he went into the cooler to get the chops he cut up and put on reserve for her. Michael was both surprised and flattered. "Yeah, that's me. How did you know?"

"I used to watch you fight. Well, my boyfriend a few years back loved boxing, and his idea of the ideal date was to grab some takeout and go to a boxing match. I saw you fight a few times. I remembered you from high school."

Michael was flabbergasted as he came out of the freezer and plunked the chops on top of the paper he laid out on the counter. He looked her over. She was sincere. More than that, there was a kind of a twinkle in her eye. He could tell that she liked him. He wanted to keep this conversation going. He wrapped the chops as slowly as possible and prodded her with "You remembered me, huh?"

Catarina smiled. "Yup. They called you 'the Hammer.' After the first fight I saw, I knew why. You pack a wallop with that right hook."

Now Michael was curious. "Which fight was it?" "The one against Kid Dynamo...David something."

"Jacobi," came the assist from Michael. He knew the exact fight she was talking about. Kid was a punk—TKO in round seven.

"That's it," Catarina confirmed. Then she moved things along with "I was sorry to hear what happened—with your hands."

Michael suddenly got self-conscious. He looked at his hands as he finished taping up the paper wrapping on the chops.

Catarina knew she'd stepped in it. She attempted to recover the conversation with "It was an accident, right? Something about moving a big marble table and it falling on your hands?"

Michael didn't want to tell her the truth, but he didn't want to lie to her either. He simply muttered, "It was an unfortunate thing, that's all." He handed her the chops without looking her in the eye. Silvio paid for them out of his paycheck, so she was free to go—but chose not to.

Catarina was upset with herself. She and Michael were having a great conversation, and she had to bring up something terrible. She knew that this tendency of hers was a cause of tension between her and her ex-fiancé Patrick, though he never admitted it. She was determined to not repeat past mistakes and try to have a more pos- itive outlook on life. She also decided right then and there that she must make things right with Michael.

"Come to dinner tonight," she said as she took the chops and put them in the canvas bag she had with her.

"What?" Michael asked. The invitation snapped him out of feeling sorry for himself about his hands, plus it was too good to be true. He wanted to make sure that he heard what he thought he heard and didn't imagine it.

"Come to dinner tonight, Michael. I insist."

"Are you sure?" Michael asked coyly. "I don't want to impose." "I'm positive. There's plenty here," she said, tapping on the can-vas bag, "and this is my meal that I'm making. I can invite whoever I want, I want you there, and I won't take no for an answer."

Michael liked the fieriness and intensity in her voice. Who was he to turn down such an offer? "Okay, yeah—I'll be there. I don't get off until six, though."

"That's fine," replied a satisfied Catarina, happy that she was getting her way. "Dinner's at seven. You can arrive a bit earlier if you can make it. But don't be late."

"I won't," Michael reassured her.

Catarina gave him a short head bow as a way of saying goodbye, then turned around and walked out. Michael hated when the sexy women left, but he loved watching them walk away.

The dinner was a pleasant one. It was just him, Catarina, Silvio, and their father since their mother was working a night shift as a cashier at the local pharmacy. This was where Michael found out that Silvio was cut from the same cloth as his father. Neither one of them spoke more than ten words for the whole dinner. This was partly because of the quiet and stoic nature of both men. It is also because Catarina—much like her mother as he would find out later—had the gift of gab and was only quiet for the few seconds it took her to shovel some food into her mouth, chew, and swallow. Even then, having to eat didn't stop her mouth from running 100 percent of the time.

Michael could tell that Silvio and his father had long ago resigned themselves to what dinner with the Russo women was like. They didn't bother trying to speak except for the occasional "Pass me this" or "I need that." Michael felt no need to resign himself to anything. He found her incessant chatter charming. He liked hearing the sound of her voice and thought the nasally sound she made when she giggled was cute. He wanted to hear more of it—without the downtrodden presence of the father or having to grin at Silvio's head shakes and eye rolls.

Once dessert and coffee were done and Michael felt like he could move again after stuffing himself so full, he complimented Catarina on the delicious meal and asked, "How about we go for a walk?" Silvio and his father muttered thanks and praises to God when Catarina accepted.

The early spring air was cool, crisp, and invigorating after a heavy meal of lamb chops, mashed potatoes, and asparagus drizzled in olive oil and coated in sea salt, followed by coffee and cheesecake. For Michael, meals this big were typically reserved for holidays. It was a good thing too. If he ate like that all the time, he wouldn't have been a welterweight for very long.

The quiet neighborhood with houses and yards in the River City suburb of Bridgeburg was a far cry from the Italian section of River City where Michael grew up. He took a deep breath of air as soon as he felt it on his skin. He was expecting Catarina to start talking right away, but as soon as they got outside, she clammed up. This was unexpected, but Michael was never one to be thrown off-balance by something he didn't see coming. "Your dad seems nice," Michael said for an icebreaker.

"Yeah, he is," came Catarina's reply. "Very quiet, though."

"Yeah, I guess. He's like my brother. Neither one of them say much."

Michael couldn't help it. He tried to suppress a laugh but wound up snorting. A baffled Catarina asked him, "What? What's so funny?"

"Nothing," Michael knew he stepped in it and the best way out was straight through. "It's just that, you're the exact opposite of them."

"What do you mean? Are you saying I talk too much?" Catarina feigned exasperation.

"No! No, not at all! I…" Michael panicked for a second. Then he looked over and saw the sly grin on Catarina's face. He started laughing.

Catarina laughed too. "I know! I can't help it. Whenever I get nervous, I talk a lot."

Michael stopped walking. Catarina did too. He squared up to her and looked her in the eyes. "Nervous? Why were you nervous?"

Catarina did all she could to look away. She fumbled for the words to say to Michael that would sound plausible without giv- ing away that she was attracted to him. It was no use, though. He was on to her ever since she invited him to dinner. An end to her shaky stream of "Uhs" and "Ums" eventually came when Michael put his lips on hers and kissed her softly. After a few seconds, Michael felt like he needed some air. He barely had time to grab some when Catarina took him by the arm and pulled him back toward her, this time kissing him—only less delicately.

This wasn't Michael's first kiss—he'd had plenty of kisses and more once he started proving himself in the ring. A lot of good-look- ing women are attracted to a man who knows how to handle himself. It was, however, the best kiss of his life. After all, this was the moment that Michael knew, without a doubt, that this was the woman with whom he would spend the rest of his life and raise a family.

The wedding of Michael and Catarina was a large affair. It took place at the River City Banquet Hall. The estimated head count was close to one thousand people. Most of these were city and state officials since Catarina's father, who paid for the wedding, did very well for himself as a contractor who got a lot of work from local government. It didn't matter to Michael, though. All that mattered was that Catarina was now his wife.

The honeymoon was in Italy and lasted for two weeks—one in Venice and one in Florence. It was in Venice on a quiet, moonlit evening over a few predinner bellinis that Michael confessed in full to Catarina about what really happened to his hands and why he had to retire from boxing. He was worried that Catarina might be upset that Michael was involved with gangsters, but it didn't bother her at all. She understood what happened and why. This helped to lay the groundwork for later when Michael himself became the head of the most powerful organized crime family in River City.

In the years that followed, Catarina bore Michael three children: daughters Michelle and Philomena, as well as the youngest, Michael's pride and joy, Leonardo, who everyone called Leo for short. This was the best time in Michael's life. He never thought he'd be happy doing anything other than boxing, but his children gave him a new lease on life. Michael was almost happy enough to forgive Boss Bianchi for what he did, and very well might have if fate hadn't intervened.

CHAPTER 13

ONE DAY, WHILE Michael was mopping the floor in front of the counter at the butcher shop, a young man burst through the door. He was panting from running so fast and grasped his left shoulder with a bloody right hand. Michael saw the drops of blood on his freshly mopped Italian white marble floor before he looked up and saw the man was covering up a gunshot wound.

"Silvio! Bruno! Come out here now!" Michael screamed excitedly. The wounded young man collapsed to his knees. Michael took a good look at his face and saw that he couldn't have been more than nineteen or twenty. "What happened to you?" Michael asked as Silvio and Bruno rushed in from the back room.

"I got shot!" The young man was getting excited.

Michael knew he better keep the young man calm before he lost too much blood and passed out. He decided the best way to do this was to have the young man tell his story. "Shot? How? By who? Tell me everything," Michael insisted.

Bruno and Silvio, who had experience in dealing with gunshot wounds from their time in the Army, went to work on the young man's shoulder, cutting away his shirt and going after the deeply lodged bullet with a boning knife sterilized by a lighter, as he told his story.

"I got in deep with Boss Bianchi…" The young man winced as the boning knife went into his shoulder. Michael winced too at the name Bianchi.

"Go on. Keep talking to take your mind off the pain. We have nothing else for it."

"Okay," the young man continued, "Well, I owed a lot of money to him for a Mongeese game I bet on. He knew I was just a student—

I'm going to school to become a veterinarian—so he said he'd take pity on me and instead of paying him back he'd have me do him a favor and we'd call it even."

"What was the favor?" asked Michael suspiciously.

"He said that if I could be a courier and deliver some money to some guys from the Duomo family in exchange for some blackmail evidence they have on the mayor—dirty pictures or something, I don't know—then that would be it."

A picture started to take shape in Michael's head. The Duomo family were Bianchi's chief rivals in River City. The two families made arrangements and divided up the city into territories as crime families do. Each family controlled about half the city. There was an uneasy truce between the two families that was ripe to be exploited.

The young man screamed in agony as Bruno edged the bullet to the surface with the knife and Silvio grabbed it with his thumb and forefinger. A tinge of jealousy shot through Michael, as he knew that his crooked fingers would never be able to grab a bullet like that. Silvio showed the bullet to the kid, who smiled in relief as Bruno got up and went behind the counter.

"Don't smile yet, kid. We're not done yet," Bruno warned.

The smile on the young man's face melted when Bruno returned with a butcher's needle and thread—the kind used for sewing up meat after stuffing. This time it was going to be used to sew up the young man's shoulder. Michael could see the young man was getting nervous, so he invited him to continue talking as Bruno worked his magic with the needle and thread.

"I made the deal," the young man continued, "but that son of a bitch Bianchi set me up. He only gave me part of the money that was needed for the exchange. When the Duomo guy counted and thought I stiffed him, he pulled a gun. That's when I took off for the nearest alley. The guy fired a shot, and it got me in the shoulder. I ran in a panic for three or four blocks but started feeling dizzy by the time I got in front of your place here, so that's when I came in and you saw me."

The young man's assailant couldn't have timed it better if he tried. As soon as the young man brought everyone up to speed, another man—older, rougher, with thinning hair and a five-o'clock shadow—burst through the door. He'd obviously followed the blood trail that the young man left behind him as he ran away.

"There you are!" shouted the man as he pointed his pistol at the young man.

Michael, reacting without giving a thought to his own safety, got up and positioned himself between the man with the gun and the young man. Bruno stopped sewing the man's shoulder and put his hands up. He was only halfway done, so the needle dangled and swayed back and forth on the thread after he let it go.

"Hold it," said Michael, calmly imploring the older man to be reasonable. "We don't want any trouble."

"Then you shouldn't have let this guy in," said the older man with a nasty snarl.

"I need you to drop that gun." "Not a chance."

"Drop it now."

"Who's going to make me?"

"I am." The voice—and the double-barreled shotgun—were Silvio's. The older man was so focused on the young man that he didn't notice Silvio crawl off to the side and behind the counter, where the gun was kept.

Michael slowly reached out and grabbed the gun from the older man as he said, "Okay—let's all calm down and work something out here. Okay?"

"Do I have a choice?" the older man asked, defeated.

"No," Michael said firmly. He looked the man over from head to toe. There was nothing particularly striking or intimidating about him now that the gun was taken away. He looked like any other middle-aged man you'd see on the street and not give a second thought. Michael shook his head and asked the man, "Why are you doing this?"

The older man looked at Michael, genuinely confused. "What do you mean, why am I doing this?"

Michael replied as gently as possible, "I mean why do you run these errands for the Duomo family?" He was going somewhere with this question, and wanted to lay down the foundation properly.

"I'm a good earner for them. They appreciate what I do and they trust me."

"I see. And killing is part of what you do?" "It comes with the job."

"If killing is part of the job, do you think that they'd have any trouble killing you?"

The older man had to think for a second. "They wouldn't do that."

"Why not?" Michael's inquisition was more of a searching nature than a challenging one.

"Because I would never do anything to cross them and make them kill me."

"Fair enough," Michael said, satisfied that he was getting the answers he sought. "But let me tell you how things are going to play out. You're going to go back to Duomo with the envelope…" He motioned to the young man to hand over the envelope with the blackmail. The young man reached into his pocket and did just that. Michael continued, "You're also going to have the money. This is good for you. It's good for Duomo. However, it is not good for Bianchi. Not only is he not going to have his blackmail, he's not going to have his money either."

"Serves the bastard right for stiffing us on the payment."

Michael chuckled. "Do you think Bianchi cares? Do you think he sees it that way? On top of it all, you killed one of his guys—or he'll think you did. We'll get to that in a minute. But do you think Bianchi is going to like looking like a loser in this situation—getting nothing and accepting the death of one of his guys?"

"No."

"Very good! What do you think he'll do? Will he retaliate? What would Duomo do?

The older man cracked a smile. "He'd get revenge."

Michael got excited. The older man was getting it. "That's right!

He'd take a life for a life. But it would be someone who Duomo really cared about. Then Duomo would retaliate against Bianchi, and Bianchi would retaliate against Duomo, and so on and so on and so on."

"What are you saying?" The older man could tell there was a point, but wasn't sure what it was.

"I'm saying that Bianchi purposely shorted the payment, knowing that you'd kill the messenger. In doing so, he could start a war that would once and for all determine who controls crime in River City. This is obviously a war he thinks he can win, or he wouldn't have provoked it. And you played right into his hands. And Duomo—at the end of the day, do you think he cares about you? Sure, he would never kill you directly, but he'd gladly sacrifice you in some stupid gang war if it meant he would win and get control of the city."

The older man absorbed what Michael was saying. He started to see how he was just a pawn in a much bigger game. His killing of the younger man would be a catalyst that starts a war on the streets of River City. He then breathed a sigh of relief as he realized, "But I didn't kill the kid."

"No—but you will."

"What?" The young man spring to his feet. Silvio and Bruno both restrained him.

Michael turned to the young man and said, "Relax. You are going back to the university. You will stay there and not come into the city again for gambling or for any reason." Michael then turned to the older man. "You'll return the money and the envelope to Duomo and when he asks what happened, say that you got shorted—as he can see when he counts the money—so you shot the kid, dumped the body in the river, and came back."

The older man looked confused. He could tell that there was a grand plan at play, but couldn't figure it out. "Won't that start a war?" "It will, between Duomo and Bianchi and their 'made' mem- bers—but it doesn't have to turn into one for you associates and soldiers. Do you know anyone in the Bianchi family? Anyone you trust?"

"Yeah, there are some guys I know. Why?"

"I want you to talk to them and tell them what really happened. Tell them to come here. Tell them to bring all of the associates and soldiers who they trust—and you do the same. Let everyone know that this butcher shop is a safe zone for both families. Saturday night, after we close at 10:00 p.m., we'll all meet in the back. I have a better solution for all of you to this war between Duomo and Bianchi. I just ask that before you all start gunning each other down in the streets, you hear what I have to say."

This seemed reasonable to the older man. There was something about Michael in the way he talked and handled himself that had him convinced. He'd been around long enough where he earned trust with some members of the Bianchi family, so it was something he could feasibly do. "Okay, I guess it's worth a shot. I'll spread the word and be here on Saturday with as many Duomo guys as I can bring. We'll hear you out."

"Good. That's all I ask."

In a surprising gesture, the older man reached his hand out to the still panic-stricken younger man. The younger man flinched before he realized that the older man just wanted to shake hands. The older man had a firm grip. He looked the younger man in the eye and said, "No hard feelings, kid."

The younger man grasped his right hand—now slightly less bloody after some rubbed off on the older man's gloved hand—in pain as the older man turned and left. The younger man then turned to Michael. "I owe you my life."

"Forget about it," said Michael. "Just keep your nose clean. Don't come back here, and finish school."

"I will. I know some day I'll just be a veterinarian, but if you ever need anything, just let me know. My name is Dominic." The young man held out his hand. Michael took it and shook it gently, sympathetic that the younger man had been through enough that evening.

"Will do," said Michael.

The young man turned and left. Bruno and Silvio patted Michael on the back. "I have no idea what you have in mind, Michael," said Silvio, "but it better be good."

"Yeah, real good," Bruno chimed in.

"It will be," Michael reassured them. Just wait until Saturday."

Before Michael knew it, Saturday was upon him. He felt a tinge of nervousness as he flipped the sign on the front door from "open" to "closed." The idea that hit him while the young man was talking to him three nights before had since formulated into a solid plan. Tonight, it was just a matter of getting the fringe members of River City's two crime families to go along with him. It would be no easy task, but he'd been rehearsing what he wanted to say and was ready.

Michael didn't have to wait long for the first arrivals. Within two minutes of him flipping the sign the older man, accompanied by two other rough-looking younger men—one in his late teens and one in his early twenties—knocked on the door. *They were watching the place and waiting*, Michael thought to himself as he let the three men in. Bruno was standing behind Michael, holding a bag.

Michael motioned to the bag and said, "Put your guns in the bag."

The two other men with the older man seemed ruffled by this request, but the older man nodded to them to comply. They did as they were told. As the older man put his 9mm pistol in the bag, he asked, "Are you going to frisk us too?"

"No," said Michael.

"That's a mistake," the older man said.

"Perhaps," said Michael, "but we all need to trust each other if this is going to work. Besides, Silvio has got things covered in case anything happens. Michael pointed to Silvio, who quickly bran- dished a .45 pistol in his right hand to go along with the double-bar- reled shotgun he was holding in his left.

"I see," said the older man, still skeptical.

The door then opened a second time and two middle-aged men entered. The older man turned to the middle-aged men and said, "Good. You guys made it. Now we can start."

One of the middle-aged men spoke up, "Yeah, we're here, Johnny—and this better not be a setup, on your word."

"It's not," reassured the older man. He then turned to Michael and nodded.

Now was Michael's time to get the ball rolling. First, he needed to know who he was dealing with. So far, he only got one of their names. He figured that he'd get started with his introductions first. "Welcome. My name is Michael Manetti. These are my associates, Bruno and Silvio," Michael said as he pointed to each of his friends. "Who are you two?" he asked, addressing the new arrivals.

The less scary-looking of the middle-aged men answered, "My name is Chaz. This is my cousin Paulie."

"Okay, Chaz and Paulie. What family are you with?" "What is this?" said a perturbed Paulie.

"It's all right," Johnny said. "Hear the kid out." "We're with the Bianchi family," Chaz replied.

"I see." This is exactly what Michael wanted. He knew Johnny—and presumably the other two—were from the Duomo family. *Johnny must have convinced Chaz from the Bianchi family to come along, and Paulie was here to back him up,* he thought. "Do me a favor, fellas, put your guns in the bag."

"Hey, no way," said Paulie, very gruffly.

Chaz looked over at Michael, who gave him a head nod to let him know it was okay. "Did these guys put their weapons in the bag?" asked Chaz.

"Yup," said Bruno, shaking the bag.

"All right then. Come on, Paulie." Chaz put his gun in the bag and Paulie reluctantly followed suit with all three of his weapons— one in the shoulder holster, one on his waist, and one on his ankle.

"Before we get started," Michael turned his attention to the older man, "I got that your name is Johnny. Who are these two with you?"

"This is my oldest son, Petey, and my youngest, Sammy."

"I see. Follow me." Michael led everyone to the back room behind the counter. On one side of the room was a freezer. The other side of the room was storage space. There were no chairs to sit on, so each man sat on a box, leaned against a wall, or stood in place. Michael wasn't sure what he was expecting for a turnout, but five was as good of a place to start as any.

Michael held up his hands and began. "I'm no stranger to your world. I used to be a boxer. A few years back, I had a misunder- standing with Boss Bianchi, and he did this to me." He paused for dramatic effect so everyone could get a good look at his crooked fin- gers, then he continued. "I'm sure that each of you know of similar stories, or have witnessed things like this—or even done something like it yourselves.

"But I didn't bring you here to talk about me. And I didn't bring you here for a lecture on how bad things can get. I brought you here— from both families—to talk to you tonight about a better way. As you all know, Johnny here was part of an incident that was a set up to spark a war between the Bianchi family and the Duomo family. Bianchi thinks he can take control. We all know Duomo isn't going to take this lying down. He will fight back. As soldiers in his army, it is you who will die.

"What if there's a better solution? One that stops the violence before it escalates. One that avoids senseless bloodshed and sees you all as more than just pawns in a greedy chess game between two warlords. Something organized that offers protection for guys like all five of you so you can go out and make a living without having to worry about taking a bullet every time you turn a corner. Would that interest you?"

The few seconds of silence after this question was asked made Michael feel tense. The release he felt when Johnny finally said, "I'm interested" was borderline orgasmic it felt so good to him.

Johnny then continued. "The reason I'm here tonight and brought my sons with me is that I'm trying to discourage them from the life. But they seem hell bent on trying to get in, no matter what I say to them. That kid I chased down here a few days ago was about the same age as Petey. It got me thinking. I wouldn't want to see Petey gunned down in the street like he was nothing. It would break my heart—and his mother's. If they get involved in the life in spite of what I say, then I at least want them to be safe. If you can do that, Michael, then I'm all for it.

Michael nodded, very pleased with the response. He then turned his attention to Chaz and Paulie. "What about you two? You're cousins, so you're family. You wanna see each other stay alive, right?"

Chaz and Paulie looked at each other and nodded. Michael didn't show it outwardly, but he was thrilled. He was reaching them.

"So how do we do this?" Johnny asked. "What's next?"

Somber and serious, Michael replied, "What's next is that we spread the word. Talk to guys you can trust. Tell them to talk to guys they trust. Tell them to come here a week from today, same time. Let them hear my plan directly from me. They can ask me any questions they want to ask. In the end, you'll all be doing yourselves a big favor."

Michael was well aware of the risk he was taking. He knew that if any of the men leaked anything about Michael and his plan to either of the bosses—or their trusted "made" men—he'd be a floater in the river before he knew what hit him. But this was something he believed in. He knew that if he could convince enough associates from these two families to back him, the city would be his—and he could get his revenge on Bianchi.

The next Saturday a dozen guys showed up. Then it was twenty the following week. Space in the back of the butcher shop was tight with twenty and Michael was worried if more guys showed up the next week. Luckily for Michael, one of Bianchi guys worked for a lieutenant in the Bianchi family who operated Marco's old boxing gym. As it turned out, Marco's widow was "convinced" by Bianchi and his two main goons to sell to her. This way, he would have more control of the fighters and incidents like what happened with Michael wouldn't happen again. The guy was trusted with a key, so it was no problem to get everyone in after hours.

It felt strange for Michael to go back to his old gym after being away for so long—close to five years. He thought about climbing into the ring to do some shadowboxing but decided against it. There were too many memories, and it would make him too sad. He needed to be on top of his game to talk to the gym full of mob associates that evening.

The pitch for his idea to organize was Michael's best ever that night. Not only had it gotten better with practice over the weeks, but he felt a fire in his belly like he hadn't felt in the butcher shop. It was almost as if Marco was there with him, and maybe he was in spirit, giving him encouragement to lay it all on the line. After he was done outlining his plan that associates of both families organize under him, he fielded a few questions. He answered them well, giv- ing reassurances that he would personally keep the peace and resolve any disputes. He also made it clear that they could operate their various specialties— gambling, drugs, prostitution, and the like—as they see fit, with no interference from him. He only asked that for his involvement, a 10 percent commission was given to him to split among himself, Bruno, and Silvio. The rest was theirs to keep. This was agreeable to all of the men in the room, given that they were used to paying upward of 40 or in some cases 50 percent of what they earned.

By Michael's count, there were over one hundred people at his first meeting in the old gym. This number doubled to two hundred for his next meeting. The momentum was in his favor. One thing his years as a boxer taught him was to take advantage of an enemy's weakness as soon as he could and strike while the iron was hot. It was on that evening that he made the decision that would change his life forever and change River City for decades to come. It was time to make the big move and take out Bianchi, Duomo, and all the loyal made members of their families.

Both hits were carried out in essentially the same way. An asso- ciate of the family would tip off Michael on where the head boss would be. It was Michael's decision on where and when to strike. At the same time the hit was to be carried out, both Duomo and Bianchi associates, who by now considered themselves to be part of the Manetti crew, would begin the process of rounding up the loyal, trusted, and made members of their families and bring them to the gym. They were given three choices: join Michael, leave River City for good, or wind up at the bottom of the river. Most chose to join, though a small percentage did choose to leave town. Wisely, no one chose the third option. For those who did join, it was made clear that there was no hierarchy in the family, regardless of previous "made" status. Everyone was equal in the Manetti family, except of course for Michael, who was boss, as well as Silvio and Bruno, who were his administrators.

Within three days of deciding to make the move on the bosses, Duomo was dead, and most of his crew had joined the Manetti family. The assassination itself was a brutal and shocking affair, plastered all over the next day's edition of the River City Gazette. The photo was of boss Duomo, sitting in the front passenger seat of his car. His head was rolled back, his mouth was wide open, and his face was contorted in horror. He saw the gunmen draw down on him and he knew those moments were his last. There was a crack where the bullet went through the windshield and struck him in the forehead. It was a clean kill, though it made for a disturbing image to go with the morning coffee.

The accompanying story was mostly from an anonymous eyewitness, who was headed to meet a date at Reggie's Crab Shack—a known favorite spot of Duomo, particularly when soft shells were in season. She didn't think anything of it when a car pulled up to the curb as she was walking down the sidewalk. Then out of the corner of her eye, she saw the driver get out of the car and run across the street, almost getting hit by a bus in the process. From behind her, two men in knit caps and long coats, with masks covering the bottom half of their faces, pushed her to the side. Both men drew guns but only one of them fired. It was just one shot. That's all that was needed and it was over in a matter of seconds.

At first, Michael was worried that Bianchi would fear for his own life after he heard what happened to Duomo. This, however, was not

Just as Anthony's eyes adjusted to the dark, Michael moved Philip's head aside and pointed the gun right at Anthony's nose. He wanted to squeeze the trigger, but he couldn't because of the arthri- tis in his hand. Instead, Michael pistol-whipped Anthony across the face, cutting his cheek.

"Back," Michael commanded, pointing the gun at Anthony once again.

Anthony backed into the room. By this time, Bruno had con- trol of Philip. He shoved Philip into the room, then he and Bruno entered.

Michael looked around. He spotted Bianchi immediately. Michael pointed the gun at him. Bruno had his gun pointed at Philip. Silvio had the drunk and bleeding Anthony covered. With his free hand, Michael signaled to the other three players in the room to get out. They scurried for the exits without even taking their chips. Now Michael was exactly where he wanted to be: in the same room with the three men who destroyed all of his hopes and dreams of a boxing career, with guns pointed at their heads. The problem for Michael was that it was a bluff. He could barely hold the gun, let alone squeeze the trigger.

Michael had a better idea anyway. He grabbed a seat next to Bianchi. He then put his gun in his left pocket, and out of his right he grabbed a pair of scissors—the same kind of scissors that Marco used to cut his gloves off that fateful night. Michael slammed the scissors on the table and in act of sheer brazenness, he pulled his mask down, looked Bianchi square in the eye and asked, "Remember me?"

Bianchi did all he could to keep from evacuating his bladder and bowels right then and there. His eyes widened and his throat clenched. He certainly did remember the young man who was star- ing at him. "Mike 'the Hammer' Manetti," said Bianchi tiredly.

"That's right," growled Michael. He then took off his gloves and held up his busted hands. "You did this to me so I could never box again. I just wanted to thank you for that."

Bianchi sat in stunned silence as Michael continued, "I maybe had ten or so good years left of getting my head knocked around. I coulda been big, maybe—I don't know. What I do know is that since you clobbered my hands, I found a whole other calling in life. I decided that I'm going to run this city."

"You're crazy," scoffed Bianchi.

"I already got rid of Duomo. Now it's just you. All of your associates—and his—are loyal to me. We want you gone from River City."

"You expect me to just pack up and leave."

"Exactly right. Consider it a thank you present from me." The smirk on Michael's face betrayed that something was up. Bianchi knew he was in real trouble, but he wasn't sure how.

"What's the catch?" asked Bianchi.

"No catch. Except of course that you can't return here ever again. Is that clear?"

Bianchi nodded his head.

"Good," said Michael. "Now off you go."

Bianchi started to rise from his seat. He knew this was too good to be true and he was right. As soon as he got half way up he felt the crooked fingers of Michael's hand pulling him back down.

"Except for one thing," said Michael.

Here it comes, Bianchi thought to himself.

"The night that you gave me the gift of these hands, you also killed someone very close to me. He was my trainer, my mentor, and my friend. And he was killed with these!" In one quick motion, Michael grabbed the scissors from off the table, completely ignoring the pain in his joints, and stabbed Bianchi in the chest. Bianchi's eyes widened as he screamed in pain. He could feel his right lung collapse as Michael removed the scissors to stab him again and again and again.

In one corner of the room, Philip was frozen, helpless as he looked on with Bruno's gun pointed at him. In the other corner, an angry and drunk Anthony tried to make a move to save his boss as he watched Bianchi get stabbed. But Silvio was ready for him with an itchy trigger finger. Anthony made it about half a foot before Silvio's .45 went off at point-blank range, demolishing Anthony's face and painting a Slip 'N Slide promotional poster behind him with his brains.

Silvio shocked himself at what he'd done. He'd killed before, in the Army, but it was never this up close and personal. He felt no remorse, though. In his mind, it was what he had to do to control the situation. Neither the gunshot nor Anthony's demise fazed Michel in the least. He was caught up in a vengeful bloodlust, stabbing Bianchi repeatedly in the chest, neck, and face. It took a solid minute of stabbing before Michael tired himself out. He was spent. Covered in blood. But he felt good—really good. The coroner's report would later show that Bianchi was stabbed fifty-seven times, and most of his wounds were postmortem. The coroner estimated that he died after the first dozen or so stabs.

The big deed was now finally done. Michael looked around. He saw Anthony's faceless corpse on the floor against the wall and Silvio still holding his smoking gun. Michael gave Silvio a nod of approval. He then looked to the other corner of the room. A visibly shaken Philip was stiff as a board, not daring to make a move with Bruno's gun pointed at him. Michael walked up to Philip and put his mouth close to his ear, so all he had to do was whisper.

"Do you wanna wind up like your friends here?" he asked, gesturing to the lifeless bodies of Bianchi and Anthony.

"No," said Philip, shaking his head.

"Smart guy," said Michael with a grin. "Okay, then you have two choices. Join me or get out of town for good. Everyone else you know is either joining me, leaving town, or dead, so what's it gonna be?"

"I'll…I'll join," said Philip, barely getting the word out. "Good. Then we have a few things to discuss tonight. You'll come with us when we leave here." Michael was happy with himself that he could land the agreement of a close associate of Bianchi. But that didn't mean the man was loyal. At least not yet. Michael figured that once he explained the way he'd decided to run things, the loyalty would come. In the meantime, he saw that Philip could be fright- ened into obedience.

Michael went to the washroom and cleaned himself off while he had Silvio take Philip out to the car. Bruno's job was to take the scissors out of Bianchi's left cheek, where Michael last stabbed him, and clean up anything in the room that might be evidence. Once that was done, their work was over. Michael was now boss of River City.

CHAPTER 14

RECENTLY, MICHAEL REFLECTED on these early days more often. The fact that the River City Mongeese were playing terribly, coupled with his fourth-quarter cognac taking effect, caused him to drift off and reminisce. He couldn't believe that it had been almost thirty years since he took over control of the city's crime. After a dozen years, the Chinese muscled in near the docks, but Michael made a deal that kept the peace. He looked over at Silvio quietly watching the game and smiled. The early days with him and his late friend Bruno, who Michael tasked with looking after Leo once he became a teenager, were the best of his life. Now that teen son of his was all grown up and a man in his own right. Michael wasn't ready to retire, but he thought it important to groom Leo to take over operation of the family business. It would have to happen someday.

As if Leo knew that his father was thinking about him, he appeared in the doorway of his dad's office holding a duffel bag. This sparked Michael to wake up from his daze. He sat upright in his chair and motioned to Leo to come in. Silvio stood up and shook Leo's free hand as the young man entered the office.

If Leo was expecting a warm reception, he was wrong. "Leo! I'm glad you're here. I need to talk to you!" barked Michael. He then turned to Silvio, who was still standing. "Leave us alone for a minute. I need to talk to my son privately."

Silvio nodded and swiftly left the room. He knew what Michael was like when he got worked up. Michael's crooked, arthritic fingers caused him to fumble with the buttons on the remote as he turned off the television, which just made him angrier. Once he succeeded, he turned a cold gaze toward his son. Leo put the duffel bag next to a chair and sat across from his father.

Michael wasted no time laying into his son. "What the hell are you doing? The things I'm hearing…they don't make me happy," he growled.

Leo wasn't used to being talked to so bluntly. His father was one of the few people who could get away with it. All he could do was stay calm, not offend his father any further, and defend himself. "Dad, I can explain if you just give me a chance—"

"You can? You can explain to me why Paisano's closed down?" "Vice had us under surveillance, and one of our guys got pinched. Then they raided the place. It's not my fault."

That last sentence only succeeding in pissing Michael off even more. He hated it when people evaded responsibility—especially his son. "Not your fault? Of course it's your fault! I trusted you with that operation. I told you to be careful, and I told you to be smart. By being smart, I meant keep it secret and low key—not have word spread around the entire neighborhood that a pizza parlor is dealing drugs! No wonder you were under surveillance! Every school kid, soccer mom, retiree, and reject in a ten-block radius knew about the items we sold that weren't on the menu. It looks a little funny when half the customers going into a pizza place look like they're just there to get a fix."

Leo thought an attempt at humor might diffuse the situation. "Yeah, but the other half thought we made a pretty good Sicilian slice, so—"

Another miscalculation by Leo. Michael was not amused. "Don't get cute with me! This isn't the time for you to be a wiseass. That place earned me a lot of dough, and now, like that, because of you—it's gone! I can't believe how careless you are."

Michael's bark had turned into a roar. Leo knew it was time to get serious and try to give some positive news. "Dad, just let me explain. I got something else. Something better. It's earning even more cash than the pizza place."

This piqued Michael's interest. "Okay, I'm listening. What would that be?"

"You know that club I have downtown?"

Michael had to think hard to remember what Leo was talking about. Once he did, he couldn't hide his disgust. He thought the place was gaudy and weird, completely lacking any sort of class or good taste. "The old factory you fixed up to make look like the rain forest? I still think that is one of the stupidest—"

"Yeah, I know," interrupted Leo. "But the club, where the offices used to be, is only the front. There's a whole factory floor in the back." Leo had heard his father's opinion a dozen times before. He just wanted to get to the good news.

"Okay. So?" *He better get to the point quick, and it better be good,* Michael thought to himself.

"So I turned it into a casino. VIP only."

Michael knew about the club Leo opened, but the casino was news. "All right. When was this?"

"A little over three months ago." Leo braced for impact immediately after the words left his mouth.

"Three months! You've been running an operation for three months, and you're just telling me about it now?" Michael prided himself on an open family—in both the professional and personal sense—where anyone can come to him with anything. He wanted no secrets. This news was like a slap in the face.

Leo was in a hole and he knew he had to dig himself out fast. "Dad, relax. I was always going to tell you. I just wanted to do something on my own and test it out to make sure it worked before I brought it to you. We only just started making real money."

"All right. So you're making good bank with this casino you have in the back of your place?"

Leo reached down beside his chair and retrieved the duffel bag. He placed it on Michael's desk. Gesturing to it with his hand he said, "See for yourself."

Michael opened the bag and peered inside. His demeanor changed almost instantly. "All right! Now this is more like it. You keep these coming to me and you'll be all right. And if there are any problems, you come to me."

Relieved that his father opened up the door to that avenue of conversation, Leo seized the opportunity. "Actually, there is something I could maybe use your help with."

Michael wasn't expecting this. "What is it?"

"Well…" Leo started sheepishly, then sputtered out as quickly as he could, "dice and cards aren't the only things people bet on in my casino. There are also the fights."

"Fights? You got a ring set up in the middle of the casino?"

"Actually, it's an octagon, like they have for MMA."

Leo was just trying to be helpful and thorough in his details. His father didn't see it that way. "What did I say about being a wise- ass?" snapped Michael.

Leo recovered and carried on. It was time for the truth. "Point is, yeah, we have fights there, and a couple…three…times, some girls have gotten killed there."

Now Michael wasn't just shocked. He was also confused. "Girls? What the hell kind of fights are these?"

"I like watching the ladies grapple. What can I say? Anyway, Claudia—"

"Claudia? You got your girlfriend mixed up in all of this? What's her involvement? I mean, what does Claudia have to do with these fighting girls dropping dead in the ring—octagon—whatever?"

There was no easy way to say it, so Leo laid it out as matter-of-factly as he could. "She's the one killing 'em, Dad. Total accidents, you understand. She just goes too far sometimes."

"All right. That's bad. But what exactly is the problem? No one's finding the bodies, are they?"

"Well…"

Michael's eyes widened. "Oh no" came from his lips. He didn't want to hear what came next, but he knew that he must.

"They've already been found."

Exactly what Michael didn't want to hear. He put the crooked fingers of his right hand to his forehead and rubbed his temple. Michael wasn't prone to headaches, but he felt one coming on.

Leo continued, "You know the River Murders that are in the news?"

"Oh no. That's you?" Michael learned over the years that publicity—good or bad—was dangerous in his line of work.

"No one has tied us to anything yet, but yeah, that's me. It's Claudia, actually."

It was time for Michael to ask the obvious question. "Why didn't you bury them like I taught you?" Michael was lucky enough in his reign as crime lord of River City to not have to commit too many murders. They were few and far between, but they did have to happen. Betrayal was the chief instigator in underlings losing Michael's magnanimous protection and instead receiving his wrath. The funny thing was that for the handful of murders that were done at his behest over the past thirty years, none were in cold weather. Leo gestured to the big window in Michael's office that looked out into the spacious back yard, secluded from the outside world by a ten-foot-high fence and after that, a dense woodland. "Dad, look outside. It's late autumn. The ground is frozen. And I'm not going to cut them up and put them in garbage bags. I don't have the stomach for that. All I could think to do was weigh them down and throw them in the river. But now they've come up."

Images of the bloated corpses of the three young girls that he saw in the newspapers and on television flashed in Michael's head. "Yeah, they've come up all right. You should have come to me right away."

"I know, but like I said, I wanted to make sure the place was making good money." Leo was a bit annoyed at having to repeat himself on this point, but he controlled his frustration with a Zen- like mastery.

"I understand. But murder? Girls getting beaten to death? You should have come to me." He paused for a moment and looked at his son with disappointment. "Doesn't matter. Too late for that now. We can only hope that the cops have got nothin' on ya, and that they don't figure this out."

"I hope they don't," Leo concurred.

Michael leaned forward in his chair and pointed his curved index finger at Michael. He meant business, and Michael knew it. "In the meantime, if anything like this happens again, you come to me. We got guys here who specialize in the type of disposal services that you'd require. Or better yet, get that girl of yours in line so that there are no more of these accidents."

Leo couldn't deny that Michael made a very good point. "I'll talk to her," he assured his father.

"Good boy," said Michael, picking up the remote as his son got up from his chair to leave. "Now get outta here and back to that casino so you can keep the money coming in."

There was immediate regret on Michael's part as soon as he turned on the television and saw that the River City Mongeese were getting decimated even worse than before. He vented his frustration to Leo as the young man walked out through the door. "Something has to make up for how bad this team is playing." As Michael turned his attention back to the TV, a swell of disgust overcame him. He threw his hands up and shouted, "Damn! Catch the ball!"

CHAPTER 15

A S LEO GOT into his car and drove off, he thought about the conversation that just transpired with his father. Leo felt that he was at the point in his life where it was time to stop taking orders and start giving them. It was time to stop listening to his father as if his father was infallible, and instead regard his old man's position in his life as one of an advisory capacity. One piece of advice he was not going to take was to talk to Claudia—regardless of what he told his father he'd do. He didn't need that headache of talking to her, and besides, watching a death sport was the reason at least half of the people showed up. He wasn't going to mess with the winning formula.

That evening, there was a carnival-like atmosphere in the casino. He normally stayed in his office and watched the happenings from there, but on this night the energy was too strong. It pulled him in like a magnet. This night, Leo walked around the crowd absorbing as many of the invigorating vibes as he could soak up. He even said hi to a few old friends, and it gave him a chance to get a ground level view of his operation. He liked what he saw.

By the time Sarah's bout came around, the energy was at a fever pitch. Her opponent that evening was a large black woman named Colleen Jenkins who everyone dubbed Clubber Colleen. She was an acquaintance of Tina's who worked on the crew that put together the very cage she and Sarah were fighting in. Once word got to Colleen—through Tina—of the purpose of the cage and who would be fighting, she wanted in. Since he was desperate for fighters at the time, Leo was happy to oblige.

Colleen didn't know any martial arts. Though what she lacked in training she made up for in sheer brute strength. Colleen was a straight-up brawler. She didn't think about moves or strategies, she just fought. When she got mad, she fought harder. Few things scared Leo's stable of young Eastern European fighters more than the sight of a pissed-off 250-pound black woman charging at them full speed with violent intent.

It was this very violent intent that Sarah was experiencing less than a minute into her fight with Colleen. Sarah thought she could finesse her big, bear-like opponent, but nothing worked. Sarah's jabs and spin kicks just seemed to bounce off Collen. Worse, Colleen treated Sarah's assaults as an annoyance, like flies buzzing around her head. This only sent her rage meter skyrocketing much quicker.

This isn't looking good, Sarah thought to herself midway through the process of getting pummeled and tossed around like a dog's chew toy. Colleen pushed Sarah against the cage, then quickly followed up with a headlock. The big woman's grip was tight. Sarah started fading fast, losing oxygen with every increased flex and squeeze from Colleen's bicep. Sarah felt like she was going to pass out and knew that if she wanted to stay conscious, she'd better get out of this head- lock soon.

Sarah hated cheap shots. She regarded going after the easily exploitable parts of the human body as distasteful and beneath the dignity of a true fighter. At the same time, she figured to herself while the world around her was getting progressively darker, she wasn't there to win a tournament. She was there on an undercover assignment. In order keep things going, she had to win. To do that, she had no choice but to go for the goods on Colleen. Knowing she'd hate herself later for doing this, Sarah got an arm around Colleen, grabbed whatever flabby flesh she felt on Colleen's chest, and then squeezed and twisted. Some call them titty twisters. Others call them purple *nurples*. Whatever the name, Sarah's hand gave Colleen one that matched the ferocity of Colleen's headlock.

Reprehensible move thought it may have been in Sarah's mind, it got her out of the headlock. As Colleen was bent over cupping her right breast in pain, Sarah gave her a swift kick in her ample posterior.

This sent Collen reeling into a fence post—a post that Colleen herself checked for sturdiness during the assembly of the cage—and split her head open. Without wasting a minute, Sarah sped over to Colleen and started pummeling her in the head. The gash on Colleen's head got worse from the beating. A stinging, blinding mixture of blood and sweat poured into Colleen's eyes.

Temporarily blinded and helpless, Sarah's fighter instincts to take advantage of Colleen's weakened situation took hold. She bashed Colleen until the big woman's body went limp. The casino quaked as Colleen hit the mat face-first. Blood spattered on to the mat, and a small pool formed around Colleen's head.

Sarah looked at what she just did, horrified. She bent down and checked Colleen's pulse. Relieved to feel one, she used all of her might to roll Colleen over. Desperate and looking around for some way to revive Colleen before brain damage set in from the concussion, Sarah spotted Vinny by the gate, cheering her on with the rest of the extremely pumped-up crowd. The beer he'd been holding in his hand was two-thirds full. By Sarah's quick count in her head, that was easily his fourth—and possibly his fifth—one of the evening.

He's had enough already, she thought to herself as she rushed to the gate and grabbed the beer from Vinny. Visibly distraught over his beer being taken from him, Vinny expressed his displeasure with a an aggravated "Hey!" as Sarah turned around and headed back into the octagon. But there was little else he could say or do. He was in no condition to do anything about having his beer unceremoniously snatched from his grasp.

Sarah threw the beer in Colleen's face. The force of the throw sent suds gushing up her nose and running down her throat. It served the dual purpose of waking Colleen up and washing away the blood and sweat in her eyes. Colleen shook her head and wiped her face. Sarah placed a gentle hand on Colleen's shoulder and advised, "Get up slowly."

Colleen nodded in understanding and began the slow rise to her feet. After she got up, she looked down at the six-inch-diameter red stain that she left behind. Some parts of the outer perimeter of the pool of blood left on the mat by Colleen were starting to dry from the heat in the room, most of which was body heat.

Sarah got up and left the octagon as Maria and Tina entered the ring with a mop, bucket, and drying rags to go to work on the quickly drying blood. An exasperated Vinny stepped up to Sarah as she exited. She could tell that he was just going to groan about his beer. In no mood for such nonsense, Sarah lightly shoved him away. In his inebriated condition, Vinny stumbled backward and hit his head on the gate. Feeling dizzy, he sat on the stairs leading into the cage.

Vinny stayed there for a little over five minutes. After minute two, he was not so much incapable of getting up as he was unwilling. He was comfortable taking a load off and feeling alone in spite of the sea of people around him. For the first time since he got pinched, Vinny felt like he wasn't under surveillance. The crowd around the octagon was starting to disperse and either go elsewhere or go back to gambling. No one paid attention to Vinny, and he liked it that way. After forcing himself to stand and moping his way into the locker room, Vinny discovered that Sarah was in the shower. He sat on the bench, held his head in his hands, and waited for her to come out. When she finally did, the first words out his mouth were, "I think I really banged my head when you pushed me."

Sarah unwrapped the towel from around her head and replied, "You had enough to drink. I had a better use for that beer than you did."

"That's debatable."

Sarah looked past the snark of that reply and moved on from the subject. "Listen, Vinny. I need your help tonight, and you can't screw it up."

"My help? With what?"

Sarah opened her locker, took out the tracking device given to her by Jill, and held it up for Vinny to see. Perplexed, he asked, "Yeah. What is it?"

"It's a tracker. I need to slip it into the duffel bag full of money tonight. I'm pretty sure that bag is tribute money from Leo to his father. If it does go there, we have him."

Vinny saw an opportunity, and ever the opportunist, he inquired, "If I help you with this, and it nails the Mike Manetti, you'll help me get a reduced sentence?"

"You scratch my back, I scratch yours, Vinny. That is the deal. But first, this has to go right." Sarah stepped closer to Vinny and made direct eye contact. "We only get one shot at this and we can't blow it."

Vinny knew it was time to get serious. "What do you need me to do?"

"I need a distraction. I need something that's going to pull Leo's attention away from the bag long enough for me to plant the tracker."

"Like what?"

Sarah had given this some thought ever since she received the tracker, but with so much going on and so many distractions, she couldn't come up with anything. All she could do was hope that Vinny thought of something. "I don't know," she said, "think of something while I get changed. Get out of here. Go!"

Once Sarah got dressed, she and Vinny made their way to Leo's office above the casino. They entered in through the door leading from the casino, but Leo wasn't there. The office was empty, and the duffel bag was on the floor next to his desk, already zipped up. At first glance, Sarah thought they were too late. "Damn it! He already zipped up the bag," she grumbled. She then walked over and gave it a closer examination. "It doesn't look like there's any kind of a lock on it. This may be easier than we thought." She turned to Vinny. "Keep an eye out, and I'll pop the tracker inside."

Vinny stood between Sarah and the door and kept his head on a swivel. Sarah crept toward the bag. She bent down slowly and extended her arm out. Her finger tips were almost at the zipper when whoosh! In barged Leo, entering through another door off to the other side—the one that lead to the club.

Thinking quickly and not coming up with anything better, Sarah palmed the tracking device and touched her toes. She hoped that Leo didn't notice her hand near the zipper when he came in and bought her "just doing a hamstring stretch" routine. Sarah quickly slid the tracking device in her sock.

Lucky for her, Leo did not notice her. This was because, as he entered, Vinny whipped around so quickly that his head started spinning and he almost fell down for the second time that evening. This caught Leo's eye. He witnessed Vinny's drunken behavior earlier and was waiting for him to literally fall on his face again.

"Jesus, Vinny! How much did you have to drink tonight?" Leo walked into the room a little more and noticed Sarah bent in half, doing her toe touches. "And what the hell are you doing?"

Thank God—he's buying it, she thought to herself. Then she said, "Just waiting for you. I figured I'd stay loose while I waited."

"Why? Fight's over."

"I know. But it's important to stretch before and after," Sarah explained.

Leo had never heard of such a thing. Claudia didn't do this, and if she didn't do it, it was abnormal to Leo. "Okay, but don't do it here. I don't like it," he said to Sarah.

"Fair enough," said Sarah as she straightened herself up.

"I'll get you your money," said Leo as he made his way to the safe.

As soon as his back was turned, Sarah turned to Vinny and mouthed the words, "Do something!" to him. Vinny hemmed and hawed as Leo turned the dial on the safe, opened it, and took out a wad of money. Vinny straightened up as soon as Leo turned around, leaving the safe open.

"Good fight tonight. I actually bet on you myself, and it paid off," Leo said as he walked over to Sarah and handed her the cash.

"Thanks," said Sarah as she took the money.

Leo turned and headed back to finish his business with the safe.

As soon as his back was to Sarah, she once again turned to Vinny and this time was more animated and forceful when she mouthed, "Do something now, you freakin' idiot!"

Vinny was trying to avoid doing the one and only thing he could think of that might work. But he was not clearheaded enough to think of anything other than to take advantage of the fact that his evening of drinking had caught up with him in a natural and obvious way. With no other option, he spoke up to Leo and said, "Hey, Leo.

Listen, I gotta take a leak, man. Can I use your bathroom right here down the hall?"

Vinny knew that Leo would never allow him to use it. In spite of this, he strutted across the office as if to head into the hallway between the club and the office, where a small private bathroom was located. Leo couldn't believe the boldness he was seeing in Vinny. It was rare to say the least. Leo put his hand up to halt Vinny and told him, "Hell no. That bathroom is locked, and you are not getting the key. That is a private bathroom for me and invited guests, of which you are neither. Go to the bathroom in either the locker room or out in the club."

This reaction played right into Vinny's hands. Sarah started to get the picture of where Vinny was going. She shrunk away and stayed off to the side, silent. In order to sell the ruse, Vinny decided to make a fuss. "Come on, Leo, I had five beers tonight. Almost six. I really gotta go and can't hold it."

"You better hold it and get to one of those other bathrooms," insisted Leo.

"I don't like those other bathrooms. I like the private bathroom.

It's the closest one and I really gotta go."

As Leo stood frozen stiff and contemplated why Vinny would say he preferred the private bathroom as if he had firsthand knowl- edge of it—and the horror of what such knowledge would entail— Vinny walked over to a nearby ficus tree next to a filing cabinet. "Ah, screw it," said Vinny as he unzipped his pants.

Before Vinny could get any farther, Leo rushed over and grabbed him by the collar. He yanked Vinny away from the plant and violently thrust him backward, screaming obscenities at him. *Thank God he didn't take it out,* Sarah thought as she quietly watched the drama unfold.

Even better, this was just the distraction Sarah needed. As Leo wrestled with Vinny and dragged him down the hall and into the club, she seized the opportunity to secure the tracker to the top inside of the bag. She zipped the bag back up just as Leo came back in, face red and breathing heavily.

Leo looked at Sarah in utter shock and disbelief. "Do you believe that moron was about to piss on my plant here?"

"Yeah. Actually, I do," Sarah responded without hesitation. She really didn't have to think about it. Sarah had the distinct notion that peeing on an office plant was something Vinny would do even if he didn't have to create a diversion.

"Unbelievable!" snarled Leo.

Sarah had to stop herself from giggling at Leo getting angry over such a stupid thing. Besides, her task was done, and she felt good about it. She felt no reason to stick around. Holding up her wad of money and giving Leo a short salute, she said, "Gotta go" and began to head off.

Leo took a deep breath and took a beat to calm down. Before Sarah was out the door he called after her. "Oh, and Sarah—one more thing."

Tendrils of panic swirled around Sarah's insides. But she turned around, faced Leo, and said, "What is it?" with as much coolness as she could muster.

"I want you to know who you're fighting tomorrow tonight."

A great feeling of relief cleared the panic away. Leo hadn't caught on to her. He just wanted to talk about the bracket. This was fine since Sarah had been following the progress of each fighter. She knew the winner on the opposite side of the bracket to her was a twenty-one-year-old Lithuanian girl named Tamara. That's who she was due to fight. Confident in her reply and looking to show off her knowledge, Sarah said, "What about Tamara?"

Leo grinned. He was impressed that she was paying attention.

However, there was more to his grin than just joy at Sarah's knowledge. "Tamara dropped out. She's giving you a bye so that you have a shot at the big prize—one hundred Gs."

Sarah doubted the veracity of the story that Tamara just "dropped out." She could tell that the girl had a strong fighting spirit and would not give up or give in so easily. *She must have been coerced somehow*, Sarah thought. But the fact remained that the schedule had been moved up so that she'd have to face Claudia. Sarah put on a brave face. "Maybe it's time for her to take her first loss." It came across as arrogant, which is just the way she wanted.

Leo was unfazed. "Maybe. Maybe not. I'd wish you good luck, but since she's my girl, we both know that'd be insincere."

"Yeah, I know, Leo. Thanks," Sarah said as she walked away.

As soon as Sarah was out of sight, Leo turned his attention to his ficus tree. He looked it over carefully to make sure it was okay. Then he thought of what Vinny almost did to it and shook his head in disgust.

CHAPTER 16

SARAH HAD A fitful sleep that evening, for the total of about two hours that she got. She spent the bulk of the wee, small hours of the morning watching old sitcoms on basic cable. She discovered that she preferred the ones with the laugh track over the ones that were taped in front of a live studio audience. For some reason, she found the consistency of the canned laughter comforting. Then she thought about how the people laughing on the laugh track were all probably dead now, and she became morose and depressed.

Still, it was better than what was really bothering her. Sarah may have put on a strong, tough exterior in front of Leo, but the fact was that she had never faced someone as dangerous as Claudia before. Her fights were either back when she was on the circuit, with rules and referees, or with run-of-the-mill crime suspects like the River City Rapist who weren't trained to fight at all. Claudia was different. She was trained, and she was unhinged. She was a loose cannon and not to be taken lightly.

Sarah's only hope was that the duffel bag she planted the tracking device in had moved the previous evening from the Amazon Glory club to Mike "the Hammer" Manetti's place. If that happened, it was proof enough to implicate both of the Manettis. Arrest war- rants would be dished out like birthday cake, and she wouldn't have to worry about facing Claudia that evening.

She couldn't wait. Sarah knew that Jill would be at her desk getting situated at around eight o'clock. At 8:01 a.m., Sarah picked up her phone and called Jill. An eighties sitcom taped in front of a live studio audience played in the background as the phone rang. Sarah paced back and forth, waiting for Jill to pick up. Sarah was starting to come to a realization that older people in an eighties sitcom audi- ence would be dead today when, just before she thought about it too much, Jill picked up.

"Did it move?" Sarah asked immediately. It was really a plea for good news more than it was a question. Sarah was on edge. Lack of sleep and an endless parade of mind-numbing sitcoms would do that to a person. She didn't bother with pleasantries and introductions. She knew that her name and number popped up on the display on Jill's phone anyway.

"Good morning to you too," Jill replied on the other end. *She clearly slept well,* Sarah thought, *and she sounded like she might have gotten some last night. Not bad for a married woman on a Thursday eve- ning.* Sarah secretly hoped that she and Dale would do so well after so many years. But no time to think about that now.

"Did it move? The duffel bag. The tracking device. Did it move?" Sarah moved from insistent to desperate in the middle of getting out those words.

"Are you sitting down?" asked Jill.

Sarah stopped her pacing and plopped herself on the bed. "Yes. Why?"

"Because it didn't move."

"What do you mean it didn't move?" Sarah tried her best to not sound frustrated at Jill. After all, it wasn't her partner's fault.

"I mean it didn't move. The bag—wherever you put the tracker, it stayed put."

"Damn it." Sarah surprised herself with how calmly she expressed her disappointment.

Jill knew her partner well enough that she could hear the con- cern in Sarah's voice. She empathized. "I'm sorry, Sarah, but at least we have a trace. As soon as the bag moves, which is hopefully tonight, we'll know."

"Leo is probably waiting for the big fight tonight before he moves the bag. After Claudia and I go at it, he'll have a big haul for his dad."

This perked Jill up quicker than her morning coffee. "You're facing Claudia tonight? Wow—that happened fast. Are you okay? Are you ready?"

"As ready as I'll ever be." Again, Sarah put on a strong front but was crumbling inside.

"Good! Glad to hear it." Jill tried to sound encouraging but could hear the trepidation in Sarah's voice. "Hey—this is a good thing. You can put your plan into action, and I'll see you later tonight with evidence against that murderous monster of a woman under your fingernails. All right?"

"All right," said Sarah as she clicked the phone off.

Sarah sat on the edge of the bed and held her head in her hands for a few minutes. She tried to visualize and focus on what she had to do. But before she could get her head clear enough to do this, she had one more call she had to make. Sarah stood and started pacing again as she hit a number on the speed dial. This time there was no waiting. The first ring barely completed when the other end picked up. It was Dale.

"Hi, Dale," she said, deciding to keep it simple. She just wanted to talk to him, not worry him. She knew he was already worried enough.

If there was any worry in Sarah's voice, Dale didn't notice it. He was just happy to hear from her. "Sarah? It's so good to hear your voice! I've been thinking about you constantly the past couple days."

"I know, I've been busy. This case is running me ragged, as you can imagine."

"I don't think I want to imagine," said Dale, laughing it off. He was just so jazzed to hear from Sarah. "How are you doing? Are you okay?"

"Yeah, I'm fine. Great, in fact—kicking a lot of ass. It feels like the good old days, you know?"

"Yeah, I know what you mean."

Sarah could feel his exuberance over the phone. She could see his big, handsome, charming smile in her mind. She only wished that she could return the feelings, but her mind weighed too heavy with other concerns. "How are you? How are things going down at the clinic?" she asked.

"Fine, doing okay. Kinda sad," Dale answered. "I had to put down the sweetest golden retriever today, but she was so old."

Sarah was on the verge of tears and was about to lose it. She could barely contain herself. Her emotions were bottlenecking, and she had to pull the release valve before she burst. "Dale, listen, there's something I have to do tonight, and part of the reason I'm calling…" She felt a swell of tears come on and paused to get a grip on herself. She could hear Dale's intake of breath on the other end of the phone, as if he was about to say something. She started talking again before he could. "Part of the reason…that I'm calling…is to say I love you. I really, really do, and if anything happens to me tonight, I want you to know that. Okay, Dale? I want you to know I love you."

Sarah's trepidation was so strong that Dale felt it through the phone. The sound of her voice was enough to give it away. Dale shuddered to think of how much of a wreck she looked at this moment—and how she'd never want him to see her in that condi- tion. Nevertheless, he wanted answers. "Sarah? Sarah, what is it? Talk to me, Sarah."

"Sorry, Dale. I have to go. Just know that I love you, and that I'll see you soon, okay?"

He knew that was basically the end of the conversation. It was best to give his love to her and pray for the best. "Okay. Sarah, I love you too."

Sarah couldn't take any more. She clicked off the phone as soon as Dale got done saying those words. His voice resonated in her brain. After a few moments, his words started to give her hope, then strength, then encouragement. She determined that she would fight her best that night and win because she wasn't just doing it for herself. Sarah had lost sight of this over the past few days. She was fighting for Dale, earning the right to go back to him and spend the rest of her life with him. She was fighting for the three young women who washed up on the banks of the river that ran through the city. Their murders would be solved. She would get the evidence that evening. Finally, she was fighting for River City, to rid the city of all of the scumbags like Leo Manetti, his psychotic girlfriend, and his crime-lord father who had for decades flooded the streets with drugs, prostitution, and gambling. It was time for Sarah to do her part to see that justice prevailed.

By the time the fight rolled around that evening, Sarah was pumped and ready to go. Nothing was going to stop her from getting into that octagon and doing what she had to do to bring the whole crooked Manetti operation tumbling down. If she scored a few good hits on Claudia, that was an added bonus.

Vinny was more nervous than Sarah before the fight. He sat on a bench, biting his nails. Sarah was on her feet, moving around and staying loose.

"This is it—the big one," said Vinny, taking the last bit of his pinky fingernail right down to the nail plate.

"I know," said Sarah, trying to tune him out and stay focused on the upcoming bout.

"This Claudia, she's killed three girls already," Vinny continued.

"I know," Sarah continued, staying loose.

"She could kill you."

That was it. Sarah had enough. She spent most of the day, from the end of the phone call with Dale up to that point, getting herself psyched up for the fight that evening. She'd be damned if this annoy- ing little twerp was going to ruin it when she was this close. She unloaded on Vinny, "Jesus, Vinny! I know! You really do have a big mouth, you know that? Now leave me alone, I'm trying to focus and you're messing up my concentration."

Vinny slunk back in terror as Leo walked in. There was a shit-eating grin on his face like only he could muster as he said, "This is it! Tonight is the big night! Your shot at one hundred thousand bucks!"

"She knows, Leo. She's not really in the mood to hear it right now," Vinny chimed in.

"All right," said Leo, "that's fine. You can only deny reality for a few minutes more, then you're on. And to be fair: my girl is a brutal fighter. You saw what she could do a couple of nights ago."

Sarah stopped moving around and glared at Leo. She was done listening to his intimidation tactics. "Yeah, I saw." Sarah was warmed up enough and wanted the fight to start already.

Leo liked seeing the fire in Sarah's belly. He thought he'd stoke it a bit. "She's been stewing ever since then, psyching herself up for tonight. For a chance to get even with you. And I'll be honest—I think the past couple of nights, you've been lucky. But tonight may just be the night your luck runs out."

"Don't bet on it," scoffed Sarah.

"Bet on it? Funny you should mention that, since that's exactly what I did," said Leo. He then turned to Vinny and said, "Isn't that right, Vinny? You're giving me a chance to own you even more than I already do?"

Sarah thought—and hoped—that she heard wrong and was misunderstanding. She turned to Vinny in complete surprise. "You what?!"

"Aaah—don't listen to him. Everything's fine," Vinny said in a calm voice that only served to make Sarah less calm.

Leo took the opportunity to elaborate further. "That's right. Vinny here wagered double or nothing that you win tonight. So if by some miracle you do walk away victorious tonight, you get your hundred grand and Vinny and I wipe the slate clean. If not, he owes me twenty Gs and you, most likely, get carried out of that octagon."

"Don't listen to him Sarah. I'm fine, you got this," Vinny said, now with some nervousness in his voice. He was desperate for Sarah to buy what he was saying, and she wasn't buying it at all.

Leo gave Sarah a cocky nod. "Yeah, Sarah. I'm sure you 'got this,' right? See you out there." Leo turned and took a few steps with an arrogant stride. He stopped suddenly and took a deep breath. "You smell that? I love that Country Fresh Scent deodorizer. I used to have it upstairs, but Claudia is allergic to it. So I had to move it down here.

I know it's cliché, but I have to say, it smells like…victory." Then with a wink and smile, he exited the locker room.

"Holy shit, Vinny! What were you thinking?" Sarah spewed at him.

"Sarah, I believe in you. I know you can do this!" By this point, he sounded like a broken record.

"Thanks—but to risk it all when you're already in so deep?" "Yeah, yeah! I'm in deep with them. I'm in deep with you. I'm

in deep with everybody! What does getting in a little deeper even matter at this point? What the hell? Screw it!" This was the first time that Sarah saw Vinny stand up for himself. She was surprised but liked it. She respected him now as more than just a weak, weaselly little pushover.

Vinny took a moment to regain his composure. He continued, "These past few days helping you out…at first, I felt like a snitch, like a rat, like it was wrong of me to do. But after that first night when you stopped Claudia from killing that girl, it made me realize that this is good, and what we're doing here is the right thing to do. I'm behind you 100 percent—all the way. This is my way of showing that to you."

Sarah was a bit taken aback by Vinny's forthright sincerity. "Okay, I get it. Thank you, Vinny."

"You're welcome, Sarah. Now go clobber that bitch!"

Sarah smiled at him and got back to staying loose. She stayed by the door, knowing that she would be called out to the octagon soon. She planned on making a spectacular entrance.

Within two minutes the penultimate fight of the evening was over, and Claudia was in the middle of the octagon, arms raised above her head, basking in the cheers and adulation of the spectators. She was also basking in about a gallon of sweat. She glistened from head to toe. To anyone who could see her look of determination, there was no doubt about it: Claudia was superpsyched and itching to lay a beatdown on someone.

Claudia took a deep breath and projected her voice like an opera singer. "So here we are. The moment you have all been waiting for.

And let me tell ya, I can't wait to bring this one out. Without further delay, heeere's Sarah!"

The normal thing for a fighter to do was walk to the ring, soak- ing in the cheers of the crowd. But this night Sarah was so pumped up and ready to go that she couldn't wait to get to the octagon. She charged at it, going full speed down the narrow path that led to it from the locker room. Sarah had her game face on. She was more than ready for the fight ahead.

Sarah flung open the door to the octagon. The metal-on-metal ping sound as the door smacked against the cage rang throughout the casino. Sarah did a lap, arms in the air, feeding on the good vibes from the crowd. Once she had enough, she turned and walked over to Claudia, who was standing in the center of the ring watching Sarah put on her show, amused by the spectacle.

Sarah and Claudia stepped close to each other. Neither woman was going to back down. Their chins were down, their eyes were up, and their foreheads were no more than three inches apart. Claudia spoke first. "Tonight, I end you."

"There's an end coming tonight, Claudia—but it's not mine." "Enough talk. Let's do this!" Claudia grabbed Sarah, and the two women grappled. After a couple attempts to overpower one another, they split apart.

Sarah and Claudia traded blows—kicks, punches, jabs, round-houses, leg sweeps. They threw all they could at each other. The fight was brutal, and the two women were pretty evenly matched.

Sarah finally landed a punch to Claudia's nose and stunned her. She used Claudia's moment of weakness to do a leg sweep. Claudia fell on her ass and got the wind knocked out of her.

For a follow-up, Sarah put Claudia in a leg lock. Slowly but surely, Claudia clawed her way to the fence. She was in agony the whole way but made it. Claudia grabbed on to the fence and used the leverage to help wriggle out of the leg lock.

Sarah got up and threw a jab at Claudia. Claudia ducked in the nick of time. Sarah's fist hit a fence post. Sarah grasped her hand in pain and turned away, doubled over.

Like some kind of combination of ninja and monkey, Claudia jumped on Sarah's back, got her in a head scissors, and took her down to the mat. Sarah punched at Claudia's legs. The blows had little effect. Claudia's strong, muscular legs barely felt the awkward punches.

Sarah's face was red as Claudia's leggy vise grip got tighter and tighter. Soon, the punching stopped. Sarah's body started to go limp. She was almost passed out. Her eyes were almost closed.

Seeing Sarah going limp, Claudia grinned devilishly as she maintained the head scissors. She squeezed harder.

This just pissed Sarah off even more. She'd be damned if she was going to let this grinning, murdering thug beat her in a fight. Sarah got a second wind—and then some. Her eyes snapped wide open— they were red and bulging. Her breath was short and fast. No other word for it—Sarah was angry.

Letting out a fearsome war cry, Sarah dug her nails deep into the sides of Claudia's legs. Claudia bellowed out in agony as Sarah raked her nails down Claudia's legs.

Claudia released her head scissors and rolled off Sarah, track- ing blood on the mat. Face flush and pulsing with adrenaline, Sarah jumped on top of Claudia and let loose a flurry of punches. Once Claudia was punch drunk enough, Sarah put her in a choke hold.

Claudia squirmed and tried to wriggle herself out of it, but to no avail. Within seconds, she was unconscious. Sarah was victorious.

But Sarah wasn't even close to stopping. She placed her hands on Claudia's head as if she was going to snap her neck. Sarah held the pose for a beat. Then, as if being jarred back to reality, she looked up at the crowd, who were now on their feet.

Sarah then looked up at the office. Leo was peering through the window. Sarah could clearly see, even at that distance, that he worried about what she would do. She couldn't bear to look at him. As Sarah looked away she spotted Vinny in the crowd, shaking his head to indicate to her to not go through with what was her clear intention.

Sarah let go of Claudia's head. Claudia crumpled to the mat, out cold. Sarah bolted out of the octagon. She didn't head into the locker room though. She ran right past Vinny without saying a word, and straight through the exit.

Sarah rushed out the main door to the club and on to the busy street. She headed down the sidewalk, walking briskly for two blocks until she came to the main door of her apartment building. The speed of her walk helped to keep her warm, but once she stopped, she began to feel the creeping cold sensation of the autumn air. Instinctively, Sarah reached into her pocket for the key only to remember that she left straight from the fight. She didn't stop at her locker to get her things, and therefore didn't have her key.

"Shit!" said Sarah as she walked to the side of the building and headed down an alley. Sarah looked up at the fire escape. The ladder hung just low enough where if she stood on a nearby dumpster she could jump up and grab it.

Being careful to not disrupt the evidence under her fingernails, Sarah put her palms on the dumpster. She was about to push herself up when he heard a deep, loud voice behind her yell, "Hey!"

Sarah whipped around and found herself face to face with a large, muscle-bound man in his midthirties. The man was dressed in jeans, work boots, and a hoodie. He looked like he was returning home from the local corner bar after a night of heavy drinking and was feeling brave. *He probably thinks he's the one-man guardian of this neighborhood*, Sarah thought to herself.

"You sneaking up the fire escape to rob somebody?" the big man asked her.

At least he was giving her a chance to explain. Sarah decided that honestly was the best policy. "No, I promise you I'm not robbing anybody. I live here. I just don't have my key with me."

"Bullshit!" the big man interrupted, now getting aggravated at thinking Sarah was lying to him. "You're a thief. I'll show you what we do with thieves around here."

The big man lunged at Sarah. She already had a long night and was in no mood for a fair fight. She punched him in the nose with a flat palm as he tried to grab her. It was the only way she could punch for fear of tarnishing the evidence under her nails.

Taking a few steps back, the big man gurgled in pain. Sarah thought briefly about what to do next. She knew that she'd hate her- self for taking the cheap and easy route with a mostly innocent civil- ian who was only trying to protect his neighbors, but he left her little choice. She needed to get into her apartment and secure the evidence literally in her hands as soon as possible. Against her better, kinder, more decent nature, Sarah reared back and propelled her right leg forward as quickly as she could. The pain-stricken, busted-nose big man received a swift, well-placed kick to the balls. Not knowing or expecting what came to him, he was caught completely off guard. If he had hit the pavement any harder, he would have cracked it. Sarah looked down at her handiwork and knew he wasn't getting up anytime soon.

As Sarah made her ascent up the fire escape, the pangs of guilt started to hit her. She knew he'd be okay eventually, but she hated that it came to that. She wished she'd found another way. But she did what she had to do in the moment. At least that's what she told her- self. The problem she had was in convincing herself that she wasn't completely full of crap.

The window that led out to Sarah's fire escape didn't lock. This was actually a good thing in this scenario. She used it to gain access into her apartment. As a soon as she got inside, the warmth of the heat from the electric radiator greeted her with a comforting embrace. This helped to calm Sarah down as she made her way to the bathroom and took a pair of rubber surgical gloves from the medicine cabinet. Sarah put the gloves on to ensure the integrity of the evidence under her fingernails. As she did, she noticed a bottle of melatonin that she brought with her. They were ten-milligram tablets and always did wonders to help her take the edge off and get a good night's sleep. She downed one with a glass of water and crawled into bed. She was asleep within ten minutes, the evidence she collected safe and secure inside her gloved hands until the morning.

Back at Amazon Glory, Leo was far from resting comfortably. Sitting at his desk, counting out that evening's take—half a dozen or so enormous stacks of bills—he should have been happy. However, he was not happy. He was seething. It didn't help matters that Vinny walked in with a sure strut and a cocky smile—payback for Leo's equally cocky behavior in the locker room before the fight.

"All right! Look at all the money you made! Hell of a fight tonight, huh?" Vinny said enthusiastically.

Leo was in no mood for small talk, and Vinny's chipper attitude only grated on his nerves. "Yeah. It was," he reluctantly conceded.

"Awww, come on. Don't be sore. That's what happens when you challenge a pro. Now I want to hear it from you to be sure: we're even now, right?"

"Right, Vinny."

"Great," exclaimed Vinny, relieved that he could finally move on with his life. The great weight of the debt he owed to Leo was now lifted off him, and he felt a surge of euphoria. "I'll be on my way now. Be sure to save a hundred Gs of this for Sarah," he said, gesturing toward the stacks of money. I'm sure she'll be by soon to get it, hehe. Later!"

Vinny was halfway to the door when Leo shouted, "Hold up!"

Vinny turned, slightly annoyed, He wanted to go out and party the rest of the night away to enjoy his newfound freedom away from Leo. He still had the cops to contend with, but he knew that would be over soon. They were less of a problem to him than Leo. "Yeah, Leo. What?" he asked, trying to mask his displeasure.

"Did you just say that Sarah is a pro?"

Vinny was legitimately confused. He was so happy that he had no idea what words came out of his mouth. "Huh? No—I don't think I said that."

"You just did. You just said, 'That's what happens when you challenge a pro.' So I'm going to ask you this only once: is she a pro?" Vinny knew he was in deep. He did what came to him instinc- tively and tried to bluff his way out. "Look, Leo—what I meant is, she fights like a pro. That's all."

Leo wasn't buying any of it. "But is Sarah a pro? Don't bullshit me. I'm not in the mood, and I wanna know: is Sarah a pro? Is she or isn't she?"

By this time Leo was right in Vinny's face. Vinny had his back to the wall with nowhere to go. He cracked. "Yes! Okay, yes. Jesus. Yeah, she's a pro. She spent a little time on the regional pro circuit years ago. But she's been out of it for a long time."

Leo's mood went from bad to worse. He was beyond furious. "Unbelievable! You bring a ringer to my club, then place a bet against me? You fixed this!"

Vinny's knees started to feel weak. He didn't like the murderous look in Leo's eyes one bit. He tried to defend himself and deescalate before things got violent. In a clear, calm voice, he stated, "No, I didn't fix it. I thought she'd be a good contender, so I brought her here, that's it."

"That's it, huh?" "Yeah, I swear."

Leo wanted to believe him, but he had an instinct for liars. He smelled that something else was up. "You know what I think? I think you're lying to me. I think there's more to this than you're telling me." "No, Leo—there isn't, I swear," Vinny pleaded. He started to get the feeling that the violence he feared was increasingly becoming inevitable.

"And I'm going to find out one way or the other." Leo socked Vinny right in the gut. This instantly knocked the wind out of Vinny, and he fell hard. The next thing he saw before the world went black was Leo's size eleven-and-a-half leather-soled lace-ups coming down on his head full force.

When Vinny finally came around, he was down in the casino. It was totally empty. As he gained more of his senses, he discovered that he was inside the octagon—and was chained to the fence. He pulled focus and saw Leo and Claudia having a conversation off to the side. Claudia was badly bruised from the fight with Sarah. The scratches on her legs were untreated, red, and swollen.

In spite of her appearance, Claudia was as nimble and as blood-thirsty as ever. As soon as she saw Vinny move his head around, she walked over to him and started punching his head and torso. Vinny cried out in torment. His screams of pain echoed through the empty, cavernous casino. Claudia finally stopped after giving him a fence-shaking uppercut to the abdomen, which caused Vinny to spit up some of the beer he'd downed hours before.

Disgusted, Leo urged Vinny to come to his senses. "You can make this stop. All you need to do is tell me the rest."

"I don't know any more. I swe—" The statement was cut off by a jab across the jaw from Claudia.

"Let me ask you this," said Leo, "you say she was a pro years ago. What's she been doing between now and then?" He could tell that the blows to Vinny's abdomen and jaw were affecting the volume of his speech, so he walked up to Vinny and stood next to Claudia to make sure he had no trouble hearing.

"I don't know. She's the one who came to me."

Leo punched him in the ribs. "Liar! There's something off about this girl. Something's not right. I can't put my finger on it. It's more than her being a pro, though." Leo was flush with rage. His face was red and he stared daggers at Vinny. Quickly moving his mouth close to Vinny's right ear, he screamed, "Who is she?"

Vinny closed his eyes. Claudia went to work on his chest and abdomen some more. She was tiring out, and her punches were getting weaker but still effective. Adding intensity to the situation, Leo kept his mouth close to Vinny's ear and yelled, "Tell me, Vinny! Tell me, Vinny!" with each pulverizing punch from Claudia.

After a few seconds of brutal pounding and being screamed at, Vinny relented—he couldn't take it anymore. "She's a cop!"

The beating stopped. Claudia and Leo stepped back, horrified. It was something they were both thinking but dared not say for fear that it might be true. Now it was confirmed. Their blood turned to ice water.

Vinny knew the cat was out of the bag. His only hope was for a quick death if he was honest and told them all they wanted to know. "I'm sorry, okay? But she's a cop. I got pinched."

"You said you made bail," Claudia said, still in disbelief. "I didn't. I made a deal."

"You freakin' rat!" fumed Leo. "What kind of deal? Why is she here?"

"It's for the bodies of the girls Claudia killed in here. I told them about all of it, and they sent her to collect evidence." Vinny couldn't believe how easily the truth poured out of him. He knew he was the kind of guy who would eventually crack under pressure, but he always thought that when push came to shove, he could keep his composure and maintain at least some dignity. The blood-infused drool and the fact that he was on the verge of tears said otherwise.

Now Leo was very interested. He'd heard the magic word. "Evidence? What kind of evidence?"

"Evidence linking you to the murders. That's all I know." "What did she get?" Leo was trying to subdue his rage long enough to extract much needed answers from Vinny. "That's all I know," Vinny replied.

The lid on Leo's rage was starting to slip. "Tell me what she got, Vinny!"

"I don't what she got. The cops just asked me to help her with the investigation. I have no idea if they even got anything or not."

Leo stepped close to Vinny and leaned in. "You better hope they didn't get anything for your mother's sake." A horrified Vinny looked at Leo as he turned to Claudia and coldly informed her, "Okay, I'm done with him."

With a sinister grin on her face, Claudia slowly walked over to Vinny. He pleaded with her and Leo to spare him and leave his mother alone as she placed her hands on his head and snapped his neck. Vinny's body went limp, held up only by the chains.

Leo admired his girlfriend's handiwork. "Good riddance."

"Do you think he was telling the truth?" Claudia was doing everything she could to not have to face the reality of the situation she and Leo were in.

"I think we get most of it. I still don't trust him, though. Better lay low for a while." Leo gestured toward Vinny's lifeless body hang- ing on the fence. "Plus, we gotta do something about this. I better call my Dad."

CHAPTER 17

SARAH WOKE UP early the following morning, excited to face the day and put this case behind her. She hadn't slept that well in days. The thought of getting back to Dale and living a more normal life put a spring in her step as she got dressed. Jeans and a sweater were the outfit of choice. In spite of the sweaty stench still lingering on her, she didn't shower or even wash her face. Even though she still had the gloves on her hands, she didn't want to take any risks that the precious evidence under her fingernails may get tainted. After putting her hair up in a ponytail, Sarah got into the beat-up, fifteen- year-old rust bucket that the precinct lent her for the assignment and headed down to the station to return it and pay a visit to the lab technician.

The lab technician's name was Ernesto. He was originally from Honduras but came to the United States on a student visa. After exceling at chemistry and biology at the university, he graduated at the top of his class. While he missed his mother, father, and three younger siblings, the thought of returning to Honduras depressed him. He decided that he wanted to stay in the United States. He applied for training in the River City Police forensics lab and was accepted. With a job and a residence of his own in River City, he applied for citizenship, which he achieved after four years. Shortly thereafter, he achieved the role of supervisor in the lab.

Sarah always liked Ernesto, but she found him a bit too serious for her taste. At first, she thought it was a language-barrier issue, and that was why he didn't get any of her joking around. After a while she figured it out that it was just who Ernesto was—he cared more about the microorganisms sitting under a microscope than he did about the person sitting in a chair across from him.

This was all just as well. Sarah could save her good mood for those around her who truly deserved it. As she sat in a chair and had Ernesto carefully remove her gloves and dig under her nails, she said nothing. Rather, she pretended like she was getting a manicure— something she'd not done in ages. Her fantasy was short-lived. Jill and Busby got word that she was in the lab and busted in to see her.

Busby wasted no time. "What have you got?"

"Hi, Lieutenant. I was going to come see you when I got done here."

"What have you got?" Busby insisted.

"Some of Claudia's skin under my nails," Sarah replied. "That's why I'm getting them done. Ernesto here was just about to bring out the emery board."

Ernesto just gave Sarah a cold look. He was unamused. *It was worth a shot*, Sarah thought.

"Looks like you scratched the bitch good," observed Jill. "Yeah. There's probably more skin under my nails than there is

on her legs," said Sarah, cracking a satisfied smile.

Busby was pleased. "You did good. If the DNA in these samples matches what's under the nails of the victim we pulled out of the river, we've got our murderer."

"Yup," said Sarah. "Between this and the eyewitness testimony from Vinny, she should be put away for life, easy. I have to say, I didn't like the little rat when we first started, but after a while he grew on me."

"We're not sure if there's going to be any testimony from Vinny," said Busby.

His forlorn expression let Sarah know that there was more to the story. "What? Why not?" she asked.

Busby turned to Ernesto and asked, "Can you give us a minute?' This was not a conversation for any ears that didn't need to hear it.

"Sure. I have enough here anyway," Ernesto replied. He then turned to Sarah and commented with the utmost sincerity, "Great job, Detective. Good to have you back safe."

As Ernesto got up from his stool and moved to the other side of the lab to begin work on the samples, Busby leaned in close to Sarah. "In the early hours of the morning, Vinny's tracker went clear across town, into an alley, and stayed there."

"Oh no," was the only commentary Sarah could muster. She had a sinking feeling that she knew where this story was going.

Busby continued, "We sent a black and white to investigate. The patrol officer found Vinny's leg in the dumpster—ankle bracelet still on it."

"Shit."

Jill tried to be reassuring. "This doesn't mean that—"

Busby picked up where she left off. "It doesn't mean he's dead, necessarily. But we're assuming the worst."

Sarah was more confident in her assessment of Vinny's fate. "He's dead. There's no way an animal like Leo Manetti would have kept him alive if he knew. Damn it!"

Busby knew she was right. "This means he's probably on to you too. Did he know about the apartment around the corner, or did you give any indication about who you were or where you're from?"

"No, I didn't," Sarah answered quickly. She knew she was super careful.

"That's good," said Busby. "I wouldn't go back to the apartment though, so I hope you took everything you needed to with you when you left this morning."

"I did."

"But if he has no idea who you really are, then it should be okay for you to go home."

These were the exact words Sarah wanted—and needed—to hear. Still, she wanted to make sure that the case against the Manetti family was airtight. "What about the bag? Did it move?'

"It moved last night," said Jill, giving Sarah a thumbs-up.

Busby was pleased too. "Even if Vinny did give up that you're a cop, he didn't tell them about the bag."

"So you have what you need on both Leo and Mike 'the Hammer' Manetti, right?"

"We do," said Busby with a smile. I plan on paying the Hammer a visit personally this morning. Wish you could come." Busby was glowing with the mere thought of cuffing Michael Manetti himself. "Me too," said Sarah, only half meaning it. She really just wanted to get home to Dale more than anything else.

"You earned it. But you also earned some time with your fiancé. Go home to him," said Busby as he gently laid a reassuring hand on her shoulder. "You should be proud of what you did. I'm proud of you."

Jill placed a hand gently on Sarah's other shoulder. "Me too."

The drive from the downtown precinct to the home of Mike "the Hammer" Manetti in the wealthy River City Heights neighbor- hood took about twenty-five minutes, traffic permitting. Lieutenant Busby himself led an entourage of four other police cars, each with two officers in them, as they made the journey down Riverside Boulevard, the most direct route to River City Heights. Busby rode alone. It gave him time to reflect on his past history with Michael Manetti that went back two decades to when he was first promoted to detective.

*****

Busby's first partner was Ralph Mendelson, who at the time was a twenty-year veteran of the River City Police homicide detectives. Mendelson's own partner, Benjamin Grady, who at ten years older than Mendelson was in his midfifties, was forced into retirement. The official diagnosis by the police department physician was cor- onary thrombosis. It was determined by the doctor that if Grady wanted to avoid open-heart surgery, he needed to clean up his diet, start a light, low-impact exercise regimen, and avoid stress. While those first two things were bad enough for Grady, the last one meant that he had to give up the job. The long hours and grieving family members looking to him to solve their loved one's murder was a bit too much for someone in his condition. Even for homicide detectives in perfect health, the load was a stressful one.

Grady was offered a desk job. It was something administrative, answering phones and processing paperwork. Sure, it had stresses of its own, but nothing on the level of a homicide detective. Grady would have none of it, though. In his mind, if the blockage in his heart didn't kill him, shuffling papers across a desk and dealing with the bureaucrats in city hall was going to do the job. He knew he could retire with a full pension, so that was what he decided to do.

This left Mendelson without a partner but only for a short while. Within two weeks of Grady's retirement, Busby was assigned to be his new partner. Mendelson took Busby on without complaint, even though he hated the idea of having any partner other than Grady. But the fact of the matter, as he knew, was that he had no choice.

Busby was excited about his first day on the job with Mendelson. The reputation that he and Grady had around the department was unparalleled by anyone else. In their twenty years of working together, the two had a homicide solve rate of 65 percent—leaps and bounds above any others, all who were below 50 percent. Busby got one of his best suits pressed and showed up at Mendelson's desk at 8:00 a.m. sharp to introduce himself with an enthusiastic smile and hearty handshake.

Mendelson was comparably less enthusiastic. Over the course of the next few days, Busby came to find out that Mendelson was not a morning person—mostly because of the moderate to heavy drinking he did in the evenings—and it was best to not talk to him before he had his morning cup of coffee with a hefty dose of sugar. Mendelson looked at the strapping twenty-eight-year-old in front of him, stood up and took his hand, giving it a good squeeze. Busby felt and heard his knuckles pop. Mendelson didn't say a word to Busby. He just looked the young man in the eye while he squeezed as hard as he could.

"Follow me," said Mendelson as he pushed past Busby. "Where are we going?" asked Busby, chasing after him. He

wanted to massage his right hand because of the throbbing pain but decided against it. He didn't want Mendelson to see and take it as a sign of weakness.

"Car" came the reply.

"Where are we going in the car?" "Morgue."

Simple, one-word answers were common for Mendelson. The more monosyllabic the better. He believed in being a man of action, not words. This took some getting used to for Busby, who prided himself on being more of a people person.

The ride down the elevator to the parking garage was silent except for the sound of the mechanisms that made the elevator move. Looking around, Busby couldn't help but notice that the ele- vator-safety inspection certificate had expired three months ago. For a brief moment, he was very concerned about the cable snapping, sending him and Mendelson plummeting to the subbasement at free-fall speed. Busby had never before been so happy to hear the elevator ding as the doors slid open.

The car was parked five spots away from the elevator—a parking area reserved for high-ranking officers or those with a long-standing tenure. Mendelson got into the car and started it up. Busby barely shut the door and got his seatbelt on by the time Mendelson pulled out of the space.

The city morgue was a plain, nondescript building in the heart of River City. The idea for its placement was so that it would be centrally located for all police precincts in the city. However, the northside precinct where Busby and Mendelson were driving from was between three to five miles farther than the others. The silence of the eighteen-minute ride there made it seem even longer for Busby.

Mendelson parked in back, and the two men went inside. They had to flash their badges at the security guard to get buzzed in, then there was a sign-in sheet. This was Busby's first time at the morgue, and he couldn't believe the security. *Why do cadavers need to be locked up so tight?* he thought to himself. Over the years, he eventually heard the stories that explained exactly why. Each one was pure nightmare fuel that messed up his sleep for at least two nights. He eventually got to a point where he stopped listening to them.

After signing in, Mendelson led Busby down a long corridor. Offices were strewn on either side for various morgue administrators.

They then arrived at the double doors at the end of the corridor that led to the freezer room where the bodies are kept, or what the homi- cide detectives affectionately called the "popsicle stand."

Waiting to greet them was Dr. Tomomi Yamashita, a second-generation woman of Japanese immigrant parents. She was about five feet five inches tall, had jet-black hair, and high cheekbones. Like Busby, she was also in her late twenties. He was immediately smitten, but he knew work must come first.

"Good morning, gentlemen," said Tomomi as she looked up from her clipboard and placed a black pen in the pocket of her lab coat. Her greeting was warm and inviting, and Busby immediately felt at ease. She kept looking at Mendelson as she gestured toward Busby. "Is this your new partner?"

"Yup."

"I figured," she replied. Then turning to Busby, she reached out her hand and said, "Tomomi Yamashita. How are you?"

"Fine," said Busby as he took her hand and shook. Tomomi's hand was small, soft, and feminine—a stark contrast to the tight, rough-skinned grip he experienced with Mendelson earlier. "I'm Max Busby."

"Welcome aboard, Max," Tomomi said with a smile before turning her attention back to Mendelson. "I heard about Ben's retire- ment. How is he doing?"

"Fine."

"Glad to hear it," said Tomomi. Mendelson's curt and vague responses didn't bother her. She was used to them and didn't take it personally. She knew it was just his way. It was even a bit refreshing after dealing with all of the other detectives who talked her ear off. *If I wanted to blab all day, I wouldn't be working with the dead*, she thought to herself many times as various detectives droned on about nonsense or tried to flirt with her.

"We're here for cadaver number 000518-G," said Mendelson.

Busby could hardly believe his ears. It was the first time he heard Mendelson say more than two words. It was strangely comforting to him to know for sure that his partner could actually string together an entire sentence.

"Follow me, gentlemen," said Tomomi as she led them across the room to the cooler where that body was kept. She opened the door and slid the body out so gracefully that it looked to Busby like she did it all in one motion.

Busby's admiration was quickly quelled when Tomomi pulled the cover back to reveal the body of a man in his early to midthirties whose face had been completely caved in. From what Busby could see, he also had bruises from being struck about the shoulders, arms, and torso. Additionally, he had a deep, thin cut that ran from one side of his throat to the other.

Mendelson kept an eye on Busby as the body was revealed. He knew that this was his new partner's first time in the morgue and wanted to see how he handled it. Busby proved himself to Mendelson by not flinching, turning away in disgust at the grisly sight, or, worst of all, getting physically ill. Even more impressive than his reaction, though, was the fact that he took the time to closely examine what he saw and ask a question.

"Am I right that the victim here was beaten and then had his throat cut?" Busby asked Tomomi.

"That is correct, detective. It actually started down here." Tomomi lowered the cover completely down to the corpse's ankles. She then pointed to the broken knees on the body. "They first broke his knees, so he couldn't move or get away."

Busby tried his best to not glance at the genitals as his eyes made their way to where Tomomi was pointing. "I see," he said extra deeply, to keep his voice from cracking.

Tomomi had mercy on him and pulled the cover back up to waist level on the body. "The perpetrators then proceeded to beat him about the upper body. Once they were done, they slit his throat with either a straight razor or a box cutter. He bled out, then they smashed in his face after he was dead."

"What was the weapon they used for the beating?" inquired Busby.

"A hammer. Two, actually. One large mallet that they used to break his knees and work the body, then a big, heavy hammer, like a sledgehammer, was used for the final blow on the head."

"Hammer?" As a patrol officer before his promotion, Busby was keenly aware of the crime kingpin of River City, Michael Manetti, whose nickname was the Hammer. The connections raced through his head: could this be the doing of Mike the Hammer? Was this his calling card? Manetti was known on the streets for being gracious and unifying to everyone under him, giving them more power and control than previous crime bosses. It's what made it so difficult to get anyone to turn on him. Was this the start of a more violent trend?

Mendelson could see the wheels turning inside of Busby's head and decided to rescue the young detective from himself. "Thank you," he said to Tomomi. He then turned to Busby and said, "Let's go."

Busby followed Mendelson out of the popsicle stand as Tomomi covered up the body and put it away. As they walked out to the car, Mendelson decided to try to dampen Busby's excitement before he got too far ahead of himself. "Don't get too worked up, kid. I know what you're thinking, and the fact that a hammer was used is circum- stantial. We have nothing to connect Michael Manetti to this mur- der. The fact is that the body you just saw—our newest case—was found yesterday in the park by a pair of evening joggers. There was no other evidence around it, so the body had obviously been moved and dumped there."

"So whoever did this wanted it to be found," said Busby as he got into the car.

"Very good," said Mendelson as he started up the car and began the trip back to the station. "The name of this one is Jamie Munoz. At least that's what was on the ID in his pocket, and as far as we can tell through all that mess, that was him."

"So they left a body, with ID on it." Busby was feeling insight- ful.

"That must be some kind of a message to someone."

"Perhaps," said Busby, "but let me tell you something else about that ID. It had a tiny blade sticking out of it. I damn near cut myself digging it out his pocket."

"That's weird."

"There are sick people out there, kid. Munoz was one of them. You know Sergeant Ross at the desk, right?"

"Yeah, of course. The one with the scar on his neck."

"Munoz is the one who gave it to him. Now Munoz is on parole for one day, and he winds up beaten unrecognizable, but left to be found and identified."

"So this is a set up to frame Sergeant Ross? Or do you think he did it?"

"Seymour?" Mendelson was surprised that the thought crossed Busby's mind—and he didn't like it. "No, I don't think Seymour is the vengeful type. Though I wouldn't blame him."

"But who would frame him by killing this Munoz guy?"

"I don't know. That's what we have to figure out. We need to start by talking to Seymour—Sergeant Ross—when we get back to the station. See if he has any enemies who would do something like this."

"Sergeant Ross is such a nice guy. I don't see it," said Busby. "Those are the ones you really have to watch out for," Mendelson

said in the calm, wise, tone of a mentor dispensing pearls of wisdom. My goal here is to see if Seymour can give us any leads, and since you brought it up—clear his name from any of this wrongdoing."

Mendelson would never say it out loud to a young, idealistic, brand-new partner, but as far as he was concerned, once Seymour Ross was cleared he was done trying to solve this case. Sure, he'd do the minimum amount of work to look like due diligence was done, but in his mind, whoever beat the hell out of this drug-dealing scum- bag who tried to kill a cop did the city a favor. It was good riddance, and he could move on to solve the cases of victims whose murders actually deserved to be solved.

As he walked into the station with Mendelson, a strange feeling of guilt came over Busby. He hated the idea of having to question Sergeant Ross, who was the friendliest person on the force, if not in the city. This man never meant any harm to anyone, and now he and his hard-nosed partner were about to grill him about a murder. Busby didn't walk to the front desk so much as he sauntered. His legs didn't want to propel him forward, but he knew he must.

Sergeant Ross hung up the phone just as Mendelson and Busby got to him. He looked up at them and smiled. *This makes it even worse*, Busby thought to himself. Then the most amazing turn of events happened.

"Detective Mendelson—great to see you," said Seymour, then acknowledging Busby's presence, "you too, Detective Busby."

Busby grinned in gratitude for the acknowledgment as Mendelson started to speak up. "Sergeant Ross, you may not be so happy to see me when I tell you…"

Seymour didn't hear him. He was too busy fiddling through his pile of messages to get to the one he wanted. "Here you go," he said, handing the note to Mendelson.

"What's this?" asked Mendelson, looking at the piece of paper with what Busby regarded as an undue amount of suspicion.

"Some guy called," replied Seymour. "He said he has a tip for you on the Munoz murder." Seymour gestured to the paper and con- tinued, "He said to meet him at the diner tonight at midnight and he'll tell you all you want to know.'

"I see," said Mendelson as he backed away from the desk.

Busby followed him and looked over his shoulder at the note. "I guess we don't have to question Sergeant Ross anymore, huh?"

"They promoted the right guy to detective, kid. Let me tell ya."

"So what now?"

"Well Busby," said Mendelson, "I hope you're a night owl, because we have somewhere to be at midnight."

CHAPTER 18

USBY ACTUALLY WASN'T much of a night owl, but he could stay up if needed. He started downing cups of strongly brewed black coffee at 8:00 p.m. just to make sure he was awake and alert for the evening. The diner that the mystery witness wanted to meet at was closer to the studio apartment Busby rented in River City Center, so Mendelson picked him up at eleven forty-five, and they made their way there.

It was midnight on the dot when the two detectives walked through the door of the Good Eats Diner. Busby remembered the place from his younger days of going to bars and clubs in the dining and entertainment district. He always admired the way it held on to its 1950s roots yet had modern touches, like digital jukeboxes at the tables. As soon as the door opened and the warm, soothing scent of fried eggs, bacon, hash browns, and the famous corned beef hash wafted up to his nostrils, he was suddenly transported back in time. He wished he was there to settle the alcohol in his stomach like he would have been years ago, but not on that night. On that night, he was there to talk to a witness to a murder.

Busby looked around the diner, which was about half full. The bars and clubs wouldn't close down and empty out for another two hours. "How do know who the witness is?" he asked Mendelson.

Mendelson took one glance at the tables to the left. He took another glance at the tables to the right. Then he pointed a finger to a man dressed in black in the corner of the diner. It was one of the few spots that was not directly in front of a window. The man had a cup of coffee in front of him that he kept staring at, but never touched. "That's him," Busby proclaimed with confidence.

Busby didn't even question it. He just followed Mendelson as he made his way to the table. When he got there, Mendelson puffed up his chest, tilted his head down, and said, "We got your note."

The man urgently motioned to them to sit quickly. They obliged. Mendelson did the introductions. "I'm Detective Mendelson. This is Detective Busby. Who are you, what do you know, what do you want, and why should I believe you?"

Busby got the distinct impression that Mendelson had meetings like this before.

"My name is Philip La Calamita," the man said. Then, taking Mendelson's questions in order, he continued, "I know who killed Jamie Munoz, I want protection, and I know what I'm talking about because I'm a member of the Manetti family."

Busby was excited at the prospect at nailing the city's *nume- ro-uno* crime boss, a man who generally kept his nose clean. This was a career-making opportunity—if it was legit. He needed to make sure this wasn't too good to be true. "Why are you coming forward?" "Because after ten years of being with Manetti, I'm sick of him.

I want out. Back when Bianchi ran things, I knew where I stood. But then that mangle-handed little bastard muscled in. The way Manetti runs his operation, like we're all equal and there's no structure and only him and his two best buddies Bruno and Silvio are on top, I don't like it. I held out for as long as I could, kept my head down, and tried to make the most of it, but I want out. I can tell you who killed Jamie Munoz and how."

"We're listening," said Busby, leaning in. Mendelson couldn't help showing his interest as well.

Philip cleared his throat and began. "Munoz was killed because he was a screwup. It wasn't just that cop that he slashed in the neck. It was a lot of other things—little things here and there—that piled up against him. Manetti hates killing and violence, but he's not above it. He will do it if necessary. With Munoz, Manetti felt that he was becoming more and more of a liability. He figured it was just a matter of time before Munoz got pinched and squawked to save his skin."

"So Manetti arranged his release so he could kill him?" asked Busby.

"That I don't know," said Philip, "but I wouldn't be surprised if some parole board officials were bribed. Sure, why not—in spite of Manetti's more peaceful approach to running things, he's still as corrupt as they come. Manetti could have gotten to Munoz inside as well, but he regards things like that as too impersonal and too old school. His way of doing things is more direct."

Mendelson was growing impatient. He'd heard enough of the why. He wanted to know who did it. However, before he could ask, a waitress approached the table with a smile on her face and a three-quarters-full coffee pot in her hand.

"Let me top you off," she said as she poured more coffee into Philip's cup. When she was done, she looked over at Busby and Mendelson. "Can I get you two gents anything?"

As much as the scent of scrambled eggs, home fries, and corned beef hash wafting through the air drove Busby wild, his bet- ter judgment took over and he simply replied, "No, thank you," as Mendelson simultaneously shook his head. The waitress shrugged and walked away.

Mendelson wasted no time after she'd gone. "Who did it, La Calamita? And how do you know?"

"It was Bruno and Silvio—Manetti's two right-hand goons. I know this because the night it happened, I was also at the Manetti house to deliver some tribute—his cut of the profits from my num- bers business—and was waiting outside the door to go in. I overheard Bruno and Silvio reporting back to Manetti that the job was done, and how they did it with hammers. I guess that's his trademark since he's Mike 'the Hammer' Manetti. Pretty sick way to off someone, though—to beat them to death with a hammer. Plugging someone with a gun is quicker and cleaner."

Mendelson was satisfied. "Are you willing to swear to this in court?"

"I am, as long as I get the protection that I asked for." "We'll see what we can do," said Mendelson.

"In the meantime, how do we reach you?" Busby asked.

Philip handed Busby a card. It said "Lookin' Sharp Dry Cleaners" and had an address and phone number printed on it. "This is my dry-cleaning business. Just leave a message asking about dry-cleaning a 'green wool suit with pleated pants' along with a number. I'll call you back."

Busby took the card. He and Mendelson exited the booth as Philip grabbed his coffee. He tried to look as casual as possible as he sipped.

As they headed to the car, Busby asked Mendelson, "What do you think?"

"He's legit," said Mendelson. "I think he'll help us. Plus, what he said about the method of murder—the hammers—corroborates the *coroner*'s report, so it leads me to believe he's telling the truth."

Busby slipped into a low-key state of bliss thinking about Tomomi at the mention of the word coroner. He was abruptly snapped back to reality with Mendelson's assertion to "Get in the car" followed up with "We both need to get some shut-eye. We have a big day tomorrow trying to convince the higher-ups to give this guy the protection he needs so he'll testify."

It actually didn't take much convincing on the part of Mendelson and Busby. Their lieutenant, the captain, the commissioner, and the mayor—everyone up to the governor who heard about this witness was on board that he was valuable and should be protected. Since Mendelson and Busby were the ones Philip contacted, and he trusted them, it was agreed that they be assigned to protect him. But first, Busby got to live a fantasy he'd been dreaming about since he saw Jamie Munoz's beaten and battered corpse laying on a metal slab: the arrest of Mike "the Hammer" Manetti.

It was an unseasonably cool day in August when Busby, Mendelson, and a convoy of squad cars made their way to the Manetti estate. It was Busby's first trip to that part of the city. The large houses with wrought iron gates and well-manicured lawns impressed him. He knew that behind most of these gates lived good, honest people who were upstanding members of the community. There were wealthy business owners, high-priced attorneys, in-de- mand surgeons and specialists, as well as a few Hollywood celebrities who had homes in this area of the city. It disgusted him to think that someone who makes their living on the suffering of others, like Mike "the Hammer" Manetti, could share in this opulence.

Arrest warrants were also issued for Bruno and Silvio, and uniformed officers were assigned to make those arrests at the same time. Manetti was special. He was the big fish in this pond, and Mendelson and Busby wanted to make sure that everything was done right with his arrest so that there were no issues with prosecution.

Mendelson was driving. Shortly before 7:00 a.m. he pulled up to the gate of the Manetti estate and hit the call button.

"How can I help you?" came the voice from the other side of the intercom.

Mendelson held the warrant up to the camera. "Police. Open up now." The gruff tone in his voice made it clear that he meant busi- ness. The gate opened up immediately. By the time their car traveled up the long, cobblestone driveway and arrived at the house, the front door was already open and one of Manetti's crew—a tall, lanky man with slicked-back hair who was wearing black sunglasses—was there to let them inside.

"Good morning, officers," said the tall man as he ushered Busby and Mendelson into the front foyer. Busby instinctively gave the man a dirty look since he thought he was being a wise guy, but it actually wasn't necessary. There was no sarcasm in the man's voice and no sur- reptitious grin on his face. Busby had no choice but to take the man's comment at face value. *He must have been instructed to cooperate with police*, Busby thought.

Manetti made his way down the stairs as Busby and Mendelson looked around at the gorgeous architecture and ornamentation sur- rounding them. It was like they were in a palace. Busby then turned his attention to Manetti, who had a robe on over is pajamas and was wearing slippers. *Either he doesn't know he's going to be arrested, or he doesn't care*, Busby figured.

"Gentlemen, to what do I owe this early pleasure?" asked Manetti.

"Michael Manetti?" Mendelson had to ask the question even though he knew the answer.

"That's me," said Manetti, cinching the belt of his robe tighter around his waist.

Mendelson cleared his throat. "Mr. Manetti, you're under arrest for complicity in the murder of Jamie Munoz. Turn around and put your hands behind your back."

Manetti wasn't fazed at all. He did as he was told while calmly stating, "I can assure you that this is a mistake."

A tinge of jealousy shot through Busby as he watched Mendelson place the handcuffs on Manetti. He wished he could be the one to do it. But given that Mendelson was the senior officer, he had the honors.

As he was being cuffed, a soft, high-pitched voice called out "Daddy?" from the top of the stairs. Everyone looked up to see a young boy, Michael's eleven-year-old-son Leo, standing between the bannister rails, looking confused.

"It's okay, Leo," said Michael as reassuringly as he could. "Daddy just needs to go with the officers for now but will see you again real soon." Catarina appeared behind Leo and put a hand on her son's shoulder. Michael turned his attention to her. "Get him back to bed. I'll be all right. We've talked about this." Catarina nodded and gen- tly moved Leo away from the bannister. She accompanied him to his room as Mendelson and Busby walked Manetti out the door in handcuffs.

To no one's surprise, Bruno, Silvio, and Manetti were tight-lipped. None of them confessed to anything. All three were rep-resented by Martin Boucher, a highly paid, hard-nosed defense lawyer. His surname was French and translated into English meant butcher—a fitting name for a man who 99 percent of the time made mincemeat out of the prosecution's case. Rumor was that since Manetti used to be a butcher, he chose Boucher for that reason. The truth was that Manetti liked Boucher the first time he met the man years ago when he first moved into his River City Heights neighbor- hood. "It's comforting to have a lawyer I can trust living down the street," he used to joke. It wasn't a joke anymore though. This time he needed him.

Boucher tried his usual brash, bullying, boisterous tactics, but the police held their ground. All three arrests were clean and by the book, the suspects were made aware of their rights, the case against them was air-tight, and they had a witness. The prosecution was ready to ask the judge to deny bail on the grounds that all three men posed a flight risk, and it was strongly insinuated to Boucher that he talk his clients into cutting a deal. They knew they had him by the balls, and it felt damn good.

The very next day, Mendelson and Busby took Philip to a safe location. The choice was a nondescript, single-story house on the low-income side of town with paint peeling off the siding and shin- gles missing from the roof. It had been condemned by the city three years ago, then rebuilt just enough to make it habitable for use as a safe house. It had been a while since its last usage though. The living room reeked so strongly of mothballs that the first thing Mendelson did was open all of the windows and turn on a fan, which he promptly pointed out a window to air the place out.

Busby thought it was a miracle that the place had electricity. The television barely picked up a signal, but it was watchable. When there was nothing to watch on either the four national channels or four local stations, the three men passed the time playing cards. Before they knew it, dinnertime had come, and the three hungry men needed to decide what to eat.

"How about pizza?" suggested Busby.

"Sounds good," said Mendelson. "How about Paisano's?" "Ick," Phil chimed in. "That place isn't any good anymore. It's a damn shame too. I like this other place better. It's called Faranelli's. I know the owner, Jimmy Faranelli. He's a good guy. How about we go there?"

"Do they deliver?" asked Mendelson, as serious as ever. "Yeah, they do."

"Okay, then let's do it," said Mendelson. "I'll look up their number in the phone book and place an order for a few pies. In the meantime, Max, how about going to the corner gas station a few blocks from here and getting us some drinks—sodas and waters, things like that. No beer or anything. Remember that we're on duty here."

"Will do," said Busby. "I'll be back in a bit." He turned and left as Busby grabbed the phone book and Phil slouched down on the couch, making himself comfortable.

Busby was gone for forty-five minutes. This was the day that he learned that a lot can happen in forty-five minutes. Within a block and a half of returning to the house, he saw the flashing blue-and-red police-car lights in the distance. Busby's blood ran cold as he thought the worst. *It can't be*, he thought as he shook his head and continued forward. But the closer he got, the closer he saw: the lights were coming from the safe house.

Busby dropped the two bags with the drinks he was carrying. All of the containers were made of plastic, so they landed with a thud and nothing shattered. The twist top of a two-liter bottle of lemon-lime soda—his favorite, particularly with pizza—popped off and sprayed his ankles as he took off toward the house at a full sprint.

A uniformed officer saw him approaching and put a hand up. Busby stumbled through his pockets, and after what felt like five minutes instead of five seconds, he found his badge and flashed it at the officer. The officer stepped aside and let him pass. The door to the house was wide open, and Busby ran right in.

The first thing he laid his eyes on was a grisly sight. It was Phil La Calamita, sitting where he had left him on the couch, shot dead. The dark-red blood that ran down his blue shirt was still half wet and glistened in the light. The portion of blood that dried created a dark maroon stain that was spread all over his torso like some kind of demented ink-blot picture.

Busby quickly assessed that two bullets struck Phil and it looked like a professional job: one in the torso and one in the head. He surmised that whoever did this shot Phil in the chest first to keep him in place. The shooter had good aim and hit him center mass, right through the heart. Phil was more than likely already dead, or at least very close to death, by the time the shooter moved a bit closer and squeezed a round of lead into Phil's head to make sure the job was done. That bullet struck him in the left cheek, and because of the angle of Phil's head, lodged in his brain. Either bullet was a kill shot.

Whoever did this knew what they were doing and definitely wanted him dead, Busby thought to himself.

Seeing that there was nothing that could be done for Phil, Busby continued into the house and made his way into the kitchen. Mendelson was seated at the head of the table. Sitting next to him was a medic, who had just finished stitching up his shoulder and was now wrapping it in a thick, beige bandage. Busby pulled out a chair at the other end of the table and took a seat.

"La Calamita's dead," said Mendelson as he winced in pain. "I saw," said Busby. "What the hell happened?"

Mendelson took a deep breath. "It all happened so fast that I'm not totally sure, but here's what my statement is going to be when I give it, and it's the truth as far as I know: I called in the pizza. They told me delivery would be in thirty minutes or less. About twenty minutes later, I heard the doorbell. I thought it was the pizza delivery. I didn't think it could be anyone else. So I open the door, and next thing I know I have a hole in my shoulder big enough to stick your index finger in. I fell down and back and hit my head on the wall. The shooter stepped over me. I heard two more shots, then I heard the gun fall to the floor and the shooter left. I heard a car peel away. That's it. It was all over in seconds. I crawled over to the radio on the side table in the living room and radioed it in. Next thing I know, the squad cars and the ambulance are here. And now you're back too."

Busby snapped out of his stunned silence with a "Damn." Realizing that was an incredible understatement after hearing that story, he followed up with "You're lucky the shooter didn't kill you too."

"This was a pro. My gut tells me that he shot me in the shoulder on purpose to get me out of the way so he could get to his real tar- get—La Calamita. I think Manetti was smart enough to instruct this hit man to not give him the headache of any dead cops. He knows what kind of heat that could bring."

"Right," said Busby. Now that the shock of everything was sub-siding, he was starting to see the big picture of what this all meant. The state's star witness was dead. "The case against Manetti was based around La Calamita. Now the DA has nothing."

"Nope," said Mendelson, sighing in relief as the medic finished the bandaging and collected her things. "I wouldn't be surprised if the charges are dropped tomorrow. Without a witness who can tes- tify and point the finger in the Munoz murder, they've got nothing."

"Son of a bitch!" Busby slammed his hand on the table.

Mendelson remained cool. "Son of a bitch is right, kid. Son of a bitch."

The following day, Mendelson was proven right. He couldn't be at the courthouse when the DA dropped all charges against Mike "the Hammer" Manetti as well as Silvio and Bruno because he was still in the hospital under mandatory twenty-four-hour observa- tion. However, Busby was there as the three men walked free. They were led out of the courthouse by their lawyer, Martin Boucher. Of course, the press was there, and ever the self-promoting glory hound, he stopped to make a statement in front of all the cameras and microphones.

"Today is a bittersweet day," said Boucher for an opener. "On the one hand it's a happy day. My three clients, who have always been innocent of these heinous accusations leveled at them by the state, are walking free. However, this freedom comes with a price. That price is the life of a close friend and business associate of Mr. Manetti by the name of Philip La Calamita. The state asserts that Mr. La Calamita was going to testify against my clients. Whether or not this is true, we will never know. My only hope is that the River City Police Department stop persecuting innocent men like my clients and start using their resources to find Mr. La Calamita's killer and bring that person to justice. That is all. Thank you."

It was short and sweet and lawyerly. It also served to take the spotlight off the three men who deserved it and pointed it at the River City Police Department, as if they made it a habit of accusing the innocent and weren't interested in solving Phil's murder. *What a crock*, Busby thought to himself.

As he listened to Boucher's statement, Busby fixated his gaze on Manetti. The mob boss did his best to try to look somber and depressed. He almost pulled it off, except for the fact that as soon as Boucher finished his statement and started walking down the court-house steps, Manetti followed him with a grin. This rubbed Busby the wrong way. Then to make matters worse—and what really stuck in Busby's craw ever since—was when Manetti looked off to his side, saw Busby, raised his misshapen hand to his brow, and gave him a salute with his crooked fingers. That was all Busby needed. Manetti was as guilty as hell of not only the murder of Jamie Munoz, but also the murder of Phil La Calamita and the wounding of his partner. Busby's blood boiled standing there that day in the hot August sun, and he swore that come hell or high water, one day he would pay back that bastard for what he did.

*****

A little over twenty years later, that day finally came. Thanks to Sarah, enough hard evidence was collected to link Mike "the Hammer" Manetti to the Amazon Glory nightclub owned by his son, and to the three bodies put in the river because of him.

This time, it was Busby who flashed a freshly signed arrest warrant to the camera at the gate. He couldn't help but notice that it had been upgraded to a wireless, digital system since the last time he was there. Same as before, he and the rest of the police cars were allowed to pass through with no issue.

Once everyone had parked and exited their vehicles, Busby gathered them around and instructed, "Everyone stay here, and stay sharp. I don't expect there to be any issues." He held up the arrest warrant like a treasured prize he'd just won. "I'm going inside now, alone, to serve this warrant on Michael Manetti for complicity in three murders in our city. I've been waiting twenty years for this, but I don't expect it to take long."

With that a member of Manetti's crew opened the door. As he passed by the man, Busby recognized him as the same tall, lanky man who opened the door for him and Mendelson twenty years ago. The man was still tall of course, and still had the slicked back hair, though it was thinner and grayer than in the past. The biggest change was in the man's overall body shape. Busby couldn't help but notice how much harder it was to squeeze by the man's protruding belly. *Eat a salad every once in a while*, Busby thought to himself as he turned slightly to his side to get by.

This time Michael Manetti was already awake. He'd taken to waking up earlier in his older age. Instead of coming down from his bedroom in slippers and a robe, Manetti was already sitting at his desk. He was hardly working though. The TV was on, and he was watching the highlights on the morning news from the River City Mongeese game the night before.

Manetti was unfazed when he saw Busby enter the room. He didn't bother to turn off the TV or even lower the volume. With barely a look at Busby, he smugly asked, "Lieutenant Busby—to what do I owe the honor?"

Busby gingerly placed the arrest warrant on the desk so Manetti could see it. Manetti chuckled when he looked at it. The memories of his previous experience of being under arrest—and going free— came rushing back to him like a tidal wave.

Busby cleared his throat. He wanted to make sure this was stated perfectly and could be heard over the low-key babbling of the talking heads on the television behind him. "Michael Manetti: you can do me—

as well as the citizens of our fair city—the honor of putting both your hands flat on your desk and standing up slowly. You're under arrest."

Manetti was incredulous. "Arrest? I barely ever the leave the house. What could you possibly have to arrest me for?"

Busby pointed to the duffel bag sitting on the floor next to the desk. "Is this your bag?"

Manetti looked down at the bag. "Yeah. What of it?" "Mind if I look inside?"

"Be my guest."

Manetti leaned back in his chair as Busby picked up the bag and rested it on top of the arrest warrant on the desk. He unzipped the bag. It was empty. Manetti flashed Busby the same grin that he flashed him on the steps of the courthouse twenty years earlier. Busby returned the grin as he reached his hand into the bag and felt around for a few seconds. Busby grabbed a hold of something from inside the bag and yanked. He removed his hand from the bag and held up the object for Manetti to see.

"This is my tracker," Busby declared proudly. "The GPS records on it indicate it went from your son's Amazon club last night, to here."

"Yeah, so what?" Manetti had an idea as to where Busby was headed, but he was trying to play it cool.

"So the club is under investigation for illegal gaming, not to mention some dead girls that have turned up in the river, which we can connect back to your son's fight ring that he has there." Busby felt good. He paused for a beat to watch Manetti soak in what he just told him.

Once it all came together in his head, "That stupid little shit" was all that Manetti could say.

"Speaking of, where is your son at? We went to arrest him and his crazy girlfriend this morning too. I got notified on the radio on my way here that neither one was home. Do you know anything?"

Manetti was so disgusted he wanted to spit. But he knew spitting on a cop would just add to his troubles, and he wasn't going to expectorate on his floor or furniture. He swallowed hard, then spoke. "I have no idea. And even if I did know, I wouldn't tell you."

This was exactly the reaction that Busby expected. "Fair enough. But we'll find him. And we'll bring him in too."

Busby removed the hand cuffs from his belt. "It's time, Manetti. Stand up slowly and keep your hands on the top of the desk." Manetti did as he was told.

As Busby walked around the desk to get behind Manetti, he continued, "You know, I've been wanting to do this for a long time. Ever since you gave me that little salute with your mashed-up hands twenty years ago. I've been thinking about this moment since then. I told myself that once we got enough on you, I'd come here and put the cuffs on you myself. Somehow, I knew it would feel good."

Busby used his right hand to grab Manetti's right wrist and brought it behind him. He looked at the hand that taunted him so many years ago. It momentarily repulsed him to be so close. As Busby used his left hand to grab Manetti's left wrist and bring it behind him, he thought of the jealousy he felt when Mendelson got to cuff him two decades ago. Now he was the senior officer, and it was his turn. As the cuffs clicked into place, Busby let out a deep breath of extreme satisfaction. He leaned in close to Manetti's right ear and stated simply, "I was right."

Busby walked Manetti out the door and into the throng uni- formed officers waiting with bated breath to find out how things were going. They all breathed a collective sigh of relief when Busby walked out with Manetti in cuffs. The arrest was made without incident.

Busby took Manetti to the nearest squad car and placed him in the back. He stepped away as the two officers in charge of the car got in to drive off. Inside the car, Manetti shook his head and then took a look at his big, beautiful house. A sick feeling welled up inside of him at the thought that he would never see it again. He then looked over at Busby, who was standing around ten feet away from the car, star- ing at him. Manetti didn't like it. He liked it even less when Busby raised his hand to his brow and gave him a salute as the car sped away to take him to jail.

CHAPTER 19

S ARAH WAS EXHAUSTED by the time she got home. All the sleep she got while undercover was tainted by stress. She never got any deep, restful sleep. As soon as she got up to her and Dale's room, she dropped her belongings and crashed on the bed. It was comforting for her to be lying on her soft, warm blankets again. She could smell Dale on the sheets. He was already at work, but it felt like he was there with her. She breathed his essence in deeply as she nodded off.

By the time Sarah woke up, it was almost six o'clock, and she had been asleep for nearly nine hours straight. She knew Dale would be home from his veterinary clinic soon, so she decided to go downstairs and turn on the TV while she waited for him to get home. The local six o'clock news was just starting. The lead story, as read off the teleprompter by the overgroomed and finely tuned anchor, was about the arrest earlier that morning of River City's mob kingpin Mike "the Hammer" Manetti.

In spite of the fact that the news was about a case that she was directly involved in, none of the words really registered with Sarah. She barely even blinked at the footage of Busby walking Manetti into the station as reporters bustled about, sticking their microphones in their faces for a sound bite they weren't going to get. Sarah was beyond it all now and totally over it. She was thinking about Dale and couldn't wait for him to get home.

It wasn't long before she got her wish. Dale opened the door. Sarah snapped out of her trance as soon as she heard the all-too-fa- miliar creak of the top hinge. Before he was even halfway through the door, she had her arms around him, tight.

Dale was thrilled and couldn't believe it was real. He hugged her tightly back and exclaimed, "Sarah! This is a great surprise! Are you back for good? Is your case over?"

"Yes!" Sarah replied enthusiastically, then pointed to the TV. The on-the-scene reporter covering the arrest remotely was just wrapping up. The all-caps words "MANETTI ARRESTED" written on the chyron at the bottom of the screen was all Dale needed to see. "That's great! I'm so happy you're finally done!" He smiled and gave her a long, passionate, open-mouthed kiss. Sarah gave in kind. When they finally took a breath and got some air, Sarah said,

"So am I. And I meant what I said. I'm done with undercover work." "Yeah? You mean it?" Dale didn't mean to sound skeptical—it just came out that way.

"I'm going to go in tomorrow and tell Buzz that I am glad to help provide any testimony and take point in the search for the oth- ers involved—"

"So you didn't get everybody?" Dale asked, a bit confused. "No. There are two who got away," Sarah stated matter-of-factly.

"We're still looking for Manetti's son Leo and his girlfriend Claudia, who we suspect is the one who did the actual killing."

Dale's confusion melted into concern. "They're both still out there? Sarah, this isn't good."

Sarah cracked a smile. She understood Dale's concerns but also knew that he had nothing to worry about. "Relax. Neither of them have any idea about my real name or where I live. We're completely safe."

"Are you sure?" Dale was halfway to being convinced.

"I am. We're going to find them and we're going to catch them, and once we do, this will all be over for good. Okay?"

That brought Dale the rest of the way there. "Okay," he replied with a nod.

With that conversation over, Sarah turned her attention to other, more pressing matters. "Now what are we having for dinner? I haven't had a decent meal in days, and I'm starving."

At the same time in midtown River City, the setting sun caused long shadows to fall on the streets. The gargantuan buildings that loomed over the luxury high-rise district blotted out the sun as the hustle and bustle continued down below, ever increasingly illuminated by streetlights.

One of these monuments to wealth and power was under construction by Fine Lines Construction LLC. The company was started by Bruno early on in his criminal career as a front company for his illegal-arms trafficking, but was swiftly taken over by Silvio after Bruno's untimely demise. Way up high in the penthouse of this work in progress sat Leo and Claudia, who had been hiding there ever since they found out Sarah was a cop. Workers were instructed by Silvio himself to not enter the penthouse under any circumstances, or they'd find themselves taking the shortest route possible to the sidewalk hundreds of feet below. The only ones allowed up were Tina and Maria, who brought meals with them. A generator supplied elec- tricity for a stove, refrigerator, and TV. The plumbing was not yet working, but that was the purpose of the empty spackle buckets.

In spite of the fact that she had no way to shower, Claudia worked up a sweat by doing push-ups. She was super pissed off and needed an outlet for her aggression now that she didn't have a supply of Eastern European young women to wail on.

Leo was more of a brooder. He stood at one of the thick floor- to-ceiling windows overlooking the street below and scowled. He had nothing but contempt for the city and the people in it. His thoughts wandered about all of the tyrannical destruction he would inflict on the city if he had the power. Just as he started really developing his idea to bus drug-addicted vagrants all over the city to turn every neighborhood, no matter how upscale, into a cesspool of vomit, nee- dles, urine, and feces, Tina and Maria walked in and interrupted his train of thought. He was angry at first, but only at first. He reasoned that they didn't know he was concocting a master plan for citywide destruction, plus he was anxious to hear any information they had to bring him along with dinner.

Claudia stopped her workout and ran over to Tina, who was carrying a bag of Chinese takeout from Jade Empire, her favorite place.

As someone who prided herself on being in shape, Claudia normally avoided fried foods, but she made an exception for the egg rolls from Jade Empire. They were just too good. Claudia snatched the bag out of Tina's hands and began greedily rummaging through it, looking for the egg rolls. Tina knew there would be hell to pay if the egg rolls weren't there, so she made sure they were there and on top. Claudia found them almost immediately.

Leo wasn't thinking about food. He was barely even hungry. His desire was for the update he asked Maria to get for him. "What did you find out?" he asked bluntly.

Maria could tell that Leo was fired up. She was a bit scared that he might shoot the messenger—literally—but there was no point in not coming out and saying the plain truth. "We talked to that beat cop we have on the payroll like you asked, and he said he didn't know."

To Maria's surprise, the outburst came from Claudia. "Didn't know? We pay him to know! When I get outta here I'm break his freakin' neck!" Her arms flailed about so widely that the egg roll in her hand was in danger of flying across the room.

Maria didn't look at Claudia. She knew doing so would only draw her ire. She continued to address Leo. "He said that the under- cover operation was kept under very tight wraps. There's no way he could have known."

"Was he able to give us anything?" Leo inquired desperately. "Well, now that the case is busted wide open and your dad is

in jail, the whole station is talking. He gave us the name." Maria was relieved to be able to give some good news. "Her name is Sarah."

"At least she was honest about that," Claudia snorted. "Sarah Kolchek."

Leo smiled widely and rubbed his hands together. "Okay, now we're getting somewhere. What's the story with this 'Sarah,' whoever the hell she is?"

"We asked about that too," Tina chimed in.

"It's probably best for you to see for yourself," said Maria, taking her smartphone out of her back pocket and activating it with her fingerprint. She gently maneuvered her finger around the touch screen, tapping a few times to play a video. She held up the phone for Leo and Claudia to watch. On-screen was the MMA fight from

Sarah's dream. The title of the video said, "MMA Hall of Shame: 'Big Mel' Gomez." Sarah looked younger but was recognizable. They watched to the end of the fight where Melinda's elbow was dislocated and Sarah got sucker punched. Claudia grinned with satisfaction at seeing Sarah get defeated. Even though it happened years ago, it felt like a well-deserved comeuppance.

"This fight ended both of their careers," informed Maria.

Tina tried to contribute with "Sarah went into law enforcement—"

Claudia abruptly shut her down with "No kidding." Her fuse was short, and she was not suffering fools—or those who stated the obvious as if it was a major revelation—gladly that evening. She was more interested in the other woman in the video. "And Melinda?"

Maria answered, "She wasn't too hard to find. She's a trainer at a gym called Super Fitness, only about half an hour away from here."

This was the best news Leo had heard all day. "I like it. Someone who we know can take this bitch down—and I'm sure she has a score to settle." He thought a bit more then continued, "Plus she's a trainer. She should still be in good shape."

Claudia liked what she was hearing. She even managed to crack a smile as she caught Leo's drift and saw where his thoughts were headed. It cooled her off a bit and made her less tense. Addressing both Tina and Maria, she commanded, "Find her. Offer her what- ever it takes. It's payback time."

Tina and Maria turned and left immediately. As soon as the door closed, Leo, who felt like he just got a new lease on life, snared Claudia in his arms. "I love it when you're all hot and sweaty and pumped." He kissed Claudia intensely on the mouth while simulta- neously putting both hands on her firm, well-exercised butt cheeks and lifting her up. Claudia wrapped her well-toned, somewhat muscular legs around

Leo's waist. The newly formed scabs that cov- ered the scratches down her legs stung for a second when rubbed against Leo's shirt, but she didn't let it bother her. Leo made his way to the mattress on the floor in the corner of the living room that served as their bed.

Leo was completely hard by the time they made it to the mattress. He held on to Claudia as he got on his knees and lowered her on to the bed, being careful to not disrupt his throbbing erection.

Claudia's workout clothes—yoga pants and a thong—were easy enough to pull down. Leo knew that if he entered Claudia right now, he'd climax quickly. He prided himself on making sure his woman received pleasure if he was also going to receive some, so he plunged his head between her legs and started licking and sucking her clit and labia. Claudia's crotch was especially sweaty from the intensity of her workout, and it drove him wild. The smell and feel of a young pussy, slippery and glistening from a combination of perspiration and sexual arousal, turned him on like nothing else. Claudia moaned with pleasure and approval as Leo got faster and rougher.

Leo was careful to not let his supersensitive tip rub up against anything since it would only stimulate him even more, but after a few minutes Leo was on the brink of letting loose all over the floor. Satisfied by the sounds of ecstasy Claudia was making, he felt as though he'd pleasured her enough. It was his turn. With one smooth movement, Leo arched his back and thrust his rod into Claudia's well-primed and eagerly awaiting vagina. It was a good thing he plea- sured her earlier because after three pumps, he was done. His penis went almost immediately flaccid as he pulled out of Claudia and laid beside her. He took his girlfriend in his arm and the couple spooned as they drifted off to an early night's sleep.

The next morning was business as usual at Super Fitness. The clanking and whirring of weights and cardio equipment punctuated the insistent beat of the Top 40 hits station piped in through the speakers. At 6:00 a.m., most of the handful of people present that morning were there to get in their workout before they headed off to their jobs. Tina and Maria, not dressed in workout clothes or car- rying a bag, slipped by the half-asleep twenty-year-old at the front desk—who looked like she was hungover and just wanted to be left alone anyway—and headed into the gym.

"You called last night, and they said Melinda is scheduled to be in now, right?" asked Tina.

"That's what they told me," replied Maria, defensively.

Tina and Maria looked over at the throng of people in the car- dio area with the exercise bikes, elliptical machines, and treadmills. They walked slowly down the two long pathways and not-so-sub- tly looked at the face of every woman. None of the women seemed bothered, though, being too wrapped up in working out and pay- ing attention to whatever they were watching or listening to in their earbuds. Once satisfied that Melinda was not in a cardio area, they turned their attention to the weights.

Amid the dozen or so people occupying the free-weight work- out area, one stood out from the rest. The first reason was that she was the only woman working out with free weights that morning. The second and more compelling reason was that it looked like she was putting up a substantial amount of weight on the squat rack, and grunting loudly while doing so. There was no mistaking who this woman was, even though her hair was shorter and she had a few crow's feet in comparison to the video Tina and Maria watched the previous evening. This was "Big Mel" Gomez. Just one look at her in person, and both of them understood that it was a well-earned nickname. The two approached Melinda as carefully and as casually as possible.

"Are you Melinda Gomez," asked Maria, even though she knew the answer.

Melinda didn't look at her, or at Tina, or even stop her work- out. In between grunts she inquired, "Who's asking?" as she greedily sucked in air and squatted down, getting ready to thrust into the next repetition.

Tina jumped in with "We have a proposition for you." Melinda paused at the top of her squat and looked them over, one at a time. After a few seconds and with a grimace, she shook her head and said, "No, thanks. I'm straight."

"Cute, but we're serious," insisted Tina, though she was mildly insulted.

"So am I," retorted Melinda as she continued with her squats. Maria decided to try a different approach. "Does the name Sarah Kolchek ring a bell?"

Melinda grunted extra loud at hearing Sarah's name. This got her attention. She racked the weights and, after a few deep, heavy breaths stated, "Yeah, that name rings a big bell. Why?"

"We shouldn't do this here," Maria noted.

"Do you have somewhere that we can go and talk?" asked Tina. Melinda nodded. "Yeah. Let's step into my office."

Melinda led Maria and Tina to the back of the gym and opened a door that led to a hallway. Lining either side of the hallway were doors to small offices. Melinda hung a left into one of the offices in the middle of the hallway. Tina and Maria followed her in.

The office itself was small and cramped, an effect made even more pronounced by the fact that she didn't have a window. On one side of the office was a bookcase with various texts covering every- thing from exercise to nutrition, as well as more technical, scien- tific books on subjects like biology, anatomy, and physiology. The books looked new and unread, judging by the number of them that had unbroken spines, as if they were purchased just for show, to fill the shelves. The only furniture in the office was a cheap metal desk, a fairly well-padded and comfortable-looking desk chair, and two less-comfortable plastic chairs for guests to sit in.

Melinda took a seat in the desk chair and leaned back. "So what is this proposition that you two ladies have involving Sarah Kolchek?"

Now that they were alone, Maria felt comfortable being more frank. "We're here on behalf of Leo Manetti."

Melinda shifted position from leaning back to leaning forward. Her mouth was agape as she rested her forearms on the desk and clasped her hands together. "Leo Manetti? The cops are looking for him. They just brought his dad in. It's all over the news."

"We know," grumbled Tina, still feeling slightly stung that Melinda wouldn't be interested in her if she was a lesbian, which she wasn't but it bothered her anyway.

Maria explained, "Here's what the news isn't saying: the Manettis were infiltrated by an undercover cop. One who was pretending to be an average street fighter—but she wasn't."

"It was Sarah Kolchek," said Tina, feeling the need to spell it out for Melinda.

Maria continued, "Leo Manetti wants to get some payback on her. We figured you were a good candidate since you faced her before. Plus, after that punch to the back of the head you gave her, we figured you don't have a problem acting outside of the rules. Were we right?"

Melinda leaned back in her chair and moved her forearms to the armrests, gripping the edges of them tightly, wanting to tear the leather-covered foam padding right off as the memories of that fight raced through her mind as clear as day. She calmed herself enough to say, "Maybe" and then to asked, "what's in it for me?"

"What do you want?" asked Maria.

"See this gym we're in?" replied Melinda. "You want this gym?" scoffed Tina.

Melinda didn't appreciate her tone but chose to ignore it. "No. But I want a place just like it. Somewhere not only with workout equipment, but also with an octagon, so I can be a part of that again."

Maria thought about it for a few seconds. After determining in her mind that this request wasn't too out of line, she said, "I'm sure that if you come through for Mister Manetti, he will grant this request."

Tina shot out, "Anything else?" She was looking to end this conversation and get going as soon as possible.

"Yeah," said Melinda, her little grin morphing into a big smile. "When I face Sarah, it's one-on-one, no-holds-barred, and it's not over until I say it's finished."

"I think we can definitely do that," agreed Maria. "All right. I'm in."

A swell of excitement rose up through Tina. "Great. We'll be in touch with the details."

Maria and Tina got up as Melinda stayed seated. Not knowing what else to say as they left, Maria simply said, "It was a pleasure" as she and Tina took their initial steps to leave.

"Believe me, the pleasure is all mine." Melinda cackled as she rested her head on the back of the chair. She was looking forward to her rematch.

CHAPTER 20

DALE GLANCED OUT the window as the sun crept up over the horizon to mark a brand-new day. He appreciated it in a way he never had before. It looked different, brighter somehow now that Sarah was back. He thought about her, about the life they had already built together, and about the life they were going to have in the future. He felt so euphoric that he decided against having the usual cup of coffee that he typically relied on to get him started in the morning. *This is what people mean when they say they're high on life*, he thought to himself.

Even though Dale wasn't having any coffee, he brewed some for Sarah. She entered the kitchen just as the BrewMaster 1000 that they bought together at local department store Brannigan's when they first moved in together was relinquishing its final drops. Her hair was a tangled mess, but she looked well rested—about right given the wild yet exhausting night they both had the night before. "You're up ear- lier than usual," she observed with a smile that matched Dale's.

"Yeah, I know," Dale concurred. Then after clearing his throat, he continued, "I forgot to mention: I have a conference today across town. I need to get in early to take care of a few appointments, then I'll be gone for the rest of the afternoon."

"Oh, okay. Should I wait up tonight?"

Dale felt bad as he shook his head sympathetically. "I probably won't be home until late, so no."

"Aww. I just got you back, and now you'll be gone tonight." Sarah was disappointed but flirtatious. She was determined that nothing spoil the good mood she was in.

Picking up on the vibe, Dale walked away from the window and put his arms around Sarah's waist, telling her, "I know. I miss you too when you're gone. But I really want to go to this conference, and I promise I won't be any later than I have to be. Is that better?"

"Yeah, a little…I guess," said Sarah as she grimaced a bit.

"I'll still see you, but it will be late tonight." He kissed her intensely, but before he got worked up to the point of starting a repeat of the previous evening, he pulled away. "Gotta run."

Dale scurried into the living room and grabbed his coat to head out into the cool, crisp morning. He knew he'd have to warm up the car and scrape off some frost before he could drive away, which he found to be an annoyance. Sarah let out a soul-crushing sigh as the door shut, then shuffled her way over to the kitchen counter to pour herself a cup of hot, fresh coffee. She remarked to herself on how lucky she was to have such a thoughtful man as she took her first sip and looked out the window to watch the sun finish elevating over the horizon.

After showering and getting dressed, Sarah decided to drive to Brannigan's for some clothes shopping. She wanted to dress to impress as she transitioned into her new role behind the scenes of the police department, or potentially, went out on interviews for another job. She wasn't set on leaving the department, but had it in the back of her mind recently as an option. Now that she was done with undercover work and had her fill of being a law-enforcement officer and dealing with other people and their problems, she didn't feel the least bit bad about focusing on her own life for a while. That life of course included Dale, who she loved more than ever. *As a mat- ter of fact,* she thought at that moment, *I'm going to tell him so. He left so early this morning that I didn't have a chance. I don't want a single day to go by where I don't tell him that I love him.*

Sarah hit the hands-free button on her steering wheel that connected to her cell phone and when prompted, said, "Call Dale." After four rings, his voice mail picked up. Sarah was a bit bummed that he didn't answer, but in no way deterred from her intention. "Hey, sweetie, it's me. I'm just calling to say that I love you. This under- cover work made me realize how much I miss you and I can't—" a bolt of pain split Sarah's head open. She could barely focus on the road as she tried to drive and talk at the same time. "I can't wait to… wait to…see you… again…"

As she reached over to the passenger's seat to grab her medication, she realized that in all of the chaos and excitement of being back, she forgot to put more pills in her purse. Now in total agony, Sarah put one hand on the steering wheel and another hand on her forehead. She tried in vain to massage the pain in her forehead away. The hands-free was still activated and a fiercely determined Sarah eked out the final word of her sentence, "Soon…" before trying to pull to the side of the road. The street, however, was lined with cars and there was nowhere to pull over. She tried to find a place to park through half-open eyes, but before she could find one, she noticed a fairly thick maple tree careening straight at her. Luckily no one was hurt when her car jumped the sidewalk and struck the tree, though there was a close call with a Pomeranian on a long leash being walked by a woman who was walking four other dogs of various sizes at the same time.

As Sarah woke up and came to, she looked around and didn't recognize her location. After pulling focus and taking in more of her surroundings, she realized that she was in a hospital. Looking to her left, she saw Jill sitting in a chair, reading a gossip magazine. Some teenage pop star who she didn't recognize was on the cover. Moving her eyes down to the foot of the bed, she saw a doctor—short but thin, with graying jet-black hair and a mustache that overwhelmed his face— scribbling some notes on a clipboard. Wanting to talk to him, Sarah sat up straight but did so way too fast. Her head spun from dizziness as Jill put a steadying hand on her shoulder.

"Take it easy, Sarah. You were in an accident," Jill informed her as softly as possible.

Sarah was puzzled. The last thing she remembered was being in the car, leaving a message for Dale. "Accident? Oh, damn it. Is the car totaled?"

"No, just banged up. I had it towed here for you. The keys are with your stuff in the closet, along with the parking space number."

"Thanks for doing that. How'd you get here?"

"The officer at the scene recognized you and called me right away. I rushed over here as fast as I could."

Sarah slowly swiveled her head left and right, scanning the room. Finally, she asked, "Where's Dale?"

"We don't know," replied Jill. "He's not at home, and I called the clinic, but they said he's out for the afternoon at a conference. We tried his cell too. It went to voice mail. I left him a message."

"Yeah," said Jill, the memories of her conversation with Dale at sunrise flooding back to her. "He is going to a conference today. He's probably on the road and doesn't want to answer the phone. I hope that's the case. If anything's happened to him…"

"Relax, Sarah," said Jill, gently squeezing Sarah's hand. You're in no condition to get this worked up."

"Listen to your friend," said the doctor as he finished scribbling and attached the clipboard to the foot of the bed. He then turned to Jill and asked, "Can you give us some privacy, please?"

"Sure," said Jill, relinquishing her grip from Sarah's hand and rising from her chair. The gossip magazine she was reading was rolled up and in her other hand. She looked down at Sarah and told her, "I'm heading back to the station now. As soon as I hear from Dale, I'll let him know what happened and send him here. Okay?"

"Sounds good. Thank you." Sarah felt a rush of gratitude to have such a loyal partner and helpful friend.

"Try to get some rest. I want my partner back soon!" said Jill, trying to muster as much enthusiasm and optimism as she could.

As Jill left the room, the doctor walked around to the side of the bed and sat in the chair that she previously occupied. He gave Sarah one of those stern, fatherly, yet judgmental looks that can only come with years of practice.

"Good morning, Sarah. I'm Doctor Anderson," he said in a smooth, low voice.

"Good morning, Doctor," replied Sarah. She felt like a little child who just did something bad and was about to get a lecture.

"You suffered some small injuries from the accident—basi- cally just a bloody nose and minor whiplash from where the airbag impacted with your head. It looks like your face was a bit closer than normal to the steering wheel when it went off."

"That's right," said Sarah, some more of her memories from just before the accident coming back to her. "I had a splitting head- ache—I get them from time to time from an incident a long time ago—and I think I was slumped forward more than usual as I was dealing with the pain."

"That makes sense," commented Dr. Anderson. "We'll keep you here until tomorrow morning to make sure there is nothing else too serious going on, then you can go. Of course, I also have to call the offi- cer at the scene today. He's going to want to come in and ask you a few questions, okay? As a police officer yourself, I'm sure you understand." "I do." The conversation was going better than Sarah thought it would. *This isn't so bad*, she thought to herself.

"But before I leave and give him a call, I do have something else to ask," stated the doctor politely.

"What is it?" Sarah was mentally kicking herself for letting her guard down. She waited for the bomb to drop.

Dr. Anderson took a deep breath and then he began. "There's no easy way to say this, and I've found over the years that the best thing to do is just come right out with it. There are bruises all over your body. This…Dale—is he your boyfriend?"

"Fiancé. We live together." Sarah gulped. She had an awful feel- ing about where this was headed.

As gently and in as calm a tone as possible, Dr. Anderson leaned in toward Sarah and asked, "Does he ever…hit you?"

Sometimes Sarah hated being right. She knew this question was coming next. "No! What? Jesus—no!" she shrieked emphati- cally, having a hard time keeping her voice down. "These bruises aren't from

Dale. I can't tell you where they're from, and if I did you wouldn't believe me, but trust me, it's not him."

Impressively, the doctor kept his cool. In the same calm, even tone he let her know, "Sarah, you don't have to protect him."

By this point, Sarah found his friendly, matter-of-fact tone irritating. "It's not Dale!" she snapped. "I can't give you any more details, so you're just going to have to trust me. It's not him."

Dr. Anderson knew this was the end of the road for these questions. He did his job and asked. He wasn't sure whether or not to believe her, but that didn't matter. If there was something going on with Dale, he couldn't do anything about it unless she let him know about it. "I see," he said, rising from his chair. "The best thing for you to do right now is rest up and take it easy. And if Dale does show up later, we'll be sure to send him in to see you. I know you two will have a lot to talk about."

Sarah decided to take some deep breaths to calm herself down before responding, "Thank you." As the doctor exited the room, Sarah slumped down in her bed. After she calmed down some more, she suddenly felt exhausted. Her plan for the afternoon was to take Dr. Anderson's advice: get some rest.

Out in the hospital parking garage, a previously despondent Jill was feeling optimistic. Her worries about Sarah's mental health and overall physical well-being evaporated with each step she took toward her car. She genuinely felt good as she removed the keys from her purse. That feeling disappeared in an instant just as she was about to hit the unlock button on her car fob.

A nondescript black van screeched to a halt behind Jill. The double back doors flew open. Maria and Tina burst out of the van, and before Jill could assess the situation, they'd each grabbed her by an arm and were dragging her toward the van. What they didn't know about Jill was that she was feistier than she looked.

Jill wrestled her arm away from Tina's grip. Taking advantage of the fact that the keys were in her free hand, she swiped at Tina and cut her cheek with the key. As Tina wailed in pain covering the gash on her cheek with her hand, Jill seized the opportunity to kick her in the cooch. Tina doubled over, holding her lower abdomen. Suddenly, she had worse pain than the wound on her cheek to con- tend with.

This all happened in a matter of seconds. Maria couldn't believe the fight inside of Jill. She and Tina both underestimated her. Needing to gain control right away, Maria slipped in behind Jill and put her into a full nelson. Jill struggled, but to no avail—Maria was just too strong.

Tina straightened up with a grin on her face. She saw that Jill was in a helpless state, and she decided that it was payback time. She uppercut Jill in the abdomen and knocked the wind out of her. That was it for Jill. She was down for the count. Tina and Maria dragged Jill, who at this point was dead weight since she couldn't walk, and brought her to the back of the van. When they got to the back, they rested her arms and upper body on the floor of the van, leaving the rest of her dangling over the edge. In a coordinated effort, Maria grabbed Jill by the waist, Tina grabbed Jill's legs, and the two of them together pushed Jill all the way into the van. Tina climbed into the van, all the while keeping an eye on Jill. Maria closed the back doors to the van and then ran around to get into the front passenger's seat. As soon as she climbed in, a loud voice bellowed, "We good?" It was Melinda, sitting in the driver's seat.

Maria returned the tone of voice. "Yeah, we're good. Drive!"

Melinda floored it. Jill looked up to see if she could get a good look at the driver, but she couldn't. She did, however, spot an uncon-scious man lying next to her, his back pressed up against the side of the van. It took her a brief moment to realize that it was Dale. He was bound, gagged, and a bit bruised. *He must have put up a hell of a fight too*, Jill thought to herself. *Good for him.*

Several hours later in her hospital bed, Sarah woke up from her nap. She looked around for Dale but didn't see him. Equal parts dis-appointed and worried, she reached for the phone by her bedside and dialed his number. As the phone rang, she thought about how smart she was to always make sure she memorized important numbers and didn't rely on having them programmed into her cell phone.

Once again, Dale's voice mail picked up. In a bit of a panic, but trying her best to stay positive, Sarah left a message. "Dale—it's Sarah again. Where are you? Call me. I'm getting worried."

She hung up and looked over to see a figure standing in the doorway. Who the person was didn't register immediately, then she heard the voice, as deep and devious as ever, say, "Looking for someone?"

Sarah's immediate reaction was shock and horror. This was an unexpected—and unwanted—blast from the past. "Melinda Gomez? Why are you here?" Then after taking a couple of seconds to put a few puzzle pieces together, she demanded, "What do you know? Where's Dale?"

Melinda walked toward Sarah. Her gait was menacing. Her form was imposing—Melinda had put on a lot of muscle since their last meeting. Melinda kept a frosty stare at Sarah as she walked toward her, but Sarah refused to blink or back away. Finally, Melinda was standing right next to Sarah's bed. Sarah wasn't sure what Melinda was planning to do, but whatever it was she was ready to put up a fight.

As if a switch flipped inside of her head, Melinda broke her gaze at Sarah and looked off into the corner of the room. "You know something—at first I was worried."

Melinda's change in demeanor threw Sarah off for a split sec- ond, but she quickly regrouped and asked, "Worried about what? What are you talking about?"

Melinda's upper lip curled into a sinister grin. She looked over at Sarah lying in her hospital bed. Her countenance was cold and contemptuous. "I thought you retired. I thought I'd never get you in the octagon again. Then out of nowhere the opportunity came my way. But then I heard about your accident, and I didn't think I'd get a chance for payback."

"Huh?" Who are you working with, Melinda?" "Some ex- acquaintances of yours."

Sarah's blood ran cold when she came to the realization of exactly who Melinda was talking about. "Manetti."

Melinda leaned in closer to Sarah. She narrowed her eyes. "I want a rematch with you, and I want it as soon as you're out of here."

"What makes you think you'll get it?" replied Sarah defiantly. "You heard from your boyfriend lately?" This was the moment Melinda was waiting for. She was done toying around and eagerly wanted to see the look on Sarah's face with what came next.

"He's my fiancé. And no—why?" A feeling of dread suddenly overtook Sarah. "What have you done with him?"

"Relax, he's safe—for now," Melinda teased.

The feeling of dread quickly drained from Sarah and was immediately replaced by a white-hot rage. She wanted to pounce on Melinda right then and there, but her better judgment prevailed. "I swear, if you've done anything to him, I'll tear your liver out with my bare hands" said Sarah, seething.

"There we go! That's the fighting spirit." Melinda's attitude was cocky, and her tone mocked Sarah and her predicament. "Oh, and don't worry, Lacey—Cagney is safe too."

Not the most original comparison. Sarah and Jill heard it hundreds of times over their years together as partners. She knew exactly what Melinda meant. "Jill! You have Jill too?"

"You two will be back together tomorrow—as long as you show up."

Intrigued and done with the mind games Melinda was playing, Sarah was now looking for nothing from Melinda except for straight answers. "Show up where?"

Melinda got serious. "To our rematch. The big rematch I have been waiting years for." She tossed a folded piece of paper on Sarah's bed. "Here's an address. Be there tomorrow at noon. That should be enough time for you to check out of here and get there." Melinda then leaned over and brought her face close to Sarah's face, taunting her. "Come alone, and be ready for a fight." As she straightened up again, she said,

"You should get some rest. You're gonna need it." She meant it as more than just a suggestion to Sarah. It was a warning: come prepared.

The two women stared daggers at each other in the barely lit hospital room. Neither one broke eye contact until Melinda got to the door. "Tomorrow at noon," Melinda reminded Sarah as she ges- tured to the folded piece of paper with her chin. Sarah picked up the paper as Melinda left. She unfolded it and looked at the address. She didn't know exactly where it was, but she knew enough to know that it was in the luxury-living district of River City. She was confi- dent that she could find it easily enough the next day, which couldn't come fast enough.

Sleep did not come easy to Sarah that evening. There was too much going through her mind. She wondered how Dale and Jill were doing and what Leo Manetti and his insane girlfriend were doing to them. She said a silent prayer that they hang in there until she could get to them tomorrow. Until then, there was nothing she could do but worry.

Hours that seemed like days passed by. The sun rose, and Sarah watched every minute of it from her bed, thinking of the sunrise of a mere day ago when she came down the stairs and saw Dale staring out the window, doing the same thing.

She tried watching some morning-news programming to take her mind off things, but it was no use. A lot of time was still being spent on the monumental arrest of elusive mob boss Mike "the Hammer" Manetti, and it only fueled the fire in her to get out and prepare for what she had to do later in the day. Mercifully, about ten minutes after eight, Dr. Anderson walked in and checked her over. Sarah assured him with all urgency that she felt fine. He noted her improvement from yesterday, but he was still skeptical about her other bruises. He kept it to himself, though, since he already did all he could.

After Sarah checked out of the hospital, she briskly went to her car. Jill had left a note with Sarah's car keys to tell her where the car was parked and she found it right away. It was a little banged up from the accident but thankfully ran just fine. Sarah wasted no time in going straight home, speeding the whole way.

When she got home, Sarah burst through the front door, stone-faced. She was a woman on a mission. The first thing she did was run upstairs and head straight into her room.

Sarah threw open her closet door and dug around on the floor. She grabbed a box and flung it on the bed, then ripped open the lid and whipped out all her old clothes and gear from her fighting days. Sarah quickly got dressed, then headed to back to the closet.

Tucked away on her side of the closet was a small cabinet. She unlocked it and opened the doors. Inside was an assortment of 9mm, .45 ACP, and .38 Special handguns. Sarah loved handguns and men- tally kicked herself for not taking a seller up on a deal for a .357 Magnum last summer, but she quickly dismissed the thought since this was no time to think about such things.

As Sarah loaded up a duffel bag with some handguns and ammo, she glanced up and saw some painkiller bottles on her dresser. They were reminders of what Melinda did to her the last time they fought, and the sight of them infuriated Sarah. She hated being dependent on them. Angrily, Sarah grabbed one of the plastic bottles and squeezed it. The dozen or so round little white pills that were left inside burst out all over the floor.

Calming down, Sarah looked at the pills scattered on the floor and realized that she was pointing her anger in the wrong direction. It wasn't the pills she should be mad at, it was Melinda. If anything, the pills were a huge help in dealing with the pain and dizziness of her head injury. Sarah was not about to take a chance that she would have another one of her spells today. The prescribed dose was one pill, but Sarah ignored that and took two, just to be sure. She built up enough of a tolerance over the years where the side effects of things like cramps and nausea were minimal. She wanted to stay focused and feel no pain.

After taking the pills, Sarah headed back to the duffel bag. She zipped it up and raced back out the door.

With traffic, it took about half an hour for Sarah to get to the luxury-living district from her house. It was around 9:15 a.m. by the time she got to the area, and it took another fifteen minutes or so until she saw the address Melinda had given her. It was a building under construction. There were trucks and vans for a company called Fine Lines LLC parked on the site. A big crane stood on top of the building. However, there was no movement. No one was working on the building that morning, which was strange for a weekday. *Someone gave the crew a day off*, Sarah thought to herself. *They knew I was coming.*

Now that Sarah found the place, she needed to find a place nearby to hang out for a couple hours. She knew that sitting in the car was no good. She needed to move about and stay loose, but with- out wearing herself out. Three blocks away was the brand-new River City Design Center. It housed hundreds of the finest and best-known commercial and residential retailers in the United States. Sarah spent her time walking from shop to shop looking at furniture, fabrics, tiles, kitchen and bath displays, curtains, and rugs. In her head she dreamed of one day having enough money to buy the material she liked to create her dream home. These thoughts kept her motivated, because she wanted that home to be with Dale. She would do any- thing to make sure that happened. She was ready to kill today if it came down to it.

When the time came, Sarah got back into her car and drove to the construction site. She was fifteen minutes early but okay with waiting from here on. She wasn't taking any chances. To her surprise, Melinda was already there—also dressed for a fight—and standing next to Leo. They were both standing next to the van that was used to kidnap Jill and Dale the day before.

Sarah parked about fifty feet away from the van and turned the engine off. As she got out of her car, the doors to the van flew open. Her attention caught and now on high alert with a supreme level of situational awareness, Sarah honed in on Claudia inside the van with Jill and Dale. They were bound and gagged next to her. Unable to control herself, Sarah called out, "Dale! Jill!" before turning one sincerely pissed off stare toward Leo. "Okay, you bastard. I'm here. Let them go!'

Leo signaled to Claudia, who unceremoniously removed Jill's gag and cut her free. Once Jill was loose, Claudia pushed her out of the van. Jill landed on her feet at first, but then she stumbled forward and landed facedown in the dirt.

Claudia laughed at Jill lying facedown, wincing and moaning in pain. Seeing this just ticked off Sarah even more. Jill wasn't too happy about it either. Jill got up, dusted herself off, and walked to Sarah. When she was safe, Sarah called out, "Now Dale."

"Dale?" Leo called out, feigning confusion. "Oh no—I don't think so."

Sarah was beside herself with rage. "You lying son of a bitch! That was the deal! I show and fight Melinda in exchange for the both of them!"

Leo took a strong exception to being called a liar by Sarah. This set him off, and his rage matched hers. "Lying? You're calling me a liar? You're the one who snuck into my place, got me to trust you—no thanks to that piece of garbage Vinny DiGrazio—then ruined everything I worked so hard to build. No way, cheeky bird—you don't get to play that card. That's a case of the pot calling the kettle black if there ever was one." Leo took a much-needed, deep, and calming breath, and then continued more rationally. "No. This is the deal: you get your partner here for showing up. She can be in your corner while you and Melinda fight. If you win, Dale goes free. If you lose…well, if you lose, all three of you die. Got it?"

Sarah knew that Leo held all the cards when it came to Dale.

She had no real choice. "Yeah, Leo. I got it."

Leo clasped his hands together with excitement. "Good! So let's get on with it."

Sarah, Jill, Melinda, and Leo moved toward the apartment building in progress. Claudia stayed in the back of the van with Dale. As they walked in, Leo looked back over his shoulder and shouted, "Sit tight, Claudia! This won't be long."

Sarah grinned with confidence and muttered, "You got that right" under her breath.

CHAPTER 21

AS THE FOUR entered the half-done lobby, Sarah took in her surroundings. Drywall was up, plastic tarps were hanging and lying all around the area, and there were various tools and power equipment strewn about. She could see where the center of the lobby was going to have a giant fountain, but at that moment all that was there was the foundation where the fountain will be. Coincidentally, the cir- cular shape, which was indented about two feet into the lobby floor, was just the perfect size for a fighting ring.

Sarah and Melinda entered the ring and immediately started circling each other. Each woman sized the other one up. "You ready to start this?" taunted Melinda.

Undaunted, Sarah immediately replied, "I'm ready to finish it." Sarah readied herself. Melinda readied herself. Fierce fighting stances on both. Sarah was ready to get this going and end it as soon as possible. She narrowed her eyes at Melinda. "Come at me, bitch!"

Melinda let out an ear-piercing war cry and charged at Sarah, who braced herself for the impact. The two women grappled. Melinda was stronger than Sarah and thirsted for revenge. Sarah's adrenaline was pumping harder than it had in a long time—possibly since her last meeting with Melinda—and all she could think about was Dale and making sure he was going to be safe. Each tried to get dominance over the other, but to no avail. After half a minute of each woman trying their hardest, they both realized they were evenly matched. They broke apart after Melinda pushed Sarah away. While Sarah was off-balance, Melinda delivered a cheap shot to her jaw.

Sarah reeled back, stunned. Before she could shake it off, Melinda charged at her.

With beastly strength, Melinda wrapped her arms around Sarah, picked her up, carried her out of the ring, and pinned her against a nearby stone pillar. Sarah screamed as she was thrust against the unyielding Italian marble. Melinda dropped her and then started immediately pummeling her in the abdomen.

Jill and Leo stood to the side watching the fight, their attention laser sharp and undivided. Leo grinned. He loved the way things were going. Jill was frantic. She knew this wasn't looking good for Sarah. "Come on, Sarah!" she yelled out, doing her best to sound more encouraging than desperate.

Jill's voice gave Sarah a rush of strength. She used her adrenaline burst to parry Melinda's last blow. Melinda's hand went past Sarah's body and slammed hard into the pillar. She shrieked and grasped her hand in pain.

Her torso was throbbing, but Sarah did her best to ignore it. This was her opportunity to gain the upper hand. She grabbed Melinda by the hair on the back of her head and kneed her in the face. Melinda stumbled backward. Sarah swept Melinda's legs. Once Melinda was on the ground, Sarah jumped on top of her and pounded her mercilessly.

Jill's nervousness started to vanish. "Go, Sarah!" she cried out. Leo's happiness faded into deep concern. "Come on Melinda—get out of there!" he yelped as distress crept into his throat.

In the midst of the flurry of punches being unleashed upon her, Melinda managed to get a leg up and around Sarah's upper torso. She barely managed to kick Sarah off.

The two women stood up, collected themselves, and faced each other down. Dirt, sweat, and blood covered both of their heads, arms, and hands.

Leo felt a slight tinge of sexual arousal. This was normally the kind of thing that did it for him. Putting those thoughts aside, he called out, "All right—time for round two!"

Sarah and Melinda moved back into their makeshift ring. Melinda nodded her head approvingly at Sarah. "I'm glad to see you stayed in shape. Now when I beat you, I'll have the satisfaction of knowing you were a worthy challenge."

Sarah, defiant, let Melinda know her thoughts. "News flash, Melinda: that's not going to happen."

Meanwhile, Leo grew impatient and perturbed by all the chit- chat. "Hey, ladies!" he said boorishly to command their attention. Sarah and Melinda turned their heads to look at him. As soon as they did, he implored to them, "Will you two fight already!"

Melinda turned her head back slightly faster than Sarah. This split second made a huge difference. She ran in and popped Sarah with a quick jab. Sarah reacted just in time to put her head down so Melinda hit her forehead. This allowed Sarah to easily shake off the blow. The two combatants traded blows—punches, kicks, knees, elbows. It was all lightning quick. These two fighters went at it with immense passion and ferocity. Neither had an upper hand over the other one until Melinda landed a huge surprise uppercut that sent Sarah careening back. She barely managed to stay on her feet. Melinda jumped and came down full force with a punch to Sarah's cheek.

Sarah fell down flat on her face, barely conscious. Melinda got on the ground and put Sarah in an arm bar. Melinda had been wait- ing five years for this payback, to give Sarah a taste of what Sarah gave to her at their last fight. "How do you like it? Huh?" she taunted as Sarah let out a head-splitting shriek. The pain for Sarah was excruci- ating. Melinda taunted some more. "Give up! Come one—give up! I have you beat and you know it."

Sarah heard Jill shouting cheers and words of encouragement to her, but she tuned them out. She tuned out everything until she willed herself to hear nothing. The pain she was in vanished along with sound. She was in her own space. In the silence she thought of Dale. He was the reason she was fighting, and he was worth fighting for. In that moment, she knew she had to leave her quiet, pain-free space if she wanted to see him again. The pain came rush- ing back along with the sounds of yelling, mixed with Melinda's grunts and groans as she applied pressure to Sarah's arm. Reaching deep inside, Sarah pulled out every last bit of strength and determi-nation inside of her. "No, Melinda. You never beat me—and you never could."

Sarah thought back to her training and remembered an escape move called the coffee grinder. It was her only chance to break free. Sarah twisted her body and pumped her legs. Before Melinda even knew what happened, Sarah was in the dominant position. She turned Melinda over and forced her head into the ground.

Jill was thrilled, cheering as vigorously as she could. Leo, on the other hand, couldn't believe his eyes.

Both women rose to their feet. Before Melinda could turn and face Sarah, Sarah punched her in the back of the head. Melinda flew out of the ring. She wasn't expecting that two could play the payback game. "How do you like a sucker punch to the back of the head?" quipped Sarah.

Melinda whipped around just in time to notice as Sarah drop-kicked her and sent her stumbling backward toward some scaffold- ing. Sarah sprinted at Melinda and bear-hugged her. Feeling super- human strength in every part of her body, Sarah lifted Melinda in the air and tossed her into the scaffolding. The scaffolding collapsed like a house of cards. It fell on top of Melinda, along with all of the buckets of plaster and various trowels that were resting on it. Melinda lay under it, partially buried, unconscious, and immobile. Sarah took a close look and knew that she was still alive but wasn't getting up anytime soon.

Furious, Leo picked up a nearby brick and cracked Jill over the head with it. Hearing her friend tumble to the floor, Sarah ran to Jill as Leo headed out the door.

"Jill! Are you all right?" asked a concerned Sarah.

Jill shook off the pain in her head as if it was nothing. "Yeah, I'll be okay. Let's just get that son of a bitch!"

Sarah helped Jill get up on her feet. They ran outside just as the van peeled away. "Damn it! They still have Dale." Sarah pointed to her car. "Get in!" Sarah ran to the driver's side as Jill hopped in the passenger's seat. Without wasting a second, Sarah started up the car and floored the gas pedal as hard as she could. The tires screeched as the car darted out into traffic and barely missed getting T-boned by a taxi. The driver honked his horn. Sarah was already too far down the street to hear the string of expletives that followed.

It was lunchtime. The streets and sidewalks were loaded with pedestrians. This didn't stop Leo from driving like a maniac. Claudia was in the passengers' seat, saying silent prayers that they wouldn't get into a deadly collision as he blew through stoplights and swerved into oncoming traffic. As he looked in the rearview, he could see Sarah's car—unmistakable with the front bumper dented in—gain- ing on him.

Sarah was in hot pursuit and wished she had a siren on her car. She stayed as close as she could to Leo's van. She was a bit more care- ful and conscious of pedestrians, but she made sure that she didn't lose sight of the van. Jill gritted her teeth and held on as Sarah deftly maneuvered through automobile and pedestrian traffic. In the back of her mind, Jill was impressed at Sarah's driving skills. The pair had never been in a car chase before, and in spite of the natural worry that came with being in the situation, she liked the way Sarah handled the car as she weaved and skidded to keep up with the van they were chasing.

"Do you know where he's going?" Jill asked, hoping it was somewhere close so this situation would be over.

Sarah took her eyes off the road to take a quick glance at her surroundings. "I think I know. And if I'm right, we'll be there soon. See that bag in the back?" Jill turned and looked. She saw the duffel bag sitting on the back seat. "Grab it," instructed Sarah, "We're going to need it."

Jill grabbed the bag. Mass amounts of relief swept over her when she unzipped it and saw what was inside. "Good thing you brought these." Jill rifled through the sidearm selection and chose the one that was perfect for her.

Sarah grinned as Jill loaded a clip into the .45 she selected. "I like to be prepared."

As they got closer to the destination, Sarah got the confirmation that she was right. Leo pulled into the Amazon Glory parking lot and drove right up to the entrance. Claudia rushed in as Leo opened the back of the van and grabbed Dale, dragging him into the nightclub as Sarah pulled in right behind them. She grabbed a .38 from her bag and loaded as quickly as possible.

Inside the club, the fish tank was lowered. Maria was behind the bar, feeding a stack of cheap cuts of meat to the piranhas. Tina was polishing a table. Both women jumped with fright as Claudia burst in and immediately turned around, waiting for Leo. Seconds later, Leo rushed in and barked at them, "We're being followed! Get the guns, and shoot whoever comes in here after us," as he continued straight through the back door, pushing Dale ahead of him and with Claudia following closely behind.

In immediate compliance, Maria pulled a shotgun and a hand- gun out from under the bar. She tossed the handgun to Tina, who caught the gun and cocked it in one swift motion. Spotting a good hiding spot behind the giant tree with the anaconda, Tina got into position. Maria pumped the shotgun and waited behind the bar. Both women were primed and ready for whoever came through the door, but they had a good idea on who it would be. Tina thought about Jill and wanted payback for the cut on her face.

They didn't have long to wait. Sarah kicked open the door. Sensing a trap, she immediately stepped back and grabbed cover off to the side. Smart move on her part. Maria and Tina unloaded straight away, peppering the doorway with bullets. The shooting only stopped when they ran out of bullets and had to reload. Sarah and Jill seized the opportunity and made their move. Sarah bust through the door, staying low, with Jill close behind. They toppled over a table and hid behind it in prone position.

Sarah looked at Jill to make sure she was okay, then gave her a nod. Jill nodded back. No words had to be spoken. Each woman knew what this meant. They rose up simultaneously from behind the table and opened fire. Sarah concentrated on the bar. The stack of meat exploded as ammo rounds crashed into it. Jill concentrated on the tree, forcing Tina to stay behind it to avoid getting hit.

Once their guns were empty, Sarah and Jill ducked back behind the table to reload. Maria and Tina came out from their hiding spots and unleashed a hail of bullets. The table barely provided cover for Jill and Sarah, but they were low enough so they didn't get hit.

Maria was the first to run out of bullets. Sarah didn't waste the opportunity. She rose up and fired at her while Jill gave Sarah covering fire on Tina. Bullets ripped into Maria's chest and sent her flying backward. She tried to catch herself on the glass shelves behind her, but they were flimsy and unreliable. The shelves shattered under Maria's weight and sent her plummeting into the fish tank. This was fresh meat like the piranhas have never had before. The frenzy started immediately. Maria screamed and gasped and gurgled as razor-sharp teeth ripped her apart. She was dead in a matter of seconds.

Tina was incensed. Raging out of her mind, she stood out in front of the tree and wreaked havoc with her handgun. "You bitches! I'll kill you!" she screamed as she fired wildly at the table that Sarah and Jill were once again hiding behind. Pieces of the table exploded all around Jill and Sarah. They lay flat on the floor but were losing cover fast.

Feeling brave, Jill looked through a gaping hole in the table. Squinting to try to gain focus in the smoke-filled room, Jill looked up and noticed the thin wire bolted to the ceiling that held the big, fake anaconda's head up. Even better: Tina was standing right under it. Aiming carefully, Jill fired off a round at the wire. She hit it. The wire snapped, and the anaconda came tumbling down—right on top of Tina.

For anyone who didn't know any better, it looked like Tina actually got swallowed by a giant snake. Half of her body was in its mouth. The rest of the big snake collapsed, as did Tina—still in its mouth—right along with it. Jill scurried over after Tina got swal- lowed and stopped shooting. She observed her handiwork. "She's not going anywhere anytime soon," Jill called over to Sarah, who was surveying the damage.

The place was completely trashed. Tables and chairs were broken, splintered, and shot full of holes. The pictures that didn't come crashing down off the wall were hanging crooked. Sarah made her way over to the bar and behind it, noticing that the fish tank was a frothy vat of liquid crimson. She looked closer but then had to immediately turn away. Maria's shredded-up, half-eaten body made her sick to her stomach. Sarah signaled for Jill to follow her. The two women headed through the same door to the back that Leo went through moments earlier.

Sarah led Jill down the narrow hall and past the offices. Jill's mouth dropped open as she followed Sarah to the casino floor. The operation was larger and more impressive than she ever imagined. As she was following Sarah and taking in the grandeur and enormity of what she was seeing, Jill slowed down. Snapping out of her brief moment of mesmerization, Jill suddenly realized that she was falling behind. Sarah was already making her way down the stairs to the octagon.

Jill managed to take two steps to run and catch up with Sarah when a pointy-toed boot appeared from out of nowhere and kicked her in the face. The gun flew out from Jill's hand and disappeared in the rows of seats. Before she could gather her senses, Claudia was kicking her in the ribs and stomping on her chest and abdomen.

Sarah didn't notice that her friend was no longer behind her. Her attention was entirely focused on the octagon. In it, Dale was chained to the fence. Next to him was Leo, brandishing a knife. Sarah raised her weapon. She kept it pointed at Leo as she entered through the gate into the octagon.

Leo raised the knife to Dale's throat. "Drop it! You drop it, Sarah, or I'll slit his throat. You may kill me, but he dies too."

Sarah knew she was stuck. There was no way she was risking Dale's life for any reason. "Okay! I'm dropping it." Sarah tossed the gun out of the gate and closed it behind her.

Leo flicked the knife down. It stuck into the mat near Dale's feet. Feeling pumped and ready for action, Leo ripped off his shirt. He readied himself in a fighting stance. "Let's finish this."

Sarah readied herself. The two fighters circled and sized each other up before they commenced trading blows. Sarah was more than warmed up by this point and not feeling the least bit of fatigue. If anything, being this close to rescuing Dale gave her a second wind. She held her own well as she and Leo went punch for punch and kick for kick, blocking and dodging as needed. Her years of training took over and she acted mostly on instinct, with very little thought on what she needed to do.

Back in the stands, Claudia had the upper hand, kicking the hell out of Jill. One kick sent Jill down the stairs. Claudia walked down after her. She felt no need to run. She was like a predator stalking her prey. She felt cocky and more than a little self-assured.

Jill got up as soon as she could and booked it into the locker room. Frantic and battered, Jill hid in a stall. She stood on top of the toilet and crouched down so as to be out of sight if Claudia looked under the door. On the back of the toilet, she noticed an aerosol spray can of Country Fresh Scent air deodorizer. She picked it up and grasped it with both hands with her finger on the spray button. Taking her time, Claudia strutted in like the queen of the locker room. "I know you're in here…you can't play hide-and-seek for long!" she taunted.

Jill bit her tongue to keep from screaming with fear. Claudia started kicking in stall doors. The trepidation built in Jill as each door was forced open with a loud thump and crash. Finally, inevita- bly, Claudia kicked in the door to Jill's stall. She saw Jill standing on the toilet, petrified.

"Gotcha!" bellowed Claudia. She took a moment to gloat at her helpless prey before she made her move toward Jill to finish her off once and for all.

As if suddenly jolted out of her state of frozen terror, Jill extended her arm and sprayed a copious amount of deodorizer right into Claudia's eyes, nose, and mouth. Claudia thrashed about. She could practically feel histamines being released as her body's immune system sprung forth with its allergic reaction. Her facial muscles con- tracted. Capillaries dilated. Claudia couldn't see. She could barely breathe.

Now it was Jill's turn. She launched off the toilet, headed right at Claudia. Claudia was defenseless as Jill gave her a pounding. But Jill's blows had little effect. She was not a trained fighter, plus Claudia was strong and knew how to take a beating.

Her situational awareness heightened, Jill spotted a plunger lingering in the stall with the corner of her eye. She picked it up and with one smooth motion smashed the wooden handle against Claudia's head.

Claudia fell to her knees, facing the open stall. Jill straddled Claudia, picked her up from under her arms, and dragged her over to the toilet. With all her might, Jill lifted Claudia's torso just high enough to get her over the rim of the bowl. Jill then grabbed a hand- ful of hair on the back of Claudia's head and shoved her head into the toilet.

Claudia gurgled and struggled. Jill held her head down, taking sadistic glee in watching Claudia squirm under her. Claudia was on the verge of drowning until Jill remembered that she was a cop, so she flushed the toilet. Jill let up on the pressure she was putting on Claudia's head. Claudia picked her head up to get some air.

Claudia got one gasp before Jill grabbed the back of her head with both hands and slammed her face into the side of the porcelain bowl at full force. Blood streaked down the rim of the toilet bowl as Claudia's unconscious body fell on the floor next to the toilet.

"Stay here with the toilets where you belong, you piece of shit," said Jill as she backed out of the stall and admired her handiwork.

In the octagon, Sarah was in the midst of taking a serious beat- ing at the hands of Leo. He was totally in control, and there was little Sarah could do to fight back. After a few punches and kicks, Leo picked up Sarah, held her over his head, and tossed her against the fence. The cage reverberated with the force of the impact. Sarah's body hit the floor of the octagon with a thud. It looked like she was out cold.

Leo laughed a smug, self-assured laugh. He turned his attention to Dale. "You know, you need to see the bright side. It's good that you're both in here. This way both of you can die together and won't have to live without each other for too long."

This set off Dale in a major way. He raged at Leo as hard as he could, and while he couldn't do much more than that while bound and gagged, his intention was clear—he wanted to pulverize Leo into dust.

Dale's impotent protestations made Leo want to make it hurt even more. "But don't worry. I'm going to kill you first. That way, she can watch. I'm gonna carve her up last because when I do, I really, really want to take my time doing it."

Ready to put his words into action, Leo reached down to grab the knife at Dale's feet. What he failed to notice, however, was that Sarah did not get knocked out cold. She sprang to consciousness after a couple of seconds—just in time to hear Leo tell Dale about them dying together.

Operating on pure, white-hot rage, Sarah quickly crawled up behind Leo while he mocked Dale. The split second before Leo grabbed the knife sticking out of the floor, he saw a hand reach between his knees and grab it first. Sarah got a firm grip on the knife handle. She turned it toward Leo and plunged it into his thigh. Leo howled in pain and fell down on his side.

Sarah ripped the knife out of his leg, jumped on top of him, and put the point of the blade up to his eye. As much as she wanted to blind and mutilate him right then and there for revenge—or would it be justice?—Sarah knew she couldn't. A scared and injured Leo yelped at what he thought was coming, then Sarah turned the blade up and pointed the handle of the knife at Leo's head, raining blow after blow to his skull.

Leo was unconscious in seconds, but this didn't stop Sarah. She was a woman possessed, bashing Leo's face in. Jill rushed into the octagon just in time to stop Sarah from going too far by grabbing Sarah's wrist before she could strike one more blow, and she gently pulled her off Leo.

Sarah stared at Leo's limp yet luckily still breathing body with a mix of horror and amazement. Winded and panting, she composed herself after a few seconds and managed to say, "Thanks, Jill. I… don't know what…came over me" between deep breaths.

Jill smiled at her. "Hey—that's what partners do."

Jill got to her feet and held her hand out to Sarah. Sarah took it, and after Jill helped her get to her feet Sarah asked, "Whaddaya say you help me unchain Dale, and then we can chain up this scum sucker in his place?"

"Sounds good," replied Jill, "but I do have one more to add to this chain gang."

"Oh?"

"Yeah. I'll be right back. I dropped something in the toilet."

As Jill ran out through the gate, Sarah checked Leo's pocket and found the key to the lock on the chain. After grabbing it, she rushed over to Dale and pulled down his gag. "Are you all right?"

The gag made Dale's mouth dry. He smacked his gums to get some saliva on his lips and tongue before he replied, "Yeah, I'm all right."

Sarah hurriedly freed him from his chains. As soon as Dale could move his arms, he turned to Sarah and cradled her sweaty, blood-streaked head in his hands. He didn't care. To him, she glowed. "We're all right, Sarah. We will be forever." For Sarah and Dale the octagon, then the casino, then the club, then the city, and then the world all melted away as they kissed passionately.

*****

Two months later, in the bright yoga studio at Super Fitness gym, Sarah and Jill were stretching out in the front corner. As they did, several women entered the room, each one dressed like they'd come to break a sweat. Most of the women came in pairs or small groups, chatting among themselves while clutching towels and water bottles.

Sarah assessed the women as they entered. It would be a full class that evening.

Jill decided to break their silent stretching. "He misses you." Sarah had an idea of who she meant and was shocked. "Who?

Lieutenant Busby? He misses me? I don't think so."

"No, he does," Jill confirmed with the utmost sincerity. "And so do I. Things aren't the same down at the station without you there.

"Well, I wish I could say I miss it too—but I don't. Sure, I miss you, and I miss ol' Buzz too. But…I don't miss any of the rest."

"So teaching these classes here at Super Fitness is better?" prodded Jill.

Sarah beamed. "Sure. They had a job opening after Melinda disappeared, so I figured I'd offer my services. Plus, they have an excellent maternity benefit here." Sarah's smile was radiant. Her skin and hair looked shinier and healthier than a mildly jealous Jill had ever seen it now that the mountain of stress Sarah was under was gone.

Jill was intrigued by Sarah's last sentence. "Oh, you and Dale are still trying?

"Still? We never stopped. As a matter of fact, he and I tried again last night." Sarah chuckled and nudged Jill, who cracked up too.

After a few seconds of giggling, Jill changed the topic. "I'm just glad I signed up for your class. They got me breaking in a rookie, and as you know, those streets are dangerous enough as it is without having to babysit fresh meat. I don't want to take another butt whooping like I did with that crazy bitch Claudia."

Sarah straightened up and got serious, remembering that eve- ning. "She's right where she belongs now."

"Damn right!" Jill exclaimed assuredly. "That awful bastard Leo Manetti too."

Sarah gave a quick nod. "He and his dad will have a lot of time to catch up with each other."

"Thank goodness that scum is off the streets. But there's more out there."

"I know. And I'm here to teach you how to protect yourself from them. You ready?" Sarah quickly rose up.

Jill sprung to her feet, stretched out and rearing to go. "Ready!"

Sarah stepped away and in a loud voice addressed the room. "All right, ladies—time to start class. Everyone line up."

The women all broke from their individual minihuddles and quickly formed some rows. Jill took her usual place: front row, center.

Sarah continued, "Today we'll warm up with some left/right alternating jabs. Ready?"

The women all assumed a fighting stance and responded in unison, "Ready?"

"Begin!"

The class followed along enthusiastically with Sarah, who was grinning from ear to ear. She finally found her vocation. She was helping people, but in a different, less stress-filled, and much-less dangerous way. She was truly happy. Dale was thrilled that he didn't have to worry about what would happen to her on the streets any- more. This was more than where she wanted to be. This was where she belonged.

ABOUT THE AUTHOR

IN ADDITION TO writing, Andrew Hudak is an avid movie watcher who also enjoys cooking a great meal at home. *Takedown* is his first novel. Andrew was born and raised in Connecticut, and is where he currently resides.